More praise for
THE SIZE OF THE WORLD

"To illustrate what [Silber] calls 'the elusive connection between place and happiness' requires perfectly calibrated psychological insight and near-photographic descriptions of daily life in far-flung places, and Silber is a genius at this." —Howard Norman, *Washington Post Book World*

"Without heralding, Silber covers all the big themes: morality, culture, paradise lost and found, longing, for-given... much to admire here."
Globe

the very marrow of the novel. Vast shifts in time or place no longer feel strange or jarring. Instead, we come to expect them." —Karan Mahajan, *San Francisco Chronicle*

"While her characters struggle with their demons, she draws their lives out with ease and tenderness, generously leaving the reader with what evaded them: their own private Walden, for a few moments at least."

—Lenora Todaro, *Bookforum*

"In unadorned prose that takes tremendous psychological and geographic leaps, Silber offers a dizzying array of insights as she cuts back and forth between stories set in the U.S. and Asia." —Conan Putnam, *Chicago Tribune*

"Silber offers an intriguing network of characters in shared settings, but, ultimately, the book's strength lies less in its unity than in the interesting digressions found within each story." —Brad Hooper, *Booklist*

"Silber's sixth book again showcases her intricately crafted narrative style. . . . The characters within the book's delicate web illustrate how inescapable are the consequences of any human action, rippling from one generation to another across continents in this 'great, swarming world.'" —Thailan Pham, *People*

"Joan Silber writes novels that act like tidy galaxies of stories. She writes stories that act like poetically compressed novels. Regardless, each one describes orbits, then more orbits, patent or subtle. The orbiting of concentric tales, details, and vocal tones is what holds Silber's fiction together and is also what makes it move."

—Molly McQuade, *Bloomsbury Review*

"Silber illuminates how we are bonded by our differences."

—C. C., *More*

THE SIZE OF THE WORLD

Joan Silber

THE SIZE OF THE WORLD

a novel

W. W. NORTON & COMPANY

NEW YORK LONDON

For information about permission to
reproduce selections from this book, write to
Permissions, W. W. Norton & Company, Inc.
500 Fifth Avenue, New York, NY 10110

For information about special discounts
for bulk purchases, please contact
W. W. Norton Special Sales
at specialsales@wwnorton.com or 800-233-4830

Manufacturing by RR Donnelley, Bloomsburg
Book design by Barbara M. Bachman
Production manager: Anna Oler

LIBRARY OF CONGRESS
CATALOGING-IN-PUBLICATION DATA

Silber, Joan.
The size of the world : a novel / Joan Silber. — 1st ed.
p. cm.
ISBN 978-0-393-05909-0
1. Americans—Foreign countries—Fiction.
2. Homesickness—Fiction. I. Title.
PS3569.I414S59 2008
813'.54—dc22
            2008001342

ISBN 978-0-393-33489-0 pbk.

W. W. Norton & Company, Inc.
500 Fifth Avenue, New York, N.Y. 10110
www.wwnorton.com

W. W. Norton & Company Ltd.
Castle House, 75/76 Wells Street, London W1T 3QT

1 2 3 4 5 6 7 8 9 0

In memory of my brother, Ralph

CONTENTS

THE SIZE OF THE WORLD

ENVY

Toby

I.

I USED TO MAKE my father repeat the names of where he'd fought on the Pacific Front. The complicated contours of those syllables intrigued me (Makassar, Badung, Sunda). My father said war wasn't the best way to see the world, whatever the Navy said in their recruiting ads. But I could trace the battle lines on maps for any number of wars. That was the sort of hobby I had then.

I liked getting lost in projects. I was a Navy brat, moved from post to post as a kid, and I got used to occupying myself without company, with a surprising degree of contentment. I liked doing things on my own. The things changed, but my habits were steady. Ernst was the one person I ever met who was better at this than I was. I was an amateur of aloneness compared to him.

I might have turned out more like Ernst. There was a spell in my life when I made an effort to. I admired him, and in many ways he was admirable. After I settled in Bangkok, I used to write to Ernst every year at Christmas. I wrote him summaries of what I was doing at work, what my wife and kids were up to. Ernst never wrote to me—he never wrote to anyone. Why would someone who hardly spoke in person get gabby on paper from thousands of miles away? It was hard to imagine him doing such a thing, but I always hoped he would. It didn't matter that I knew better.

WE WERE BOTH IN our twenties when we met. Bydex was my first job, right out of engineering school, and Ernst had started a few years before me. The guy who hired me said he was putting me on a project with the company genius who was not a social butterfly, was I okay with that? When I walked into our shared office, Ernst raised an eyebrow and nodded while seeming to look over his shoulder. He shook hands, went back to whatever he was writing, and that was the end of our first meeting.

But he loved the work. Once he'd sized me up, he made a point of taking me across the hall to meet the guy who was designing the electronics for a laser range finder that measured the distance from an airplane to the ground for accurate bombing. He thought I'd just want to see the beauty of it. I did.

Almost everyone in the company was married except us. This was in the late sixties, in a sedate outpost of that era—we were in Phoenix, then a dusty town in the middle of nowhere. Ernst and I didn't know what to do with ourselves. We played ping-pong in our married friends' furnished basements, we played pinball in roadhouses off the highway, we drove for miles with nothing but static and Bobby Darin on the radio, we went to a shooting range and killed the shapes of ducks. No women worked on our project—we were devising tests for the guidance systems on military aircraft—or were anywhere outside the typing pool. I was so lonely I used to make surprise phone calls at noon to my high school girlfriend, who had a husband and a baby.

Ernst and I were summoned one day to a large inner office with ugly maroon drapes, where a project manager told us what everyone knew, that Bydex systems were letting planes go off course in Vietnam, a place you definitely didn't want to get lost over. And how would Ernst and I feel about seeing the world? Following the equipment into the field, being the company's tech reps over there? "We can't send mediocre drones on this," the manager said. "We need our best, which is you." I knew he was flattering us into believing it was a reward to be flown into a war, but I was immensely flattered anyway. I said I'd think about it, but Ernst knew right away. He tilted his head and gave his small crooked smile and murmured, *Why not?* It wasn't a jaunty question—it had in it his private satisfaction that as a rule situations were as crappy as he expected.

Saigon was not a combat zone. That was what I told my family, although they could see how jittery I was. It was a city near the bottom of a country at war—the ground fighting was mostly in the countryside (I hadn't yet heard anyone say *in-country*) around villages farther north or down in the Delta. It was true that the Viet Cong had invaded Saigon during the Tet Offensive some six months before, but they hadn't held it very long.

I don't know what Ernst told his family. He had one sister—who was out marching against the war, he said she'd always been an airhead—and he had a mother and father. His father owned a dry-cleaning plant. That was all I knew about them. He didn't act as if he needed a family or understood why anyone did.

WHEN WE CHANGED PLANES in Anchorage, I called my folks from the airport, while Ernst sat reading a Nero Wolfe mystery. The cover had a drawing of a corpse bleeding onto a carpet. My mother got very emotional, and I knew it had been a mistake for me to call. I envied Ernst, absorbed in his book. Our flights were on commercial planes filled with soldiers, and on the long middle route to Japan there was a group of Marines behind us, telling the world's dumbest dirty jokes. But Ernst slept like a baby. His sinuses made his breathing loud—this new intimacy did not please me.

Tan Son Nhut Air Base was teeming with soldiers. They looked very young, even to me, under their hats and helmets. As soon as we landed, I was looking for wounded ones on stretchers, or battle-weary groups covered in mud—I wasn't hungry for horror but I had prepared for these sights the way I'd tried to learn a few words of the language. *Cam on.* Thank you. *Phong tam o dau?* Where is the bathroom? And then I did see two men carrying a heavy duffel, end by end, across the runway, and they moved with such focused deliberation that I understood this was a body bag, and I stopped in my tracks. Ernst was behind me. "Just walk," he said.

SAIGON WAS LOUD with traffic and smelled of exhaust fumes and hot asphalt and something faintly vegetal and pleasant. I did not see how our driver could make his way through the headlong flow of bicycles and cars. I hadn't understood that it was a real city, with broad avenues and big boxy modern buildings and pink French colonial palaces, at the same time that it was a sprawling bazaar with people in conical straw hats carrying sacks of rice on shoulder poles and hawking packs of cigarettes and magenta fruits.

Our car moved slowly and was like an oven. Since my dad was in the Navy, I'd lived in some hot places in the U.S.—San Diego and Corpus Christi and Key West. Saigon was definitely muggier than any of them. Sweat was running down Ernst's face as if his pores were weeping.

"*They* look cool," Ernst said, looking through the window. The women on the street were all in long-sleeved tunics and shirts (for modesty, the driver said) and did not seem to be sweating much, standing over their piles of auto parts and bananas and steaming vats of soup. Every item of the First and Third World was set out on the pavement—Bic lighters, bottled beer, sugarcane. In the midst of this jumble of enterprise, the vendors' faces were distant and closed. I couldn't tell if they were resigned or infuriated or just exhausted. It was too soon to even guess. Some of the women were very beautiful. Not the men, who looked bony and fierce-eyed to me. Even then I didn't know what to make of the men.

THE GOVERNMENT HAD bunked us into an old faded-glory hotel, a tiered white hulk with a soldier on guard outside. The lobby held a stiff arrangement of dark lacquered wood settees inlaid with mother-of-pearl, and we sat on these and waited with our luggage while someone checked us in. Across the marble floor, a man whose trousers were tucked where a leg had been cut off at the hip was crawling, begging from anyone who happened to be there. When he tapped my knee, I fished an American quarter out of my pocket to give him. One of his eyes was milky and vacant. Even Ernst gave him a dime.

Our rooms were not bad, with their big rattan headboards and the windows X'd with duct tape to keep them from shattering. Over my bed was a woodblock print of a happy native paddling a boat under a willow tree. Where was *that* kingdom? It took about ten minutes for me to notice that nothing could make me cool in that room, not the ceiling fan, not the blinds drawn down, not mugs of ice brought up from the bar.

From the first morning on, we worked very long hours at the air base, and when we came back to the hotel after dark, I went upstairs and lay down on my bed and listened to the noise of the street. Some of it was our noise—convoys and trucks and boisterous American voices—and some of it was theirs, the shrill and glottal syllables. I knocked on Ernst's door to see if he wanted to go out. "You mean now?" he said from behind the door. He didn't sound eager but he came out right away. At home he'd been like that too.

Once we were on the sidewalks, people kept calling out to us. Men's voices said in their half-swallowed English, "Where you going? I can take you cheap. Not safe to walk. You like young girls, how young? I can take you now, cheap for you." They didn't stop, no matter what we said or didn't say. They trailed us across the avenue, around the square. "I see you before, I know you," a girl of about fourteen said. "You looking for me?" So we took a cyclo—our two big Western bodies in a cart pushed by a skinny old man on a bike—to a bar that the corporal who was our driver had told us about. We walked into a dark basement lit by purple lights and full of soldiers and Vietnamese girls playing pool at a table in the center, with Mick Jagger singing "Under My Thumb" in the background. It took about a second to see that we were out of place in our seersucker suits and not welcome either.

So we walked back to the hotel bar, where we drank glasses of beer with American civilians who were older and richer than we were and we let them brag to us about what they knew. "Never trust anyone. First rule. Get it tattooed on your chest over your heart." This hackneyed lesson was intoned by a chemist who'd been setting up ice-cream factories for the troops. "But the French restaurants are good, I'll tell you which ones." A construction engineer who'd been in the country for years, carving up new harbors, kept trying to tell us about the huge motorcycle he'd bought for a song. He described every part of its mighty carcass, one of the few things likely to interest Ernst. I got a little jolly from the beers and the talk, but Ernst went silent, frozen (I later realized) in contempt. In the elevator I asked if he'd had a good time, and he said, "Not really. I'm not very crazy about profiteers."

I wiped, as my mother used to say, the smile off my face. Now I saw what he saw, how the men all looked a little oozing and overripe. Inflated and blustering.

THERE WERE PLENTY OF other bars in other hotels, and our first nights were spent going from one to the other. And women found us, as it was their job to do. Two pretty teenagers asked us if seats at our table were taken. "You always so tall?" one of them said to Ernst. She was delicate and long-waisted, with a rough voice. The softer, plainer one picked me. Mine could speak a little English but not a lot, and it unnerved me later that night to have her small, pliant feet above my shoulders and her scent all around me and have so few words of hers I could follow. What was she saying, was she saying anything? And I didn't even like, not really, the jolt of pleasure that arrived in the midst of my not wanting anymore to be there.

And where was Ernst? I'd last seen him led by his girl into one of the other rooms. There'd been a tiny, awkward smirk on his face. A man like other men, I'd thought.

Now he was waiting for me on the inner stairs of the building where they'd taken us. "Everything okay?" I asked.

"Hurry up," he said. "It's late."

"How was it?" I said. "You liked her?"

He didn't bother to answer.

Someone earlier that night, a man who was very drunk, had told me he knew Ernst was in the CIA. "He has that spook look," he said, "that expressionless look. I'd know it anywhere."

Certainly no one was better than Ernst at keeping things to himself. Before we left the States, a few people we worked with had pretty much voiced the same opinion. But what did the CIA do? It gathered information, didn't it? If this involved asking anyone questions, Ernst was not your man. He was notably incurious about other people and had no practice in exacting even a sentence. And CIA work would have required lying and disguise. Ernst hated even the small white lies of most social exchanges (*Good job on that* or *Nice house you've got*) and was famous for never uttering them. He had no tolerance for falsity. "Phonies," as he (like Holden Caulfield) called them, made him shudder in disgust. The widespread habit people had of humoring each other was why he mostly chose solitude.

———

WE SPENT A LOT of time at the airfield. Ernst's hearing had already been damaged at home by the roar of engines, so I wore ear protectors, which he laughed at. The soldiers also found me hilarious. We watched the planes take off and we rode with the pilots on practice runs. Everything we checked out worked fine. We spent a lot of time rerunning the checks. Ernst was methodical.

I was never very comfortable going up in those planes. I had enough sense to keep this sentiment to myself. Fear had settled in me as soon as we arrived. A week after we got there, a bomb went off in a nightclub in our part of town, a place I'd been to, with walls of mirrors that were now piles of slivered rubbish. My high school girlfriend, Kit, had started writing to me. *Please take very good care of yourself, Toby*, she said. *All of us at home are thinking of you.* I was thinking of me too.

The Air Force pilots hated us. They liked to tell us the grisliest stories they could—mutilated soldiers who'd screamed the whole trip back, deadly bamboo snakes in the cockpit, kids on bikes throwing satchel charges into American trucks—and said we should talk to the infantry guys if we really wanted to hear stuff. GIs with necklaces of ears, eight-year-old girls luring men into ambushes, had we heard about those? I said, "Jesus. Holy Christ." I thought they were overdoing the list for me (these weren't wartime clichés yet) but Ernst didn't flinch.

"Planes go back out there into the thick of it every

morning," the pilot said, "early, like when you're buying your croissants for breakfast."

"But we love our planes," the copilot said. "You love this one?"

"I do like these, actually," Ernst said.

The two pilots gave each other a look, and we were swooping down nose first. Only our seat belts, digging into our bellies, kept us from being thrown into the cockpit. Even Ernst was yelling, "Fuck! Oh, fuck!"

And then we were gaining altitude too fast, our heads jerked back. The plane did a jarring, nauseating loop and then another lunge—the ride wouldn't stop. I was shouting, "Right now, cut it out!" which probably egged them on. I thought they were going to kill all of us— why would they do that? I managed to stop yelling, "*Cut it out.*" I sounded like a first-grade teacher. But why wouldn't they stop?

"Enjoy that?" the pilot said when we were level again. "Either of you shit yourselves?"

We hadn't. Ernst was white and sweating. "Interesting," he said. "Very interesting."

I envied him. Everyone in Vietnam had to go through a process of hardening; even the civilians working for American contractors talked about how green they'd been in the beginning. But Ernst arrived with his own crust.

"THOSE GUYS ARE CRAZY," he did say, when we were back on the ground having coffee (a beverage then thought to calm you) in one of the air base canteens.

"*Why* did we come here?" I said. "We didn't have to come."

I thought he was going to say there was a war on. We worked in the defense industry, it went without saying we believed in the necessity of wars generally. You could not allow certain people to get away with certain things. Ernst thought the world consisted largely of such people, but he especially hated the Communists. No one could tell him they had a few okay ideas. "They're bad news," he said.

"I wanted to travel," he said now. "When Bydex hired me, they said I would travel."

"This is travel?"

"You get to see people," he said.

He did? What people? It was true he walked around with a camera, a fancy, complicated number with extra lenses, and he used a light meter. But he mostly took pictures of buildings, as far as I'd seen—the post office, the opera house, the American Embassy with its flank of giant flowerpots. The post office had been designed by the same guy who did the Eiffel Tower and it had a very handsome arched ceiling. So what?

And how many Vietnamese had I talked to? How many conversations had I had? My circle of local acquaintance was notably narrow. I had talked to the hooker who called herself Miss Mai, the bellhop, and the crippled beggar who came every night to the hotel, with his one sealed eye and his slurred speech.

———

INSIDE THOSE LONG DAYS, I was longing for my old girl-friend Kit. And I was thrilled when she wrote, but her letters disappointed me. They reminded me not only that she was married but also what I hadn't liked about her in the beginning. She was nice but shallow and sometimes downright sappy. I had lied about this to myself when we were together—decided she had her own kind of intelligence or was sharper than her language showed—and it struck me now that this was the sort of lying Ernst was free of. His life seemed very free to me and very clean.

ERNST KNEW A LOT of details about the war, for a guy who wasn't in the CIA—where exactly Prime Minister Diem had been murdered by his own generals, how long the DMZ actually was, and what Madame Nhu had really wanted. He said he just remembered what he read in the newspapers. Didn't I know what I saw on TV at least? His memory was pretty remarkable. He was famous at work for being able to recite the figures on any project without looking.

And he could describe every shop on a block he'd just walked through. At night, when we made our way back to the hotel, he was the one who kept me from turning down the wrong avenue and getting lost in a tangle of unmarked streets. He could always say which direction the river was in or how far we were from the brick Notre Dame Cathedral. He's more *here* than I am, I thought.

But I liked the country more than he did. I started to have more chats with Can, the bellhop who worked nights; he knew a little English and some French. He offered to sell us drugs, as did the laundress and every cyclo driver we met, but once we were off that topic, he let me ask him the names of all the plants in the courtyard. Of course, he only knew them in Vietnamese, and my attempts at repeating the tones reduced him to a very dignified form of high amusement; he cracked up without making a sound. I tried to describe Florida to him, and my mother's yard with its croton and yucca and allamanda. He probably had no interest whatsoever but he repeated the words. He had a noble politeness.

He had three kids, a boy and two girls. I asked how they liked school. "They like school, when there ever is school." I pantomimed eager students raising their hands, but he didn't understand me at first. Apparently, his kids were so good they would never rush to answer—"Don't want to make mistake, and also don't want to brag." I was tickled by this idea of comportment and reported it to Ernst. It did make me think of myself. I had been timid and modest for an American boy, much to the dismay of my family.

Can wasn't at the hotel for a few days, and I asked at the desk if he was sick. "Gone," the day manager said.

"He's okay?"

"Gone," he said.

It was Ernst who told me he'd heard Can was one of those who'd planted a bomb in an ordinary blue and yellow Renault taxi, and it had blown up in front of another hotel and taken out the lobby and part of the bakery next door. "It was a humongous bloody mess," Ernst said. "Lot of people in that lobby."

I knew that lobby, with its mosaic floor. It was a nicer hotel than ours, where visiting brass sometimes stayed. I'd been there for drinks. Can might have killed me, he wanted to kill people like me. My Can.

"Wake up, Dorothy," Ernst said.

It was an old story, but it was fresh to me. I'd had no inkling, of course, what Can believed or how strongly he believed it or that he had any capacity for sacrifice. He seemed so mild and civil and wryly entertained by the world. And Can's cadre had been betrayed by someone else (it did not pay to think what duress led to that betrayal)—that was how Ernst knew the story.

"Can's gone," Ernst said, "as in dead."

Ernst had his own phrasing, different from a soldier's. Not so hideously comic (nothing about crispy critters), cooler and flatter. And he was not about to comfort me.

BUT I WANTED TO BE like Ernst. I wrote home to Kit and to my mother—*Pilots took us for a roller-coaster ride, doing loop-di-loops the other morning. Very interesting, I can tell you!* I leaned on Ernst even more here than at home. An evening with anyone else—the other tech reps or the fat-cat contractors who hung out in the bars—always had its coarseness. At first I'd thought I was going to change in that direction; I wanted vividness, like anyone. But I wasn't a real drinker—some people just aren't—and after a while I didn't want to be out every night, with all the work we had. And I had my ambitions, unformed lump though I was. I'd chosen to be an engineer, a nerd with a slide rule, partly because I didn't like the world of business where showing off was part of the code of conduct. I was sort of interested in being a genius (though I knew I was a dark horse for this category), so that people would respect me and leave me to my own methods. I wanted to be like Ernst; I wanted praise and my own corner, both at once.

We worked very hard, in those weeks. New information kept coming in, data that contradicted itself, and we sat at our desks trying to resolve it. And I saw that I was glad to be indoors, though I had been so dazzled by the streets. The gap-toothed woman who sold pilfered American liquor and toothpaste at her stand, the shoeshine boy with his playful nasal pleading, the old man walking his bicycle loaded with rope bags of melons—they yelled at me to buy from them, to give them money. Why was I there if I was only going to walk along in my towering foreign fatness, my oblivious overfed height? Did I know they were there, did I know where I was, where was my money? I was becoming afraid of all of them. As I had reason to be.

AND WHAT WAS MAKING the planes fuck up? While we were in Saigon, four planes that flew out from Da Nang got shot down over Dak To, where they weren't supposed to be. The officer who told us said, "This can't go on. It can't." And we were the assholes who'd let the pilots go down; gone as in dead. Or captured, which was not pleasant to think about. Why were we so slow, what was the matter with us? I looked at Ernst when they called us in. He shook his head, which meant no good, no good.

We stayed at the office all through the night, trying to make some glimmer of sense out of measurements and charts and maps and whatever we had of radio logs. My high school physics teacher, Mr. Llewellyn, used to say problem-solving was just patience with your own stupidity. Ernst grunted to himself, as he did when he was concentrating. He made the sudden soft sounds people make in their sleep. He was the clearest-brained engineer I'd ever met and he should have been able to *get* this, if anyone could, the buried glitch, the needle in the haystack. It was a human error, it had to be solvable by a human.

WE GOT WORD THE NEXT DAY that they needed to send us to the air base in Da Nang. We had to look at more of the planes. I wrote my mother a long, stupidly chipper letter. Even she, who didn't know much, would recognize Da Nang as a place closer to the DMZ, a name repeated on TV in reports of heavy fighting, heavy losses.

"We're moving to a noisy neighborhood," Ernst said.

"Wasn't this just an office job?" I said. "They didn't mention any extra excursions back at Bydex." We couldn't exactly complain to the soldiers around us, since we were the pampered kittens of the war.

"*Au revoir*, Saigon," I said when we were at the airport.

"See you later, alligator," Ernst said to the city.

———

DA NANG WAS A GOOD-SIZED city too, it turned out, but we weren't really in it. Our new home was on the air base, off a dirt road near an airfield of yellow dust, with a long, low ridge of mountains in the distance. They had bunked us in what looked like a village of beach bungalows, two-story wooden huts lining the road on both sides, a jerry-built stage set.

Ernst came up with a fact while we were carrying our duffels into our rooms. "This airport in Da Nang, if you count everything in it," he said, "has the most traffic of any airport in the world."

"Big vacation spot," I said. "Wildly popular." On a garbage can next to our hootch someone had spray-painted, NOT MY HOME, JUST A PASSING THRU.

But soldiers liked us better here. We were now consultants to the Marines, not a group known for their sweet manners, but they were decent to us in the office where we worked. They had a standing joke about fixing up Ernst with a nymphomaniac nurse, a figure whose tastes for bizarre practices grew with each telling, and they liked to insult me about my wardrobe, had my mother picked it out and could they divvy up my shirts if I got shot? They called us the two brainiacs. Having come this far got us credit. We'd been issued flak jackets and helmets, we weren't just a couple of hot dogs hanging around a hotel pool sipping martinis.

We were not, of course, in the shit with them. We had by this time some inkling of what the shit was. Well, the

whole world knows now, doesn't it, what we made soldiers do. Not that I ever saw any of those villages. Around
us some of the landscape was charred from bombings, and
I was doing my best to help our planes char it—that part
was all right with me. But I got so I hated to see the men
go out from the base. At all hours you could hear overhead
the medevac helicopters bringing back the wounded and
the dead. We sent them in and then we plucked them out.

Ernst and I were working eighteen-hour days. If we
couldn't find anything wrong in the guidance systems,
maybe the bug was in the navigation systems or even in
the control systems that moved the planes around. Ernst,
who had never been one to let go of a problem, would
hardly leave his office even to eat, and he was a big eater.
I got someone to drive me to the settlement of shacks the
Vietnamese had built up west of the base on the road to
the beach. Ernst wasn't much of a gourmet but he liked
the beef noodle soup one woman made, with the green
herbs and the lime juice you threw in as you ate. Their
shantytown was quite something, with its hodgepodge of
boards and patched roofs, its crowing roosters. Someone
had named it Dogpatch, after Li'l Abner's hillbilly town
in the funnies. The soup woman had a sister who sometimes laundered my famous shirts.

I watched Ernst slurping down the noodles at his desk,
and I was glad he had me to look after him. He was probably glad too, in his way. "Thanks for the nourishment,"
he said, which was a wild burst of expressive fervor from
him. And he shared a government chocolate bar with me

for our dessert. We had our comforts, our spots of mellowness. He had bought a cassette recorder at the PX (cassettes were pretty new on the market then), and we listened to a tape of Ella Fitzgerald singing while we worked. The sound was thin and hoarse and miraculous.

THE NEXT MORNING AT SIX, when we got to our office, a lieutenant colonel was waiting outside for us in the misty brightness. "New development," he said. "There could be a reason two smart jerk-offs like you can't find anything." A Vietnamese worker had been located on the airfield where he wasn't supposed to be. He was asleep under one of our planes. Maybe sabotage was the answer here to the big mystery. Maybe monkey business had been going on all along.

I was flooded with relief—that was my first response—it wasn't my fault, it had never been my fault. Those pilots hadn't gone down just because I was an idiot. The lieutenant colonel said we might as well keep working, but they would be questioning this individual and would get back to us with what they learned.

AND THEN FOR A WEEK nobody said a word to us. Ernst kept working as if this new wrinkle hadn't turned up. I thought he just wanted to occupy himself. We heard from the enlisted men around the office that the guy they'd nabbed was the one called Chu Nam, which meant Fifth Uncle. He was supposed to be the soup lady's uncle. Maybe they were all related, we didn't know.

She disappeared too, and you couldn't blame her for making herself scarce. It was a very creepy week. When Ernst and I walked back from the office at night, I jumped at any noise, and the night was full of noises. If that guy had managed to get out on the airfield, anyone could be right next to us. "They always could," Ernst said. He was scornful of my jumpiness. "Keep cool," he said. I was thinking, not for the first time, that Bydex had picked us to send because we were the unmarried ones. I was very lonely. I hadn't known I was that lonely.

By Monday, though we never actually heard anything official, the grapevine gave us as much as we needed. The prisoner had not been cooperative. The lieutenant colonel, who had sent his own good pilots off in those planes, had not been able to get the prisoner to answer and had thrown the man out of a helicopter. The Marine who told us the story made the sort of grim joke Marines made—"He got a free ride back down to his village, express." I started coughing when I heard this— horror was choking me—I didn't know what to do in front of the others. Ernst's eyes had gone blank—I supposed the report fell into a well of darkness Ernst had in him always.

And why were we so fucking shocked? Didn't we know what kind of war this was? We knew now. I was angry that the Marine had told us. You always heard that certain things were kept secret. I had come as a consultant, not to be *in* the war. I was furious with the Marine, while I coughed.

———

WE KEPT WORKING. Ernst liked best to be lost in work, and I wanted to be walled up in that thicket with him. He had devised some new calculations, which we went over together and which suggested a new, purely mechanical solution. Ernst wanted to look inside the plane again. It took two days to get one of the men to take apart the inertial guidance system for him; any personnel who could do that were busy fixing damaged aircraft, not hanging around loose to serve our whims. When some overworked, bare-chested guy in shorts finally showed up, Ernst followed him into the cockpit while I stood outside. I wanted to stand by to shout suggestions, hot though it was in the hangar. I was about to go back to the office just when the two of them climbed out.

"Eureka," Ernst said, flatly and maybe bitterly. In his fingers was a half-corroded screw that had been in the gimbal of a gyroscope, about to cause it to split and throw the whole navigation system off. Simple as that. He held it out to me in disgust. "Cheap crap," he said. "Somebody gave the lowest bid. All the gimbals have these lame-ass screws."

And we were heroes that night—Ernst especially, though I got some of the glory, despite my disclaimers. I supposed I had helped a little. The lieutenant colonel and two other officers took us out to celebrate at a seafood restaurant along the river in downtown Da Nang. We had hardly been off the base before and kept saying how much better the waitresses looked than the jarheads who usually fed us. The murky waters of the Han River glinted outside the windows. We were toasted with bottles of beer and a speech about how no one ever thought two turkeys like us could come up with anything. The thanks were sincere. "A fucking bright spot for a change," the youngest officer said.

"Just doing our jobs," I heard myself say. The two of us were as stiff and remote as they always figured we were.

"The goddamn truth is that Ernst is more of a fucking genius than anyone even *knows*," I said. "If the Marines had any sense, they'd give him a fat, fat bonus for the kind of work he did."

"You got to die to get a bonus," a sergeant said. He was not laughing.

Ernst, who didn't eat seafood, picked at his barbecued beef without looking up. He was in a rage about how someone had cut corners to save money on the screws, how the shoddiness and sloppiness and lying cruddiness of mankind had turned up yet again. He hated the whole armed services for this, everyone at the table.

The lieutenant colonel was discussing the build on one of the waitresses. How much soup would you have to feed her till she grew breasts?

I was thinking that if we had found the trouble earlier, Fifth Uncle would still be alive. What had taken us so long? I couldn't get past that line of thought. I don't know that I ever have.

—

"THEY'LL SEND US HOME NOW," I said to Ernst at the end of the evening, when we were walking to the row of huts where our hootch was. We'd both had a lot of beer.

"Send us what?" he said. His hearing was never perfect.

"A return ticket from Adventureland here," I said.

But my voice was drowned out by a sudden clap of thunder. "Now it's going to rain," I said. "I hate this country."

There were more loud claps, one right after another, flashes of orange light, and a bunch of crackling, whistling noises—what a dope I was—they were the trails of rockets. Not a storm. We were in a fucking rocket attack. Streaks of flame were landing somewhere behind us. I looked back at the burning trees and I ran.

Ernst wasn't running with me. When I turned my head, I saw that he was standing completely still, a dumb civilian ghost in the dark. *Ernst!* I shouted at him, and then I dashed back into the smoking night and grabbed his arm and pulled him with me—*You have to move!* Ahead of us some other men were yelling. He was too heavy to drag, he was much bigger than I was. I wanted to leave him, I didn't want to die helping him. And then he began to run, he seemed to remember how all of a sudden.

I THOUGHT WE WERE okay once we got in our building, which was barricaded with sandbags on one side. Ernst at least knew to put on his flak jacket and helmet right away. His face was clenched and blank. We were supposed to go into the bunker but it seemed a better idea to stay put. I looked around for cover and I pulled a mattress down over us. We stank together under that hood.

"You okay?" I kept saying. "You okay?"

"Fine," he said.

I wondered if the kapok in the mattress was flammable. Every one of my organs was pulsing, thudding under the skin. And the other, unmoving body with me— Ernst's body—heaved in and out to get air. Ernst looked, in his sweating blankness, like a staring animal, like a bear sullenly waiting out its panic.

It unraveled me to see him as he was now. I had never thought of him as pitiable before, though other people did. I couldn't exactly stand it.

"You comfortable?" I said. I was trying to make a joke.

"Fine," he said.

People around us died all the time—I didn't know why I'd thought we were any safer. I felt like a fool, like the most naïve person in the country. I was a fool in a hole with a bear.

"If we stay here long enough," I said, "we'll be around for Christmas when Bob Hope comes to visit."

Ernst wasn't doing any smiling yet.

"Maybe Ella's coming. You think she would?"

I wasn't glad to be the one asking these questions. Why wasn't Ernst asking me? Who in the whole world did I have to lean on? Soldiers had each other in a war, but I didn't have shit.

He shook his head. His helmet nudged the mattress.

"Does she have views about the war? You know anything about her views?"

I didn't give a fuck about Ella's politics, if she had any, and the USO always had girlie shows anyway, not middle-aged black singers with glasses.

"Did she have a contract dispute with Verve?" I said. "I thought her manager owned it. Why did she leave them?"

The noises outside had stopped. We sat waiting for more.

"After ten years with one record company," I said.

I was talking to myself. What did I expect? I was the one who knew not to expect Ernst to be different.

"I hate Capitol," I said. "Why she'd go to Capitol?"

How long had it been quiet? I didn't trust the quiet.

"Money," he said.

It was a small victory for me when I heard his voice. Training my attention on Ernst, trying to bore a hole in his wall of silence, took me out of myself just a bit and gave me some relief. It occurred to me that Ernst never felt that kind of relief. Not ever.

The noise of firing had been worst to the east of us, on the other side of the airfield. "You know Ella was only twenty when she recorded 'A-Tisket, A-Tasket'?" I said. I pulled the mattress off of us—we were going to suffocate if we didn't get blown up.

"Twenty is young," I said. Ernst, in his helmet and vest, unfolded himself and stood up. Then he was walking toward his own room.

"Leaving so soon?" I said. "Leaving me to my own post here?"

He murmured, "Good night," with his back turned. I was the one who knew not to expect him to be different. But I was angry at him for not being more human. Just this once, this time of all times, couldn't he have fucking managed it?

EARLY THE NEXT MORNING, when the first haze of light was showing through the window, I heard Ernst talking, through the wall. Either he was talking to himself or he was praying. Anything was possible. ". . . *fine*," he said. There was a whir behind him. "*It's pretty hot and the rainy season is starting, which doesn't really cool things off.*" He was making a tape. "*The food is not too bad. I haven't been writing so I decided to send a tape. Maybe Susan has a cassette recorder or you can buy one. We can send tapes back and forth. Last night we had to get our protective gear out because there was a rocket attack in our area. You have the address. Signing off now. Bye.*"

He probably hadn't written to his family in years. One of the little-known facts about him was that he had trouble writing—he was a terrible speller and his sentences were always short and childish. He must have been shaken to the bone, to send them a tape now. His family would be glad and scared to get the tape.

—

I DIDN'T THINK we were going to be there long enough for anyone to answer him, but they kept us in Da Nang another three weeks. The roads on the base turned to mud when it rained, and I slipped into a crater left by a rocket and I banged up my leg—the last straw, I thought. And Ernst and I were arguing every night, when we were alone, about the war. I hadn't actually stopped being afraid of Communists—no, I was more afraid, I was properly scared of almost everything now—but I'd stopped seeing the point, I thought the point had been lost. At great, great cost. I said we were spreading evil instead of containing it. "What does *that* mean?" Ernst said. He talked about the Red Chinese and the Soviet Russians, did I know how many people Stalin had killed in the gulags? Seven million disappeared in just four years of the purges. "What does that have to do with it?" I said. We went around and around. He held (I knew) to his principles. Nothing I said about Fifth Uncle softened him. He said I was too emotional. It was hard to argue with someone who ruled out the claims of feelings. He must have thought he'd won every time.

WHEN ERNST GOT an envelope from his parents, he waited until night to play the tape, and I lay in my bunk and listened as the voices came through the wall. *Wonderful surprise to hear from you*, his mother said. *Very glad you're enjoying your work*, his father said. *The dog is getting so fat,* his sister said. You could hear they were very careful around him.

Every time I asked Ernst if he'd answered them yet, he shook his head, but he played the tape night after night. Through the flimsy wall, I got so I recognized the sequence of their voices, the different pitches in order.

BEFORE WE WENT BACK to the States, we got flown to Bangkok for two weeks of R&R. We didn't know whose idea that was, but we landed in Thailand in a state of amazement. What a palmy, good-natured city it seemed to us. The streets were every bit as hot and fetid as Vietnam, maybe hotter, but the crowds seemed wonderfully gentle and sunny. Nobody hated us, as far as we could tell. I couldn't get over it. It made me feel light and crazy just to walk around.

Our hotel had a small garden in the courtyard, and Ernst liked to sit out and drink the sweet Thai coffee they made with condensed milk. He could knock off a few hours just reading the *Bangkok Post* and the *Herald Tribune*. He wasn't up for photographing any gilt-encrusted temples or schoolchildren in uniforms—"No new data," he said—but I was restless, I wanted to wander.

It was all quite dreamlike. I got lost in the streets, I rode a ferry on the river, I fed myself on snacks of grilled bananas and seared noodles. On the third day, my leg that I'd gashed and scraped falling into a rocket crater in Da Nang began to throb and feel swollen, and I had the nasty sense that Vietnam was still claiming me. Was I a little feverish? Maybe I was. I sat down on a bench in Lumphini Park and drew up my pants leg. There was an old gauze bandage on my shin, and when I lifted a corner, the skin was oozing and gave out an odor. Why did I think I could forget the place that fast?

I was so interested in my revolting little wound that I didn't see the two youngish Thai women coming toward my bench until they called out, "You all right? We don't think you all right." I was embarrassed to be caught baring my hairy Western leg; my manners were worse here. "You hurting?" one of the women said. They did not look like hookers—they were dressed more like office workers, in crisp little blouses and narrow skirts.

"We nurses," one said. "Is okay we look? We don't hurt you."

They lifted the bandage and clucked and muttered—what a mess I was. They were quite sure that they should take me back to the hospital they had just left. "No trouble," they said. "No problem." I rode in an open-sided tuk-tuk next to their smooth-skinned, smiling selves. One of them was Bua, a girl who'd come down from the north to study here, and the other was Toon, who lived on Thanon Wisut Kasat with her family and who later became my wife.

ON THE RIDE to the hospital, when I got a better look at Toon, I was thinking what a very fine day I was having. I thought the two women were going to just drop me off at the hospital, but I'd at least have the imprint of Toon to keep, like a good wish for my future relationships in the States. *Though I did but see her passing by, / Still I love her till I die.* We'd sung that in school. I had the traveler's idea that something fleeting was blessing me.

IT WAS MORE complicated than that. My family thought I was nuts when I came home to America just to quit my job and turn around and go back to Bangkok. They thought that the war had done something to me, which it had. Hadn't my nice girlfriend Kit always tried to get me to settle down, but I was Mr. Too-Cool, Mr. Don't-Fence-Me-In? But now I wanted to nest.

It was true that Vietnam moved me toward Toon. Constant fear can make you see the real drawbacks to going through life alone. Though I wouldn't say Ernst especially took that lesson from it. He said, "If that's what you want," when I told him about my engagement, and he thought well of Toon too.

IT HASN'T ALL BEEN an idyll, of course, my marriage and my life on another continent. It's had its hills and valleys. My job difficulties have strained us and we've had problems with our son. During one of my worst times, I was seeing a therapist, a fairly smart guy from Chicago, who happened to say I was an unusually private person, which made me wonder if I was like Ernst after all. I spent some time explaining Ernst to the therapist (on my nickel) and he told me that, as far as he could tell, Ernst sounded like someone with Asperger's syndrome. A neurobiological disorder—like having a pinch of autism. Many people probably had it. "Well," I said, "there are all sorts of ways of being human, aren't there?" I wondered how Ernst would have felt about his personality having a material cause—perhaps he would have been affronted, though he did prefer the measurable world.

THERE ARE PEOPLE who say Einstein had Asperger's. I'm not sure I believe in geniuses anymore—in a superspecies of mental giants—but I think Ernst was probably brilliant. In our last days in Vietnam, we had to file reports about the defective screws (God knows what became of these reports), and Ernst wrote a few lines of tirade in capital letters against the fraud of the manufacturers. LETHAL CHEAPNESS. GREED KILLS. Bydex, who'd bought the screws for cheap, would not have been pleased. What a pure, unsullied life Ernst led, in his way.

I HAD A VERY NICE wedding in Bangkok, not big but flowery and pretty, and I sent a set of photos to Ernst, who was back at Bydex in Phoenix. I don't know if he ever received them, since he didn't send any word back. I picked the ones in which Toon looked especially wonderful and I didn't look too geeky. He didn't envy me, I knew that, but I wanted him to see.

Behold the giddy American, I wrote. What is that sucker doing? Ernst must have thought when he looked at them, at me surrounded by the smiling strangers who were my in-laws, by the unheard lilt and spit of all of them talking. I imagined him shaking his head over the smeary mess of a future I insisted on wanting. How stubborn he was. Always when I thought of him a kind of envy spread through me. In spite of everything, it just did.

II.

It surprised everyone, including me, that I was in such a hurry to marry Toon. My family in Florida couldn't understand why I was heading back to Southeast Asia, when anyone who'd been to Vietnam wanted to get the hell out of that part of the world. I had some trouble explaining that Thailand, site of rest and recovery, was to me the opposite of Vietnam. "It's *nice* there," I said. They didn't get it. And Toon didn't want to leave her home. My family thought she'd be dying to move to the U.S., but she wasn't. She had her own family.

Marrying her was a bold move on my part, and I was never what anyone would call a bold man. But the months in Vietnam put enough fear into me to make everything else small potatoes. So I was going to live in Bangkok and I didn't speak a word of Thai, so what? So I was swearing to live forever with someone I hardly knew, why not? Leftover horror made me bolder.

What did Toon think? She had reason to be wary of Americans, but she was a nurse, a steady girl. She'd seen danger and I wasn't it. She probably thought of me as some sort of lovable doofus. And then I was bleeding love for her, she could tell that early on. I was a sodden mess of leaking devotion. How had that happened to a nerd like me?

I asked myself that question every day, in Bangkok after I met her and the months I was back in the States and the strained and giddy days after I returned. She wasn't the only female I'd ever met—what was it that unsprung me? She was so calm and kind and mild that first afternoon, in the face of my smelly, festering wound and the whole sweating bulk of me. Perhaps any pretty nurse might have been the same, but actually I don't think so. "No trouble," she kept saying, though we had to wait hours in the hospital till some doctor finally released a cache of antibiotics. Bua went home. Toon was still shrugging and smiling. *Soon soon.* I felt that she could wait for days and it would not humiliate her.

It made me patient just to be with her, and when I went back that night to the hotel, I hardly knew how to be next to the exasperated grunts and sporadic mumbles that were Ernst. How had I stood it before? Hanging around with him that night, I was in exile from enchantment, pissed off, carrying my desire like a precious souvenir. When I went to find Toon the next day, I didn't care how pathetic I was.

SOMETIMES YOU HAVE ideas based on no information, and they're still right. Toon was one of those ideas. When I turned up again, she laughed softly at the sight of me.

"Hello, Mr. Toby." She couldn't talk at the hospital, but she let me come back at her break. "You eat a good Thai lunch," she said, "you never want to leave my city." We ate at a street stall and she tricked me into swallowing a hot chile, an ancient bit of slapstick that caught me off guard because she was so gentle. I had never flirted with an Asian woman who wasn't a hooker, and it made me shy, which (lucky me) was endearing.

So I became her bumbling boyish admirer, haunting her workplace, nodding at the table of her incomprehensible family. I tried to bring her gifts—paperbacks in Thai (she was a great reader) whose covers I liked, a ghost story and a soupy romance. Her own taste (I learned) was higher, but she had a soft heart and my eagerness got to her. But any touching, any kissing, had to be hidden—in a movie theater, in a car in a parking garage—and I'd go home afterward to my adult fevers, my lustful private worship of the memory of Toon. Only when I proposed did she find her way to my room at the hotel, and the astounding, sly presentation of her bared and unfolded self, the heat of her utter interest, broke me open entirely. She hummed a contented little tune as we lay in bed afterward—what a funny, peeping singer she was—and I was the one knocked out, cut to ribbons by too much sweetness.

I had to leave the next day and I could hardly remember which was my luggage or how to get in line to get on a plane. And once I was home in Florida I could not really keep track of what anyone said. Key West and Bangkok both felt like dreams to me, faded films playing exclusively in my own head. When I telephoned Thailand in the middle of the American night, Toon would say, "Toby, you okay, yes?" and I'd say, "You're there?" in idiot relief at the sound of her voice.

Maybe neither of us really thought I'd come back, but little by little, Toon brought me along. The ever-clearer outlines of plans entered our expensive conversations. How else could I have married? I had no clue really how to live with another person. Toon let me know what I was supposed to do.

It was not hard either. I had to get a job—even I knew that—and after a bunch of ragged interviews in Atlanta, I found an unexciting gig with an American soda company's office in Bangkok. It paid fine—most things paid fine for Americans in Thailand—and I was only just starting to brag about this to my Florida friends when Toon found us an apartment. Not just us, I should say. I would have lived anywhere, but this was near where she'd always lived, in an unpicturesque part of the old city, and it was big enough for her mother to have her own room and her younger sister too.

SO I HAD ROOMMATES when I first settled in, a smiling audience who formed a fond tittering garland to my happiness. Even without language I could tell her family traded little rowdy female jokes about us newlyweds. Toon would giggle and I'd pretend to preen—we were one long charade of silent-movie overacting, and I didn't mind it either.

Sometimes an aunt and uncle showed up, and the sister moved into the mother's room. I liked the uncle. He would sit with me at night while Toon was chatting in Thai with her mother and aunt. Even without much English, he taught me a basic card game called Pok Deng and he poured me shots of Sang Som (he called it whiskey but Toon said it was rum). My efforts in the game made him strike his head in comic defeat or move his hand like a snake when he was being clever himself. It was a game that rested on luck but we pretended otherwise. I looked forward to our matches at the end of a long day. Uncle Lek would glint at me in sly amusement, old rogue that he was. He won a few baht off me most nights.

Whose life was I in? Where was I? When Toon's mother said good night and the others slipped away, Toon would bring out little squares of coconut candy for the two of us to eat, and then we'd go off to our room, whispering about the day's events while we took off our clothes, and then, as if it were the most ordinary thing in the world, Toon would fold back the top sheet for us and I'd be a man in bed with his wife. I couldn't get over it, that this had been given to me. We had simple, ardent sex—neither of us was very schooled, the sheer elemental friction still stunned us—and then we lay curled around each other, bodies washed up from a whirlpool. We said tender things in both languages, and I went to sleep grateful.

I WROTE TO ERNST at Christmas: *Living well here—everything is cheap—and a whole squadron of Thai relatives is catering to my every little whim. Lord of the manor! Room for one more if you ever want to visit.*

BUT I DIDN'T LIKE my work. I was reviewing the systems that operated the machinery in the bottling plants, to make sure things were running properly and see if any procedures needed to be redesigned. I should say I was not really qualified to do this, but no one else was either. They kept wanting me to go out into the field and look at more bottling places.

"Like Dickens," I told my secretary, a Miss Brandt from Chicago. "He worked in a bootblack bottling factory when he was a child. A terrible place."

"That was a long time ago," she said. At least she knew who Dickens was. I wasn't going to any factories. Even if they were good, for Asia, I knew they had things in them I didn't want to see. Practices I didn't want to put my name to, as it were. Word spread that I was jumpy and odd from being in Vietnam.

Bydex had been easier. A place full of engineers is used to pale, cranky, obsessed guys who won't leave their desks. Here I was meant to tell breezy stories at lunch and parade my status, and I had no gift for this at all. But I was glad for the fat salary. Toon had stopped working after the wedding—I thought this was only right—and her sister still had schooling to be paid for and her mother needed an operation on her foot and some cousin was always wanting a handout.

And I was only in my mid-twenties. Every so often my

mother wrote to me from Florida, *I certainly hope your many in-laws do not just think of you as Mr. Moneybags,* or *I admire your generosity, which is not what everyone would do.* Already my mother seemed to be from another part of the planet, mingy and sour and sorely ignorant of basics. Every night I came home to my cocoon of allegiances, my web of favors and fondness. I liked my household.

AT CHRISTMASTIME, I brought Toon to the office party. "Haven't *you* adapted well?" my secretary said to me. She and a lot of the others thought I'd married a bar girl from Patpong, though Toon was wearing a staid little suit.

"Very sharp cookie," a vice president said to me after having the mildest of conversations with Toon.

Everyone assumed, at the least, that she'd married me for my money. Nobody thought this was insulting to me either. They were wrong about my marriage, which was a contract of true feeling. As it happened, Toon didn't care all that much about money and was in fact much more religious than I'd known at first.

Toon was pleasant to all and pretended to not quite follow the boorish jocularity or to care if some of the wives didn't talk to her. She was silkier than I'd seen her be. You could not have told, from the passing flashes of her shy smile, how irritating some people's questions were. It reminded me that Thailand, as all Toon's relatives liked to tell me, was the only Southeast Asian nation never colonized by the West. And why was this? "Too smart, too slippery," Toon's mother said.

Slippery was actually a recognized historical theory. A talent for compromise, a willingness to yield just the needed amount, and an avoidance of open conflict had kept the Siamese from takeover. They gave the English a nice trade treaty in 1826 and nobody needed to conquer them. The British decimated the teak forests and took out a lot of tin. But the Siamese king stayed the king.

Sometimes I thought of this theory around Toon, forthright though she generally was. We hardly quarreled—she was so gentle no opposition flared in me—and she had a dispiriting way of shrinking from me if I was being disagreeable. This was her method with the group at the office party. That night in our room she said, "Those people not worth much but could be worse."

EVERY MORNING, while I got dressed, I'd watch Toon on her knees in front of a small brass image of the Buddha, resting on his dark wood altar. It always startled me to see her touch her forehead to the floor, muttering whatever she muttered. In those moments she was sheathed in aloneness and would not have answered had I spoken. I wasn't jealous of the Buddha, but it sometimes surprised me that I was allowed to watch her. How proficient she was at this routine that was none of my business. Afterward she'd give me a reassuring smile, more polite than I needed.

MY JOB WAS SO EASY I could slip out for long lunches and catch the temple dancers at the Erawan monument or take the ferry a few stops along the river. Somebody spread a rumor that I was going to Patpong, whose girlie bars were not even open at that hour. My having been in Vietnam got this idea going. One of the higher-ups decided I was goofing off and put me on new projects any dumb clerk could do in a second. My days became hours of enraging, ennervating boredom. What bothered me was the way I handled it, attending to every miserable detail, joshing merrily with the creep who was my overseer. Probably nobody liked me better for it either.

"Someone who can't even read thinks he's *reviewing* my figures," I complained to Toon. "I'm surrounded by morons."

It had not been like this in Vietnam, where Ernst and I went about our work with full independence, with everyone making way for our critically needed brains. I could not believe I was waxing nostalgic over Vietnam. And if I liked working for the military so much I could still do it. There were seven American bases by now in Thailand, with more than a few civilian engineers attached to them.

But I didn't want to be in the war. In the last month, when Ernst and I were just hanging around waiting to go home, I'd let myself slip over into being appalled. I didn't have to keep it a secret either; there were plenty of soldiers who not only hated the war—everyone did—but thought it was the world's ugliest mistake, a what-the-fuck-are-we-doing-here bloodbath from hell. Even then there was a right and a left among the soldiers.

Ernst and I had shredded our friendship on this question. Well, it was more than a question, wasn't it? At work, they called me Toby Fonda because of my opinions. At home, my Thai relatives were too polite to speak about the war in front of me, except for Toon, who really was a good Buddhist and shuddered at all violence, and Uncle Lek, who believed in necessary force, despised Communists, and liked to goad everybody in his twinkling way.

ONE MORNING, my secretary, Miss Brandt, was sarcastic about my bad handwriting, which made me think she'd heard I was out of favor. At home I was sullen. Uncle Lek tried to jolly me with wisecracks, and I let him pour me some sustaining shots of liquor. Perhaps I would become one of those men who idled away his nights in masculine joking and cozy alcoholic distraction.

So we had our rounds of Pok Deng—two or three cards were dealt, and the closest total to nine won—it was the simplest of games, and I thought of how men all over the world played forms of this with stones or bones or coins. Lek said I was clever when I won. "Me," he said, "I'm not good with money." When he had a store, everyone stole from him. Now he still had debts. Many debts, he needed a loan. Maybe from me? When I didn't answer, he said in English, *Thirty thousand baht*. Perhaps he'd gotten a translation in advance.

This was a substantial amount he wanted, more than we spent in half a year. I didn't understand most of what he said next, a long wheedling list of all he needed. I don't have any friends, I thought. He's not my friend.

When I told him I would have to think about it, something strange happened to his jaw—it jutted out in amazement, then it lowered in cringing hatred. He got up and went to his room. The room he used in my house.

I KNEW, EVEN as I argued with Toon, that I had no choice but to pay and that my balking was coarse and unforgivable. "Talking like child, I think," she said to me. "Greedy for just you." Toon wept because I didn't understand something so obvious it could never be explained. I had never heard her cry before, and it was a painful shock to hear that helpless, mewling sound come out of her. What had I done to her? I would always be in the wrong, as long as I had money in my wallet.

"What do you *want* from me?" I said.

"No good to tell you," she said. "You don't listen. Ever."

I lay that night next to a cold and shallow Asian woman who had once been my sweet wife. She breathed her alien puffs of air, while I sweated my smells in the sheets. I could not imagine how the two of us had come to dwell in indecent proximity in the same house.

I was in a house of strangers and I would never get out, they would weave themselves around me and hold me down. Ernst would have laughed his ass off to see me. I was ashamed before the thought of Ernst. I might have learned from him and I hadn't.

———

AND I HAD TO get up early the next morning to go visit a bottling factory in the south. They sent a driver at dawn to take a few of us down there, along a highway that was ugly at first and then edged with depths of beckoning palms. The factory wasn't any worse than I had expected, except for the shrieking loudness of the machines and the tiny-bodied youth of some of the workers, their arms moving in pace with the conveyer belt's shrieks. We walked through the noise, sweating in our suits. What a big fat foreigner I was. I hated my size, my feeble friendly words in Thai, my terrified heartiness.

Nobody was interested in my questions about safety measures, and they took us for dinner in our hotel, a pink stucco hulk that had once been a tin miner's mansion. The next morning when I woke up, I noticed I really, really didn't want to go home, and I told them all I was sick as a dog—never should have had that catfish curry—and needed to rest, would take the train back later.

I SAT OUT ON the balcony of my hotel room, looking down at the town, with its vendors selling fruit and sweet drinks and its stores open to the street, and I was unspeakably glad to be alone. What would Toon's life have been if she'd never met me? She'd had one sweetheart before me, a doctor who went around performing eye operations on rural kids. A far nobler profession than being a corporate stooge, and Toon probably thought so too. He'd ditched her for another girl, and maybe I was her rebound choice, the splotchy-skinned, doltish American. Perhaps she was always making the best of it, with me.

So I thought to myself, riding the rinky-dink local bus to the national park that was not very far away at all, and why hadn't I been to the countryside here, what sort of hemmed-in existence did I have? All along the winding road was lush forest, clusters of trees with unfamiliar shapes.

When the bus got to the park, I could see that the hiking paths were muddy grooves cut through thickets of shrub and cascading branches. The silt was too slippery under my office shoes. What I wanted anyway was to take a boat out on the lake. I had always lived near water. A boy with a face like a sleepy cat rented me a canoe.

I had the lake to myself, and the water was a pearly green-blue with a faint mist hovering above it. On the banks were palm trees sticking up above a brushy grassland, and beyond the farther shore was a ridge of limestone peaks. The current was mild, I might have been paddling in a bathtub. I saw something move on the shore—somebody's dog? It was a monkey—there were several monkeys, gray-brown and lightly angular—walking on all fours, loping, chasing each other into a grove. This glimpse excited me, and I thought how much more clearly I saw things when no one was with me to block the beam of my best attention. I moved the canoe very slowly, listening to bird cries and a birdlike sound that was probably the monkeys.

Later I paddled out to a dead tree in the middle of the

lake, and, like a boy, I tied the boat to a stubbed branch and climbed the tree to look out, king of the hill. I almost fell in when I was getting back in the boat, and a burning panic went through me, but if there were crocodiles or snakes, I didn't see them. And then I paddled back while the light was still strong, and the lake had turned glassy in the glare.

When I brought the canoe back, I bought a postcard. It showed my lake, or one like it, with a blurry but unmistakably striped tiger swimming in it. Tigers could swim? I wrote to Ernst: *Who's afraid of the jungle? Behold my bathing buddy—he's a splasher. Your intrepid pal, Toby.*

IT WAS LATE IN the afternoon when the bus took me back to the hotel. I sat on the balcony, eating fish cakes with cucumber and hearing the music someone next door was playing on the radio. A station was playing Thai pop and then a familiar American tune came on—a singer with a deep, scratchy voice was oh-babying his woman to please come back, he needed her so bad. I'd listened to songs like this all my life. Love and more love; you'd think no one in the world did anything but yearn or fuck or swoon or pine every single hour. I knew all the words too, but I had lost my understanding, all at once, of why this was the only version of a full life.

What about monks? What about those stories I read as a boy featuring solitary genius inventors, working away at their crazy later-famous tasks, uninterrupted by plaguey human contact? What about the Ernsts of this world?

It did occur to me that I could get a job in the park. I didn't have to go back to Bangkok. They always needed someone who could do what I could do. I was not an engineer who knew about roads or bridges or water systems, but I could become one. I could learn more Thai. There would be years of free time to study the innumerable species of birds and monkeys and snakes. To know a mere fraction of what went on in that forest of palms and rattans and grasses would be a rich existence. I fell asleep in my chair on the pure white wing of this ambition.

WHEN I WOKE it was night, and when I stood up, one of my legs was swollen and hot, painful to stand on. I had the crazy idea that it was my old wound from Vietnam, which had long since healed. But it looked more like some kind of nasty insect bite. I went down to the hotel desk to see if they had any magic Thai medicine for it.

The boy at the desk was asleep with his head on his folded arms. "Hello!" I said. "Hey! *Sawatdee krap!*" No shouting woke him, and I tapped him on the back of the head, really quite gently. He looked up in alarm, finally— what was the matter with me? I knew never to touch any Thai on the head, not even a child, it was a sacred part of the body. I said I was sorry, in Thai, I could not think what else to say while he muttered at me. I had never heard a stranger angry here. I tried in both languages to

ask for what I wanted. I bared my leg and pointed. He had
no idea what I meant and gestured at me to keep my voice
down. I realized what an imbecile I was making of myself
and how poorly I managed in this country, how complicated it was really.

When I went back to the room, I missed America so
badly I couldn't remember why I had wanted to leave it in
the first place. I would just go home now. Back to
Florida. That was what I would do. If my leg didn't fall
off first. The simplest things were too ridiculously intricate here. Outsiders thought it was so easy but it wasn't.
My mistake had been to leave home to get married.

HOURS LATER, the sound of a car horn outside jolted me
awake. I was in a pitch-dark chamber, lying on the bed-
covers with a hard-on, thinking of Toon. Her voice with
its soft Thai lisp was in my head, the oval of her chin was
hovering over me. I was a miserable creature, a sad hairy
carcass of longing, deprived of Toon. In the damp heat of
that hotel room, I shivered with loneliness. How could I
go on this way? I couldn't. I was a fool: the oldest song in
the world.

I went down to the lobby to see if anyone knew
when the next train was. When the clerk finally found
a schedule, my phone call to Bangkok had to be on
reverse charges, and I kept shouting my name over the
reception desk telephone so that Lek, who answered,
would understand and not hang up. "Please, no shouting," he said.

TOON DIDN'T KNOW what to make of my rampant effusiveness once I was home, my constant need to clasp her to me when we were alone (I was Thai enough not to do it in front of the others). But I thought she was glad of it. When I'd slip up behind her and cross my arms around her waist, she'd dimple and laugh. In my overflow of happiness, I called her my sweetheart, my bird, my angel, my perfect girl, and then she shrugged and made a face: too much. "Okay, Toby, okay." She didn't mind any of it, but she took me with a grain of salt. For all her gentleness, she was very practical, my Toon.

It was a good time for us. And I wasted no time in giving the cash to Uncle Lek. I saw that I was forever tied to him, whatever my passing opinions; we were knotted into the same net. And every Thai knows the Buddha considered generosity first among perfections, so I gained a little merit for my next life, which it surely needed. Another positive effect of my payment was that Lek and his wife moved out. Toon's sister Supa was back in her own room when I came home one night.

At my job, I wrote a memo about the bottling plant I'd seen and how shorter work hours and more breaks were actually safety factors that would augment profits. Fat chance of anyone rushing out to follow suggestions from some newcomer punk with a touchy conscience. I came home at night tired and stupefied, sorry at times that Lek wasn't around for booze and cards. "Too much work," Toon's mother said.

I thought she meant me but she meant Lek. The old buzzard had not only paid off his debts, he'd set up another store, selling silk ties in the lobby of a hotel. I tried to ask Toon's mother how he managed that so fast. "Doing very well," Toon's mother said.

TOON SAID THE HOTEL looked like a giant lace doily but the rest of the family loved it. For a country that was proud of never falling to a foreign empire, Thailand did love its own royal charm. They took me one Saturday to visit its soaring spaces, which were really very tasteful— whitewashed colonnades and spectacular greenery. Lek's glassy alcove had its goods sinuously on display, the ties rippling with a soft metallic glow. Lek had a sheen now too, in his creamy white shirt and a very good haircut.

And he was thrilled when our paths crossed the hotel manager in the lobby. As Lek introduced me, this blue-eyed *farang* who was his nephew, he managed to suggest, in his joking way, that I was the fattest of fat cats, the world's most modest millionaire. And I felt quite happy then too, returning the manager's subtle bow of a *wai* with a little nod, a foreigner at his ease in the country. Toon thought she might be pregnant, she was surer every day. My adult life was spangled with good fortune. "This is such a very well-run hotel," I told the manager. In Thai—my Thai was better now. It was not like me but I oozed graciousness.

Lek showed up a week later at our place with a box of

expensive napoleons from the hotel bakery, exotic treats. Toon, who really was pregnant, ate hers with such abandon she came near to choking when Lek kept saying he thought her husband had already filled her to the brim with enough sweets, hadn't he? Her mother got a little bawdy too, and the bashful sister couldn't stop laughing.

WHEN I WENT TO WORK the next morning, my supervisor called me in for a "long-overdue" talk about what a major disappointment I was as an engineer. "You're nowhere near as smart as you think you are," he said. I was given a month's notice. I stared when he told me, like the boob they thought I was.

The timing could not have been worse. We had a baby on the way. The money to Lek had drained the reserves from our savings. When I told Toon, she said, "Was a surprise?"

"It sure as fuck was," I said. Her features were pinched in a stiff and tender look that I suddenly realized was pity. She had a husband who was a sap, whose flapdoodle overestimation of his genius had made him blind. It wasn't the first time I'd seen that expression on her face either. How did she live with me, then, if that was what she felt? That Toon, of all people, had to keep up a disguise—had to lie to live with me—made me think Ernst had been right about the corrupt nature of all love.

"Lots of better jobs in the world," Toon said.

I did not do well at the few interviews I had. The Bangok I moved in wasn't that big, and wherever I went, people knew I'd been fired, was married to a Thai, and had been in Vietnam. I could feel, from the questions, a fear that I was a loose cannon, a wimp who'd gotten sour from what he'd seen in combat (though I tried to tell them I had not been in combat). I'd been heard to say inflamed and bitter things about the bombing of Cambodia. I seemed to trust no one, how could I work for anyone?

I'D BEEN OUT of work for six months—watching Toon change shape, ranting about why Lek couldn't pay back a single baht, asking Toon over and over why she wouldn't think for a second about moving to the U.S.—when Lek showed up saying he had a job for me. At the hotel: I could help book day tours for Westerners. He gleamed with officious pleasure to be offering this favor.

I was an engineer—what the fuck was he saying? The two of us were alone at the table with our shots of Sang Som. *I had a fucking degree in engineering.* I wanted to throw the table at Lek, like an insulted cowboy in a western. It occurred to me, not for the first time, that if I disappeared altogether, no one could do much about it. I could slip out of this dream. Bangkok could turn back into a cloud of smoke along a ribbon of river, seen from the air. No one back in the States would blame me either. I thought this long enough to calm myself, to keep a decent coolness in front of Lek. I kept cool. I asked him what he thought they were paying for this job.

———

SO I WORKED AT the hotel, sending tourists on guided jaunts to the Imperial Palace and the Snake Farm and the ruins of Ayutthaya. The work did not pay well and we had to move to a smaller place farther on the outskirts, in Pravet, and I wasn't all that good with people, especially people whose peevish needs I had to cater to, but it was okay, after I got over being mortified. Toon's mother was always saying how lucky we were to have Lek to help.

Toon helped me through the first weeks. Her own comfort was reading the spiritual biography of a famous monk—books like this sold in the thousands and Toon actually liked them—and she'd translate bits of it to me. I was dazed enough so that this was welcome. She began with a report of how in his younger days the monk's mind would shoot out to the sky or go down to the earth when he was meditating and it was tough work for him to force it to reenter his body. So then I started asking her, "What's your monk guy doing lately?" Ajahn Mun lived three years in a cave, learning to master fear; he meditated away a painful, deadly illness and he shamed a huge black murderous spirit into behaving well. These accounts soothed me, for reasons I didn't fully understand. They were lessons in fortitude, of course, but even more than that they were examples of a stream of clear water outside the meretricious swamp I mucked around in. Ajahn Mun did not care at all who was rude to me or how much I earned. My engineering degree meant fuck-all to him too. He was elsewhere; there was an elsewhere.

I WAS SCARED OUT of my wits when my son was born. Propped up on pillows in her hospital bed, Toon had a swollen, melted face and eyes like black pits—she looked like a woman who'd been tortured, which she was, and the baby was too small to be a human. What had we done? I stood wincing in panic, but because of Toon's monk it occurred to me to try to beat down the roiling waves of fear, to fling myself against them, which I perhaps would not have done otherwise. It seemed now like a thing a person did.

Once we got him home, our son was surrounded by doting females. I could not keep my eyes from his face as he yowled or gurgled his opinions. How had a separate being just grown out of nothing like that? My son the globule of consciousness. I tried to imagine what constituted *thought* for him. What was he puzzling over, when his eyes were unfocused and he frowned at air? On the baby's one-month birthday, I sent a photo to Ernst: *See the good work I've done converting energy to matter.*

We named the baby Buell, for my father, and I had everyone call him Billy. He was a poky, contemplative little kid, absorbed in his own investigations. Our rooms didn't have much sound insulation, and wherever I went, I'd hear the others cooing and clicking and clapping to get a response out of him. He and I had a different rapport;

he'd cozy up and fall asleep in my lap because I was good at staying still. We had an excellent understanding.

I was happy with my boy, but there was too much noise, too much coming and going and chattering and crying around me, except when Billy was sleeping. I had not known the apartment would be so crowded, so noisy. I bought us a decent stereo and I'd sit in the bedroom with the headphones on, listening to Bud Powell or Ella Fitzgerald, and for a while I sort of liked Jefferson Airplane. I did what anyone asked, but I was with people all the livelong day and I didn't have much use for them by the time I got home.

I lived in a city where a student demonstration was crushed so brutally the police left hundreds dead on a college campus. Toon and her family talked on and on about it, scared and wary and too fast for me to follow, night after night—after the crackdown, a leftist cousin slipped away to a northern province—but I stayed out of it. I stayed tuned in to my music.

I believed (or wanted to believe) that Toon was not going to leave me as long as I didn't treat her badly. She had other intimates around her, she could let me be. Sharp and modern as she was, the old system served her. I floated on my own pond of separate sound, fogged in with secret noise. I did my best to be alone without leaving. In the cool of the evenings, I tried to make my own Walden. I had to.

Ernst would have scoffed at these strategies I devised,

Toby the goon with headphones. My home life and my work life too would have seemed like enslavements to him, traps that had snapped around me. We could have used more money, and Toon talked about going back to work, but I wanted her to wait until Billy was in school. He was just about to start when Toon got pregnant again. She was really very excited, and Billy was beside himself.

I WAS THINKING about Billy, how I would describe everything so he could remember, when I walked into the hospital room this time. Toon was holding the baby and telling me we had a girl, in a barely audible voice. "Hello, hello, girl," I said in English. I stroked her tiny shoulder, and when she moved her small, dimpled arm, I saw there was no hand at the end of it, just a ruddy knob of skin over the bone.

"She's fine," Toon said, in that peeping whisper. "Just one hand only not there. Nothing else wrong. Don't worry, Toby."

"Agent Orange," I said.

It was a stupid thing to say at that moment. Later I was very sorry I hadn't said how beautiful my daughter was— she had a sweet fat chin and a wispy cap of dark hair—or asked Toon how she felt or made a joke about how we'd have to convince Billy a sister was what he wanted. I was scared the hand wasn't all that was unformed or missing. How could they know what was inside her? I did remember to tell Toon I couldn't wait to get them both home. I did say that at least.

THE WAR HAD ALREADY been over for a couple of years, but word was out long since about Agent Orange. No one had sprayed it on me. But I'd hung out on airfields with planes that did the spraying, I'd been not all that many miles from the "mist drift," I'd eaten fish and water spinach from local ponds. The ponds did not bear thinking about. Who knew? No one knew. At home some guys already had cancer and some soldiers' babies were born with spina bifida, but that was all they knew. Even now they don't know much, or say they don't. So maybe it wasn't that.

Toon, who worked in hospitals and had seen much worse, said we'd never know. But I saw that the war wasn't as over as I'd thought. It didn't matter that I'd repudiated it. It was still always above me, my own smelly cloud, like the thought-balloon above a man in a cartoon. At home we played with the baby as if she were any baby; she crowed when we dandled her and got indignant when she was hungry. We hoped it was only hunger that made her scream.

I tried to watch out for Toon; that was all I could think to do. The first night home, when she wanted to bathe, I carried her into the bath. I sponged her back, I washed her hair. "Toby, is that you?" she said. "I think is someone else's husband." Neither of us had ever seen me do such a thing before. It wasn't that hard really. How worried we were then, how full of dread. When the baby cried in the next room both of us gasped and shrieked.

When Toon got up to nurse her, I tuned the radio to the crappy Thai pop station she loved and I didn't. Oopy-doopy music, I'd always called it. "Louder," she said. At least I knew one thing: in war you have to have a buddy, or you're really fucked.

WHEN I WENT BACK to work, I found myself wondering which of these executive wives I was sending on the royal palace tour was married to a liar from Dow or Monsanto or Hercules or one of the other chemical companies. All those lies for profit. Why was I being nice to these people? It made my job weirdly artificial. I wanted to wear a sign in front of all of them: GREED KILLS.

But who was I to wear such a sign? A person who'd earned an elevated salary in Da Nang, who'd gone to war without even risking his skin. And no one had made me go.

I didn't want to be afraid around my daughter. The last thing she needed was a scared jumpy father, a spooked worrier. Fear was the reason the U.S. had charged into a place like Vietnam (fear of Communists taking the world from us), fear escalating to frenzy. Ajahn Mun used to send his monks on walking meditation at night in tiger-infested forests, to teach them not to be afraid.

Meanwhile, my daughter was a bright-eyed, alert baby. Toon picked the name the monks gave her—she was Lawan, which meant Beautiful, but everyone at home called her Jiap, which meant Baby Chicken. I lived in a country big on nicknames. She hardly seemed to mind not having a left hand—as Toon pointed out, how would she know otherwise?—and waved all her limbs with the same abandon. Billy's idea was to absolutely not let anyone mention her non-hand; he would shout in a long bellowing blast if anyone said a word, a really quite effective strategy.

WE WATCHED HER CLOSELY, waiting, as Americans say, for the other shoe to drop. She learned to do things—sitting, standing, walking—in the same thrilling sequence that Billy had, and her prattling turned into speech much earlier. She was a gabby three-year-old when Toon found a job in a pediatric clinic. By that time we had Billy, who was the moody, difficult one, in a school that cost money.

Billy was the one I stuck closest to. He was intent and deliberating and stubborn. If he got mad at you, he wouldn't speak. In the fancy international school he went to, he never liked sports that involved teams (was it possible to have a kid who wouldn't suffer fools?). I taught him to swim and we'd splash around the hotel pool. He made fun of me for getting fat, though I wasn't that fat.

I wrote to Ernst: *Christmas greetings from the ever-amazing father of two. The little prodigies are working me hard. Let's hope they support me in my old age.*

They let us use the pool because although I was staff, I was Caucasian. I was ashamed of the hotel for this. I'd grown tired of my office, with its framed clichés, its photos of saddled elephants and Khmer ruins with ribbed towers and monks in orange robes, its beauties trimmed and cut for outsiders who were barely interested anyway. It had only one corny poster I could stand to look at, a lone fisherman paddling a narrow boat on a river at dusk. The boat appeared to be the sole human artifact in miles of blue. Of all the people in the hotel who had ever glanced at this poster, I was probably the only one who wanted to be the fisherman.

SOMETIMES I BROUGHT Jiap to the pool too. I walked through the glass doors, holding her good right hand, and I'd see a guest smile at us—what a cute kid, in her flounced swimsuit—and then I'd see the expression change when anyone saw the knobbed arm. *What happened? What took the hand?* I could tell you stories, I'd feel myself thinking, a long chain of stories, spiraling out to there, more than you want to know. Meanwhile, Jiap waded and splashed and thought she was cool.

I GOT A LETTER ONE DAY with a return address from Bydex in Phoenix, and I had a crazy moment of thinking Ernst had written to me at last. But it was from Rob Frye, another engineer, whom I barely remembered. He wanted me to know that Ernst Ringerman—he understood we had worked together some years ago—had recently passed away. He'd drowned in a river in Washington State, while he was camping by himself one weekend.

I was sorry that my last note to Ernst had been so idiotic and sourly cheery. Ernst must have thought I'd gone over into the ranks of the resigned, the hearty cowards of domestic life. I wanted to write him a better letter. How could he be gone? He was my phantom adviser, my invisible pal. He knew things no one else knew. It was a mean trick, to have someone I'd asked so little of be dead from me.

Only the one sister, the letter said, had come out for the funeral. He'd never married or had a dating life anyone knew about. With someone like Ernst, you had to ask yourself: When had his life ever begun? But swimming in a cool, fast-running river in the midst of a piney mountain range wasn't the worst way to go. He might have died in Da Nang, in an ugly way no one would choose, so it was possible to see his death (in a majestic landscape, when he was no longer young) as a good enough deal, not a cheat. I tried to see it that way.

Was it any kind of life? I, who'd respected him more than anyone did, felt disloyal even asking. I said to Toon, "He was only forty." I could wish Ernst a better shake on the next karmic round. I could ask Toon to. Toon said, "So sorry, Toby." I thought of the soldiers' tagline in the war—*Sorry about that*—uttered in useless, cynical shame when friendly fire killed their own. And I was thinking of Jiap's missing hand, my life's version of accidental rain on a wrong target. Toon's mother was afraid that kids in school were going to pick on Jiap because she was marked by this sign of bad karma. Ernst would've laughed himself silly at this karma crap. Toon said, "I think your friend was always glad you writing him."

—

I DIDN'T REALLY know why I missed him more once he was gone. But I had dreams about him, and I hadn't had them before. In one he was sitting at a desk designing the atomic bomb (which he probably could've done if he'd been born twenty or thirty years earlier). He was explaining it to me, but I didn't understand a single word. Nothing! When I woke up, I was sure he hadn't been speaking English.

Meanwhile, my daughter made her way through school. She was a graceful kid, quick by nature, and very good at *takraw*, a volleyball-like game mostly played without hands anyway. She could serve with her one good hand, and she swiveled and swung her leg and did pirouetting kicks and butted with her head when the rattan ball came at her. She practiced at home, to gain status with the girls who were mean to her, and Toon thought it worked, but Toon wanted to think that.

Only Toon's mother still fretted over Jiap, and her worry (it turned out) was that Jiap would never marry. "So what?" I said. Toon blanched, as if I'd insulted her on purpose, as if marriage were nothing to me. I tried to argue that Jiap could have a rewarding fate that did not involve pleasing males. I was suddenly the feminist in my family. Toon's mother suggested I try to be more optimistic.

WE HAD A BAD YEAR when Billy was twelve. He was flunking math, his best subject, out of an aggrieved boredom, which caused me to wonder why I did anything either. This was the year I went to a therapist. Toon thought this was odd on my part, and the therapist thought it was odd that I did not talk more to my wife. The therapist was American. He maybe helped a little. We could hardly afford him and he seemed to want to discuss why I had not stayed a well-paid engineer, was that a choice? "What if depression," I said, "is just another penalty for a past life? What if a person with big karmic debt—who'd been a murderer, say—should just focus on making merit this time around?"

"If only," the therapist said.

This answer got me so irritated that I went around finding some NGO, some Western foundation—of which there were many in Bangkok at this time—who needed an engineer to work in a refugee center or a reclamation project or some goddamn thing that needed doing in what my father used to call a world of shit. I wasn't an engineer who knew about roads or bridges or water systems but I could become one.

AND THAT WAS HOW I got work improving the efficiency of pit latrines and rain catchment in a slum of Bangkok, a district ever more crowded with indigent farmers come down from the northeast. Boy, did that local improvisation of a sanitation system need an overview. The hotel manager thought I was a fool to leave my job, and my kids were embarrassed when they heard what the work actually was. Toon would not let Billy go around saying I was a turd engineer, though I had made that joke myself. I thought Toon was proud of me, in her way, even though I'd managed to get yet another job with an unimpressive salary. Lek gave me dire warnings about going into that neighborhood, which I told him was safer than Miami. *Miami Vice* was viewable on the hotel TV then, so he thought I was tough when I said this.

I worked with two Dutch guys I liked a good deal, and the early days were saturated with an intensity I had not been inside for a long time. I was up till all odd hours working at my calculations and my sketches. At dawn I went down to the river, where an entire group of urbanites washed their dishes and clothes and their half-wrapped selves in its murky flow. I heard the Dutchmen tell stories of other cities' eco-messes and I chuckled knowingly, though I knew very little. How to filter the rainwater, if it was too polluted to drink? I could not sleep at night from the headiness of being useful.

Toon was afraid I was going to get terrible diseases from being around who knew what microbes; her fussing naturally led to much family kidding about my imminent collapse. Toon would say, "Remembering about washing hands, Toby?" and I'd clutch my throat and do pratfalls at the dinner table. Me! Pratfalls! Billy was amazed. He and Jiap made hilarious shit jokes in Thai, which no one would translate. Certain subtleties of Thai still eluded me. Toon tittered.

I thought Toon liked me better now. I was less depressed, less hangdog, a livelier husband than I'd been, and our life in bed had a new layer of frankness. Toon was bolder than she'd been when we were younger—her affection often had a surprising audacity. She was more apt to turn away from me too; I was a man who no longer required indulging. Though it made me wince to rethink certain past nights, I was glad we had made our way to this side, this freer, brighter spot.

ONE OF TOON'S FRIENDS from work was an American, a pretty girl from New Jersey newly married to a Thai. She came by the apartment one day to hang out with Toon, and I heard them in the next room laughing together about the habits of their funny husbands—Toby ate sardines with ketchup, imagine that. The woman, whose name was Viana, was married to a Muslim doctor from southern Thailand. Her husband didn't drink or eat pork, she said, but his visits to a mosque were mostly just when he went home to his family.

"So New Jersey's on the same river as New York?" Billy said. Billy wanted to know from Viana everything about New York—had she ever heard any of the really good neo-punk bands live? Was CBGB still there? He had always been a gentle, sulky, timid boy. Now he couldn't resist being a nervy teenager in front of an American. "Don't tell me," he said, "you actually like Bangkok."

"Ah, well," she said, "I'm here for good. I'm never going back."

Billy said, "Maybe you'll have kids *almost* as good-looking as we are." This wasn't his usual style of talking, and I thought he was flirting with her (the new Billy).

SO WHO WAS HE? No one could tell yet. He had flashes of temper between moments of unexpected dearness and was nicer to Toon than he was to me. With me he was ruder and more American. In his second year of high school, he somehow got us to buy him a small motorcycle, and he tore around the streets with the tiny fierce motor roaring—Billy, who'd been the only small boy on the planet who liked quiet.

He called his bike Spike and claimed that Spike made him get speeding tickets and skip school and forget curfew. Spike was a bad crowd in a leaky machine. It wore a fresh jasmine garland on each handlebar, like any divine figure in a shrine. Toon and I wondered if Billy had a girlfriend, since he was away so much. Jiap said, "He's probably going to marry Spike."

WHEN TOON'S FRIEND Viana came back from a family funeral in southern Thailand, Billy wanted to know if Muslims buried like Christians or burned like Buddhists. "Buried," Viana said. Billy lit a stick of incense for the dead grandfather—I thought this might be an affront, but Viana said that Zain, the grandfather, had been a very hip old guy, very enlightened, and he would have liked it. "He was above stupidity totally," she said. "In every way." But what was Billy doing—being nice to Viana or being a morbid little votary? None of us could tell.

—

BILLY DID COME HOME for supper one night with a girl on the back of the bike, a Californian from his school with a short gelled haircut and a shy face. Her name was Angela and she stayed for dinner. When Billy gave a lurid explanation of my work in shit management, Angela said, "Well. That's just part of life, isn't it?" We all liked her. Billy hardly spoke and took her home right after. He answered our nosy questions about her in irritated murmurs—yes, her parents were divorced, yes, her mother taught art at the school—and he kept company with her all that winter.

Toon and I, in our nighttime conversations, could not reach a definite guess about whether they were having sex. Toon thought no, but I gave Billy condoms anyway. I was thinking about my old happy days of sneaky sex with Kit, my high school girlfriend. Billy was embarrassed and just said, "Oh, Dad. You are so weird, Dad."

In the spring Billy broke up with her, for reasons we never knew. Angela kept calling the house, but he was not moved to relent. The phone rang through dinner. Billy told us not to bother to answer.

"Plenty fish in the sea," Uncle Lek said. "Room on the bike for new girl."

But I didn't like Billy's being so heartless. What phase was he in? He was either out on his motorbike or lighting incense in front of the shrine in the living room. I tried to talk to him about studying engineering or maybe the airier kinds of mathematics. "Physics is possible," Billy said. "Or agronomy." Agronomy?

But it turned out he had something quite other in mind. In the fall of his last year of high school, Billy announced at dinner that he planned to take vows as a novice Buddhist monk. "Very good idea!" Toon said. I didn't need to be reminded how many young men in Thailand served as monks—just for a spell of a few months, between school and getting a job. The king of Thailand had been a monk of this sort for fifteen days. But Billy was too young—you had to be twenty to ordain—he would be in with the smaller boys with no place else to go, poor kids sent by families with no money to feed or school them. "He has *us*," I said.

"Help him grow up," Toon said.

Every day on the street I saw monks in sunglasses, monks smoking cigarettes, monks stepping up to the back door of a bus. But I could not imagine Billy, currently wearing his weekend outfit of baggy jeans and a backward baseball cap, walking through Bangkok with an orange robe draped over one shoulder and his head and eyebrows shaved. Did I know him at all?

"It might not just be temporary," Billy said. "It could be a major career move. Like for good."

For good did not seem possible. Never to eat after midday, never to be alone with any female, never to let a female so much as touch him, never to handle money, never to drive a motorcycle, never to drive a car? I didn't think he could have really thought this through. I said this all night, hour after hour, and later in our bedroom.

Toon thought he might like the life. A boy like Billy.

"Like what?" I said. "He's a normal kid. He's *my* kid. He's an American citizen, for Christ's sake. He doesn't need to prove how *native* he is by wandering around with a begging bowl."

"Oh, Toby," Toon said. "Better not to say more."

"If we were home, he'd be *doing* something for money, he wouldn't be trying to *humble* himself."

"This is home," Toon said.

She blanched in outrage. I had the sense to be ashamed—what had I said? I knew what I'd said—but I was still furious at the whole continent of Asia, which seemed to be stealing my son from me, as surely as if a wave of cholera or malaria were dragging him under.

"And he'd have to chant in Pali!" I said. "A language deader than Latin. He doesn't know Pali!"

"He can do it," Toon said. "Thai boys can do it. Billy can."

Billy chanting! I wouldn't understand a word either.

"Don't we want him to have a family?" I said.

"Oh, yes," she said. "Of course, Toby."

I understood nothing. How had I lived here so long?

"Maybe he likes it," Toon said, "but then in a while he gets lonely and then he comes out. Then later he wants to go back—he could go."

"He could?"

"Oh, yes. Only not too many times. Can only leave and go back seven times."

"Seven is a lot," I said.

Seven, back and forth, in and out of the world. It seemed like a perfect life.

"You know, in the Catholic Church priests used to be able to marry," I said. I started to talk about shifts in the doctrine of celibacy, but I could see she wasn't so interested. Nothing I said held much fascination for her that night.

WE DID A LITTLE BETTER as the weeks went on. The other relatives were pleased, even Lek. "The merit is given to the parents!" he said, as if I'd just cut a good business deal. My mother in Florida, of all people, was excited and proud. "See?" Billy said.

Jiap said, "I don't know why everybody's *talking* about it so much, like it's anything so weird. It's not weird." I was looking at the hard knob of flesh Jiap had for a hand and thinking about the merit Billy was about to accrue for me, the payments against karmic debt. Like a farmer's son settling the mortgage. How much to offset the precepts I'd broken in the war, the rules against lies, greed, murder? Too much probably for even Billy. Toon would say he was doing his part. I was thinking of the phrase "forgiveness of debt."

ON THE STREET ONE NIGHT Toon and I passed a store window stocked with monks' buckets—in the old days I'd thought they were for the beach—orange plastic pails filled with flashlights, soap, sweet drinks, toothpaste, tied with cellophane bows—gifts to bring to the temple, offerings to the monks. Did Billy think he was going off to camp?

Toon and I stopped to look at the items. Could these be enough for anyone? The goods in each bucket (orange soda, liquid detergent, toilet paper, a black umbrella) were packed to overflowing, gestures of plenty. How much did anyone need?

An ache of jealousy rose up in me—how did Billy get to do this? I was sorry for myself that I wasn't him. Toon said, "Have to have a *big* party before he goes. Big fuss." She was only repeating what she'd said before, but the breathy emphasis now—the light, enchanted stress— made me hear something more. She was gazing tenderly at a window display she'd seen a million times before, touched, it would seem, to imagine Billy secluded with the monks, for however long, his days undistracted by us. It should not have surprised me that I nursed some envy for Billy. What I had not understood (hadn't I?) was how much Toon would envy him too.

We were not in a hurry to get home and we stood at the window of the store for a while, lost in looking. We were each trying to see as far we could, farther, into that glassy space of the other life—with its freedoms and its sufficiencies, the unled life—perhaps not better than this life either, but always longed for.

Anyone on the street probably thought we were just

window-shopping for alms, deciding which buckets to buy for the monks. I thought of my first days in Bangkok, when I knew nothing about anything and I felt sorry for the monks for being so skinny. I had no idea at all I'd become who I was now—settled, enveloped, private. How could I know?—a hulk of a boy loose in the world, a foreigner washed up here once by war.

INDEPENDENCE

Kit

FOR A WHILE after I was married, my old boyfriend from high school used to send me letters from Vietnam. *Dear Kit*, he'd write. *It's hot here and a little more exciting than I'd planned. I guess you're just sitting in the sun in that little white two-piece of yours.* His letters were cheerful in a fairly petrified way. He wasn't even in the army, he was there as a civilian engineer doing something to help the planes fly right. My husband didn't like my getting letters from Toby, although they were by no means love letters. Well, some had tinges. *I hope you are putting lots of suntan lotion on the tender skin under your butt that used to burn so easily.*

I liked the letters. But I was glad now that I had failed to talk Toby into marrying me right after high school. What had I been thinking? He was decent enough but secretly arrogant and frozen with everyday fears; I had always been a little too much for him. He thought I was crafty but I was really just faster, in every sense. He was the sort of boy who seemed startled when having sex. At the time his awe and confusion were endearing.

I knew I was much better matched with Doug, my husband. He was more of a bad-boy type. He came into a diner in Miami where I was waitressing the summer between my last years of college, and he flirted in a sly, half-smiling way that got me appropriately reckless. By the middle of the summer he was showing up after the lunch rush and we'd go fool around in the walk-in icebox (a sexier spot than you'd think, in that weather) just to get us both through the long dull day. He was almost done with school and already working in a Chevrolet dealership his uncle owned.

I lived with him during my last year of college, while my parents chose to think I was still in the dorm. This was the year I was tutoring in a neighborhood my dad said I'd get mugged in, and all their warnings to carry Mace in my purse kept my parents from worrying where I was sleeping.

In the late spring, just before graduation, I found out I was pregnant. How had *that* happened? It was true we had not been very scrupulous about using protection. But it seemed a great irony of nature that all the nights of heated invention, all the funky animal boldness, all the giggling and wild play, were about to chain me to family life.

I knew people who'd had abortions, everyone did. Much to my amazement, Doug was for having the baby. "I think we could do it," he said. "Stranger things have happened." It was because of the draft—men with kids weren't getting drafted. I wasn't wild about this as a reason, but I didn't want to lose my lock on Doug. I was crazy for Doug.

MIAMI WAS NOT a bad place to have a baby. When Phoebe was very little, I could take her outside and hang out with the other moms, horsing around and grousing about what work a kid was, and I'd have a pretty sociable day. If I stayed home, I might get a phone call from good old Toby from high school, on his lunch hour in Arizona. "Just calling to say hi. Hidey-hi."

"You're talking to a very busy woman who gets no sleep at all," I'd say. I was still happy then and it gave me a tiny curl of pleasure to hear the dullness of loneliness in his voice.

By the time his letters came from Vietnam, I wasn't doing so well. I wrote, *Why did you have to go there? You are brave, I know. Which is more than I can say for me. Not that there is anything interesting to say about me.* I frequently hated the way I sounded. It wasn't that I had become meek—when my husband ordered me around, I shrieked in outrage or I mocked him, and I griped about him to my friends. "Guess what he wants now?" I'd call them and say. But this complaining was nothing, a fake freedom, a vote no one was counting.

The disorder that a yowling infant brought into the house was a big disappointment to Doug. He'd imagined

I would carry off this family thing with more style. "You have to *manage* the situation," he said, a sentiment that was a spillover from his lessons in oily competence at his job. He couldn't really bully me when he sounded so dumb—when was I ever someone who could believe a sanctimonious sharpie? "Thank you, my captain and master," I'd say. My scorn made him touchier; ours was not a calm household. In bed I made efforts to impersonate my old besotted self. The lying was not good for me either.

PHOEBE WAS THIRTEEN MONTHS old when I took her to visit my family in Key West for a week. My father was a county judge and my mother's soft, fatly upholstered house, very beige and sunny, was just what I needed then. "You look positively radiant," my mother said, which made me feel especially creepy. Phoebe was in a charming phase, teetering around in her new shoes, chirruping her favorite syllables. She looked like me, a pert brunette, if babies can be said to look like adults. We hung out in my parents' yard under the huge rubber tree, watching the lizards darting around the hibiscus bushes. Key West had been a Navy island when I was growing up, but now the base was starting to phase itself out and parts of town were already run-down and shabby. On Duval Street I saw more sun-beaten, sunken-eyed guys than before— half dressed, half shaved—smugglers out for an airing, old drunks letting their features blear and melt. A few blocks from Mallory Square, near the water, things were a little brisker, with jewelry shops and T-shirt stores and dawdling southern tourists. A sightseeing trolley tootled past, honking its adorable horn. I liked my town.

I couldn't take my baby into a bar, not with my parents nearby. "Honey, if you're bored," my mother said, "you should go look up what's-his-name, your old friend." She meant Toby, who was back from Vietnam and staying with his parents.

I had a dream that night about fucking Toby; in my dream he'd learned a few new tricks. As it happened, I ran into him at the supermarket the next day.

"Here's the man! Back from his far-flung travels," I said.

"Home is the hunter, home from the hill," he said. He was never afraid of clichés.

He limped across the aisle to give me a decorous hug. I didn't want to say anything about his limp, so I said, "You look great!"

"Lost too much weight," he said. Not a word about how I looked.

"Got tanned too," I said.

"Oh, yeah, they have sun there. They do have that."

"Lots of interesting engineering problems?"

"Too interesting. I could live without that kind of interest for a while."

I was against the war, insofar as I thought about anything but myself in those days, but I hadn't harangued Toby about going. Phoebe, who was sitting very cutely in the grocery cart, began to bang on the metal. Toby patted her and gave her white-shoed foot a little tug. She screeched and burst into tears.

"Excuse me," he said. "I'm so sorry. What did I do? I didn't hurt her."

"It's nothing, it's her. She gets like that."

"I don't know how to act with babies. I'm so sorry."

Phoebe was still crying. I lifted her off the seat and held her.

"I stopped writing letters, didn't I?" Toby said. "I got very busy. You don't want to know with what. I didn't like doing the work. Well, you know what I mean."

He looked haggard and embarrassed then. What could I say? *It's all right, don't worry?* The only merciful thing I could think of doing was to get us away from him, so he wouldn't be stuck in those same agonized sentences.

We toodle-ooed out of there, and when we got home, I told my mother I'd seen Toby. "He is the smartest boy," she said. "Well, smart man now."

I was thinking of Mr. Llewellyn's physical science class in high school, when he talked about the Manhattan Project and J. Robert Oppenheimer and the geniuses who worked on the atomic bomb. After Hiroshima, Oppenheimer said, "The physicists have known sin." I thought that Toby was in a spot like that now.

At the end of the week I drove back to Miami with Phoebe in the car. We got stuck in traffic on the Seven-Mile Bridge, and the glare on the water made my neck ache. What an idiot girl I was for having had dirty thoughts about Toby. I felt immensely stupid. The world wasn't all sex, was it? Toby was in a different part of history, too horrified to be much interested in titillation.

And what did I want from Toby anyway? Nothing really, which was sort of insulting to him. Would I have swooned with helpless feeling, just out of etiquette, if he'd been interested? Did I have an honest bone left in my body? My itchiness could turn me into a joke, a horny housewife in a blue movie. If I'd known something else to want, I would have wanted it. When we got home and Doug came out to the car to greet us, I stood up and pressed my body against him full-tilt, I wound my snaky arms around him. "Whoa, girl," he said.

WE MIGHT HAVE GONE on like this even longer than we did. For a year or so I was an old-fashioned spouse, pretty and hardworking and sour, a good cook and a sarcastic laugher. But then Phoebe went through a pain-in-the-ass phase. She didn't like the *color* of her Jell-O and threw the dish at me, she wasn't going to wear that stupid *jacket* and stomped it. When I wanted to read a book in another room while she had her nap, she bellowed, "Not *going*. You *have* to stay here." She grabbed my bare shin with her tiny fierce hands, she went limp when I tried to peel her off. I whacked her hard on the arm to make her let go, a smack with some noise in it.

For a second we were both stunned. Then Phoebe,

who had been yowling, yowled louder, as if this were the very thing she was expecting, though I had never hit her before—who hits a two-and-a-half-year-old? "No more," I said, "no more, now." I didn't know which of us I was pleading with. She wouldn't let me comfort her (I couldn't blame her), and I sat in the room while she sobbed in outrage. It ended with her falling into a curled sleep on the floor. I didn't try to move her.

I hadn't really hurt her or raised a mark on her milky skin, but I was properly alarmed. I hated motherhood for what it had shown me to be. I was sorry I'd had her, sorry for what I now knew. How in love with myself I had once been. What scared me most now was my future.

In a logic that seemed simple to me at the time, I saw that I had to leave Doug and take Phoebe with me. We could go to my family. I didn't want to sneak out either, to act afraid of my husband. Doug said, "Oh, please. You have no brains, girl. What do you want really? Just tell me. You don't even know, do you?"

It was June when I got to Key West, a very hot month. My mother said, "Oh, absence will make his heart grow fonder." She thought Doug had thrown me out. Each time he telephoned, she winked at me with satisfaction. "Will you cut this crap and get yourself home already?" he said. "I've had enough." Worst was when he tried cajoling. "Have you forgotten everything, baby?" he said. I was touched to hear this, ready to say something lovey back; I could feel the white lies swelling up in my throat, the beautiful utterances. How could I turn my back on beauty? I did, but I felt perverse and grim, a pigheaded sulker.

I STAYED THE WHOLE summer in Key West, trying to figure out what the hell I was doing, a season long enough for Doug to find someone else. Who was she? "No one you know," he said. I cried when he told me, right on the phone with him. It was one of my lowest moments. What a dog in the manger I was.

But I saw it was time to move. I rented a tiny stucco hut of a house, and to my family's high disapproval I got a job waiting tables at night in a seafood restaurant near the ocean. Doug sent money when he felt like it and talked about coming to visit Phoebe (this didn't happen for months). I made friends at the laundromat near the beach. After midnight was prime laundry time. Around the machines there'd be other single moms, who were often girls I knew from high school, and there'd be a Cuban grandmother, a couple of bikers, a few hard-luck guys who owned fishing boats.

It was from Gina, who'd been in my science class, that I heard about the glories of travel. She was a skinny, pretty woman with frizzball hair and a hoarse, breathless voice. She had been to Thailand and was thinking about India or Mexico. "It's in my idea of a complete life," she said.

I had at that point a broken life. I had willed the break, but I did feel that something alive had been cut. "In other parts of the world," Gina said, "a washing machine would be like some mysterious box landed from the moon. There are more riffs on being human than we think. Like in Thailand it's rude to touch somebody's head, the head is sacred. If you don't go anywhere, you think your own way is the whole thing."

"Did you have Emmy with you in Thailand?" I asked. Emmy was her five-year-old.

"Of course. People are nice to kids. Well, the Thai were. And that slow-as-molasses thing that kids do of noticing every blade of grass is what you're traveling for anyway. That was my theory."

In the daytime Gina and I sometimes took our kids to the beach and hung out drinking beer with one of the bikers, who was really not a bad guy. He'd once been an organizer for the hospital workers' union and he liked me because I'd picketed in college. I'd always loved the beach on the Gulf side, the long white curve of land and the rippling shelf of watery blue. "I hear you're going to Mexico with Gina," he said, while she was in the surf with Emmy.

I had probably expressed this as a passing whim. I did not think I was a traveler: I liked my comfort, I was not always brave, and I was only just starting to be curious. "*Claro*," I said to the biker. "*Sí, sí.* You bet." I was kidding. Our whole purpose in sitting on the beach was to kid around.

"It's very wild there. You ready, girl?" he said. "It's a great country. Only watch your back."

———

AND I DID GO with Gina, much to my own amazement. My parents weren't happy. And Doug said, "You're a fucking nutcase," when he heard the plan, but he'd been too neglectful of Phoebe to get carried away about stopping me. I had a little cash saved from my tips—everybody told me how cheap Mexico was—and I sublet my house at a profit for the few months I thought I'd be gone.

We hit the road in Gina's VW bus. The girls were excited when we first took off. Emmy treated Phoebe like a big doll, bouncing her on her lap and carting her around at rest stops; Phoebe's face was sappy with delight. By the end of the day they were always ragged and quarrelsome, and whoever wasn't driving had to make up games and coddle them like babies. At night we all slept in the back of the van, which was covered with quilts and strewn with sleeping bags. I don't know why we thought we were safe, pulled off the highway in the buzzing dark, with the lights of cars going past us all night. But I loved the tight little unit we were. I didn't even know Gina that well, and here we were, singing made-up songs to the girls ("On top of old BACK seat, all covered with potato chips") and snorting over each other's stories about men.

It satisfied us immensely that we could do all this on almost no money. Peanut butter sandwiches and juice in the cooler, gas and tolls, the occasional beer and candy bar—what else did we need? Why had we ever thought we needed more? We were slipping out of the pointless wants that made everyone around us fat and greedy and miserable, we were speeding off to a freedom that had been there all along. We could not help being pleased with ourselves.

At Brownsville we crossed the muddy waters of the Rio Grande, cheering and hooting, and handed our tourist visas to the unsmiling Mexican officials. We had to keep driving until we got to this one great town in Chiapas that someone had told Gina about. We drove on twisting roads with viny forest on both sides and cloying heat misting our skin, and then suddenly the car was climbing into cool mountain spaces, and in a dip among these mountains was San Cristóbal de las Casas. I had a sudden wash of gratitude as we chugged into it, our rickety van huge on its streets. The houses were adobe, chalky white and pale yellow and sandy peach, with roofs of brownish tiles, and at the end of its cobbled streets a row of mountains loomed in the distance, ringed by wisps of clouds. The air smelled deliciously of pine smoke.

AND WE WERE rich here too. Within a week, just from hanging out in the town square in front of the baroque stone church, and from going to the fabulous town market, where Indians descended from Mayans stood selling piles of beans and peppers and parched corn, we'd made friends with some of the other Americans—Robin and Anthony and Howie and Fran and Fritz and Sue-Anne and a slew of others. They told us what to do, and we found a house with three rooms and a central courtyard for twenty-five dollars a month. The kids could play in the courtyard, while Gina and I, who had taken to calling ourselves the pioneer mothers, cooked meals on a brazier made from an oil drum or built a fire under the bottom of the tank that fed hot water to the shower.

I had never had much of a bent toward simplicity—I was too proud of the quirks and complications of my own civilized personality—but now I walked out every day to an older human history than I'd bothered to think about before. On our street at dawn men and women and children who'd walked miles from their villages made their slow way up the hill to the market, with sisal bags of vegetables or charcoal carried on tumplines across their foreheads. The men wore basic T-shaped tunics, the women wore embroidered blouses and long skirts. After a while I could distinguish the Chamulas from the Zinacántecos from the Tenejapas from the ones from Amatenango del Valle.

The other *gringos* came to hang out at our house—at any moment Anthony or Robin or Fritz might be at the door—and Gina had one or two flirtations going, but I did not. I was okay with this, for perhaps the first time in my life. I had other avenues of interest here, other things I craved. I could not quite get over the things people made here; I had already bought a shawl, a hammock of multicolored cotton net, a dark blue skirt that wrapped under a beautiful red-and-green-striped belt, and a heavy white cotton blouse with deep red and golden yellow satin-stitching on the bodice.

Gina had decided she wanted to learn backstrap weaving, and we went together to a Tenejapa woman who coached her in making, inch by inch, a wide strip of thickly bright cotton brocade. I kept an eye on the girls, who chased around the yard with the woman's two kids. María, who'd taught other *gringas*, had lived away from her Tenejapa village for ten years, so she had some Spanish. She was not much older than we were, and sometimes she giggled with us. She had a lovely, calm face. She taught Phoebe to wind yarn on a spool and called her Cho'oh, which meant Mouse in Tzeltal, her own language.

GINA SOMETIMES TEASED ME about my growing wardrobe of local textiles. I knew that I was only pretending, walking around in my primitive smocks, lighting our kitchen fires with *ocote*, the local pitch pine: as if I weren't wearing bikini undies made of polyester, as if I'd never seen a toaster or a refrigerator. But I was pretending like any novitiate in her robe, with the hope that mimicry could take me closer to something worth knowing.

Sometimes the shopkeepers would snicker to each other when they saw me. And once a cop—one of the grim, heavily armed *federales*—pulled at the end of my woven belt as if it were a tail. His leering amusement spooked me.

We went a few times a week to visit María, who would open the door very glad to see us. She had been married to a *ladino*, a non-Indian local, but it had not worked out. That was all we knew. She had a boy a little older than Phoebe and a girl who was Emmy's age. I asked María if she ever went home but I never quite got a straight answer. A sore subject, maybe. "I ran away," she said, "to be married."

"*My* mother always loathed my ex," Gina said. "She had a point."

The term "ex" had to be explained to María in our lousy high school Spanish. "Mr. X-Y-Z, no more name, that's funny," she said.

"They fall off the end of the alphabet, those guys," I said. I was thinking about María fleeing her village in the night, all that trouble and now no husband.

"Your parents took it hard when you picked this person?" Gina said. "Mine too."

"They don't like anyone but Tenejapa."

Gina said that was kind of narrow thinking.

"They know what they know," María said. "From their lives. When my father was a young man, he worked for a *patrón* who went twice a year between his ranch and the city, a long ride on a horse in the mountains. No highways then, no trucks. Very rocky, maybe four, five days. The wife rode in a chair strapped to my father's back."

Phoebe had heard the word for chair, one of the few words she knew in Spanish, and she ran around the room yelling, "*La silla! La silla!*"

Gina and I were silent, perhaps both hoping we hadn't heard right. I felt then how kind María was to us, us outsiders with our shallow and interesting conversation, our coins for her teaching, our blurting enthusiasms, our visits when we felt like it.

THE WEATHER GOT COOLER, but even in October I liked the evenings in our little house, when we sat on cushions in the courtyard, with candles and kerosene lanterns around us, and feasted on some elaborate combo of vegetables we had cooked. The girls liked to nestle in the hammock and use it like a swing. Phoebe liked to tell over and over which stalls we'd visited in the market—"The *frijoles* lady! The *frijoles* lady!"—which favorite café we'd stopped in for banana-strawberry *licuados* and slices of cake. Emmy paraded around in all the necklaces I had bought. Gina would say, "You think we should drive to a beach or to the ruins at Palenque or do we just want to stay put?" What lolling, royal lives we had there, we who were, after all, a waitress and a welfare mother.

Fritz, who'd been eyeing Gina for a while, came by one night with a new rumor. An American guy—no one we knew—had had a loud argument in a bakery because he thought the woman was cheating him. "Know what the bakery woman did?" Fritz said. "She had him arrested. How could she do that?"

"The shopkeepers don't like us because we're so cheap," I said. "And we don't work either. They don't get it."

The next day when Phoebe and I showed up at our favorite café, there was a cardboard sign over the glass-covered counter where they kept the pastries—NO HIPIS ALLOWED.

We were already inside—if I tried to drag Phoebe out, she'd squall. There was no excuse I could give her that wouldn't make her shriek to high heaven. So we sat down, and when we gave our order, the owner pointed to the sign. "Not us," I said in my bad Spanish. "It doesn't mean us. We are not *hipis*." The owner, a heavy-featured matron who'd always been friendly enough, walked away. I didn't know what to do, so I waited. "I'm *so* hungry," Phoebe said.

I was trying not to catch the eye of the Mexican customers. I was about to tell Phoebe we had to give up when the owner came to the table with two pieces of chocolate cake for us. Phoebe banged her fork on her plate in excitement. "Will you stop, please?" I said. "Could you, please?"

She ate her cake with her hands, very, very slowly, with the tiniest of bites. She knew something was up. "Ummy yummy yummy," she said to me in happy spite, licking her fingers.

If I told her to hurry, she would only take longer on purpose. Why did I have a kid like this? How could I have a kid like this in a place like Chiapas?

THE HOUSE WAS EMPTY when we got back. Emmy and Gina had gone to the waterfall with Fritz. I felt a little lonely. I got Phoebe to nap with me on the quilt in our room. I was dreaming about the beach at home when a banging sound woke me up. It took me a minute to know someone was pounding at the door.

People without kids never had any idea when naptime

was. It was kind of annoying. "I'm coming," I yelled. When I unlatched the door, a policeman in khaki stood before me, one of the *federales*, a man with pocked skin and a black leather holster.

"Where is your husband?" he said.

"He's away but he might be back soon."

"You have no husband," he said, and he stepped inside and closed the door.

"My daughter is asleep," I said.

"Where is your marijuana?"

"I don't smoke marijuana," I said.

"I am going to look for your marijuana."

"Nothing is here," I said. There was probably some in Gina's room. "Please don't wake up my daughter. She's only three. Almost four. Do you have children?"

He gave me a long stare, and he put his hand over my breast. "Do you still nurse your daughter?"

"No," I said. "Yes. Sometimes."

"Will you give me milk if I want it?" He was squeezing my nipple through the embroidered blouse.

"Please go away," I said. I was afraid to push him or to move. His fingers were pinching me. "I think you should go away. Please. My daughter is sleeping." A tiny, wretched spill of liquid seeped through my blouse. My body was in collusion.

He stood like that, with his curled palm clenching me—perhaps he was deciding. He could do this or he could do that. He could do whatever he wanted.

"Tell the others I was here," he said. "Tell your many husbands." He turned and opened the door and then he was gone.

GINA AND FRITZ AND EMMY came back very giddy and loud from their trip to the waterfall. "Hello, campers," I said. I didn't tell them. I had the indignant idea that they would not quite understand. I went to bed early so I could lie down and regard my terror in peace. I had not thought that I was in a place where I was hated. *Poor* people had reasons to hate us, in our well-fed idleness, but the cop was not poor. All the same, I had outraged him. In my *huipil* with its bodice of embroidered flowers I was like Marie Antoinette in her shepherdess costume to him. I was oozing money, and his country was a hobby to me.

On the street in Miami I sometimes drew from men a blind fury for being a woman in a short skirt who was certainly never, ever going to fuck them. People hated privilege, however they saw it. You could walk into a spot where the lilt of your stride was unbearable to someone. What the cop wanted to tell me was that it was his country.

I was bitter against Gina for never having told me that travel took you to this. But the cop had not only *resented* me, if you could call it that. He had wanted to cow me. At the very least. And I was thoroughly cowed now, wasn't I, a wincing American female in her bedclothes. I hated what I was.

—

"OKAY," I SAID TO Gina the next day. "Don't take this personally, but I have to go home. On the next bus. Tomorrow morning, I mean. Will you tell María I said goodbye?" Outside a rooster was crowing, though it was hours past dawn.

"This guy came," I said. Later I got much better at telling the story, but the first time I made a botch of it. I said *he grabbed my tit* and she said *what an asshole*. I saw how little language we had—Gina and I—for the deeper forms of dread. We'd done fine leaning on our hardiness before, but we were way past this right now, in another territory entirely.

"Oh, Kit," Gina said, and reached to hug me. She was a mother, after all. For about a second I liked being comforted. "I have to start packing," I said

"You know," Gina said, "I could leave with you, if you want. Except that I just started sleeping with Fritz, and I really like this house, so I couldn't right away."

"Don't *go*!" Emmy said.

Phoebe got wind of what the talk was about and she yelled, "No! No! Not going!" and ran around the room in crazy circles.

In the end I stayed because I was too chicken to travel on the bus alone with just Phoebe. That was not what I told people. I said you could not let fascist creeps like that run your life. For a week I hardly went out, though I knew I was hiding out in the exact spot where it had hap-

pened. He could come back. Even people who were trying to reassure me said that. Who could stop him, what
reason did he have to hesitate? I made Gina give away
every last bit of dope we had, the really good stuff from
Fritz and the mushrooms too, whose sacred world-
dissolving qualities I had so liked. When at last I took
myself outside, most of the Mexicans on the street did
not look much less wary than I was: it was instructive to
notice this. I supposed they had reasons to be afraid of
each other.

And I stuck close to Gina. If she was going to the
market, if she was taking the local pickup truck shuttle
to San Juan Chamula, if she was taking a hike with Fritz,
couldn't Phoebe and I come along? Our little group had
done things together before but not quite as incessantly. I
lost all savor for independence, for discovering hidden
bits of the city on my own.

I tried to keep the cop story from Phoebe, but she
heard parts of it and wailed in fright. I had to assure her
that people on the street were really *nice*, most people
were nice; I had to keep her from becoming a three-year-
old bigot.

At night in our room, I heard him outside laughing
with his friends. I heard him on the roof. I heard him
rustling through the courtyard. The relief when these
sounds dissipated did not make me forget he might come
back. What could keep him out, what bar could hold the
door against him?

The Americans who showed up at the house all had theories. Anthony said, "They hear our rock 'n' roll and they think every American wants sex all the time." Howie said, "The cop was enacting a revision of the La Malinche story, the thing where Cortés gets this Indian woman as his mistress and she betrays her people. Think of yourself as a historical reversal." I had been thinking it might be good to have a boyfriend here, but these guys, whom I'd liked well enough before, seemed young and lightweight, not much better than watching out for myself. I got a little rep in town for being snooty.

Gina lost interest in backstrap weaving, which she said was too hard—you needed a graph to follow the design and you worked for hours and you got nothing done— and she was otherwise occupied with Fritz. I was afraid to go to María's without her—worried about what I might run into on the outskirts where María lived and afraid that going there might inflame my cop, if he happened to be watching.

I WROTE TO DOUG IN MIAMI. *I wish you were here but you're not. I know I have my own fate but sometimes I wish things were easier. Oh, well, life is a struggle. Phoebe had stomach trouble for a week, but we coped. Hope you are doing well whatever you're doing. Con amistad, Kit.* I knew it was a coy and transparently self-pitying note, but I had too much longing in me not to send it. I wanted Doug feeling terrible that he'd thrown me out in the world unguarded and exposed, though in fact I had left him.

I wrote it on a postcard of Zinacántan men at a festival but I sealed it in an envelope so his new what's-her-name wouldn't see it. It was just as well he didn't answer, though I hoped he had, every time I waited for my mail in the *lista de correos* line at the post office.

PHOEBE WAS ALREADY complaining that she didn't ever, ever want to leave Mexico. Not ever. "Well, sweetie," I said, "prepare yourself." My high school science teacher, Mr. Llewellyn, liked to give his classes mock-lectures on the law of inertia. "You objects at rest out there," he'd say, "please think of me as the unbalanced force altering your state." He was English (exotic for Florida) and fetchingly sardonic, I'd thought. My boyfriend Toby had been his pet. I was missing Florida all the time now, it was from being lonely.

BY THE TIME I SAW Doug again—that winter, when I took Phoebe to Miami—I had long stopped sounding forlorn about being solo and unprotected, and I leaned instead on the bragging side of it. You would have thought I was utterly at my ease the whole time in San Cristóbal, to hear me talk about it. Even the cop at the door had become an emblem of all I now knew, an emblem of my daring, even.

I told the story so often that the outlines of it grew a shape and the elements were the same each time, not anything to shriek about. When people did shriek—"What did you *do*?"—I was the one shrugging, used to what the world was, used to trouble. And Miami didn't scare me one fucking bit now.

The winter I came back from Mexico, Doug was doing just fine. He had moved to a bigger house, a glassy ranch with a vast living room his girlfriend had decorated in white leather and apricot velvet and teak. Phoebe came in showing off a woven purse that María had given her on one of our visits, and it gave me a queer feeling to see the intricate, bright threading, the patterns of long labor, in that setting. A house like Doug's was very unusual in the world, I thought.

MY MOTHER TOLD ME that Toby had gone to live in a country in Asia. Not Vietnam, of course. Maybe Hong Kong—was that a country?—or Thailand. "You know, if you'd stayed with him," she said, "you could be living in a big house over there with servants." Since Toby had gone abroad specifically to marry someone else, this seemed like a bit of twisted reasoning to me.

"Oh, Mom," I said, "what makes you think I want a house like that?"

"You wouldn't like it? I just want you to be happy, sweetie."

I said I wasn't sure someone living as a colonial could ever really be happy, which made no sense to my mother.

"Just tell any fellow who wants to marry you," she said, "that you don't want everything too fancy or easy or better than everybody else. They'll be glad to hear it! I can hear the sounds of relief already!"

I did just that, of course, though by the time this question came up it went without saying. There was agreement on it, whatever other disputes there were between
me and the men I picked to live with. Certain leanings,
certain principles, were set in me by then. *Tell your many
husbands.*

THE MEN I LIVED with were decent people—there were
two while Phoebe was young—but it couldn't be said
that they protected me. It was too late for that. Julius,
whom I was with for three years in Miami and who
taught Phoebe to ride a bike, used to tell me I was too
independent, an odd thing to say as an insult. And he said
it from fondness, from love mixed with vanity.

What did he mean? The time my car broke down on
the highway all the way over near Naples, when I was
going to a demonstration against draining the Everglades,
I didn't call him to come get me (Triple-A came). When
my mother was in the hospital and I had a big argument
with the doctor, I didn't think to get Julius to show up
and argue for me. I forgot I could, or I didn't believe it
would help. I wasn't past all comfort, but not at the times
he thought. Julius said I didn't want him in the way,
which was not entirely wrong, though I denied it.

AFTER JULIUS AND I SPLIT UP, I worked in a day-care
center. Mr. Llewellyn, the Brit who taught me science in
high school, used to say that kids taught him the meaning
of sacrifice. In truth, I liked the feel of emptying myself

out for them, of rising to the task of letting them wear me out. It used the better parts of me.

I dressed in skinny jeans and tank tops for work, but something prim stayed with me from corralling the kids at school, and Randy was surprised to hear that I had indeed been on the back of a motorcycle before. We met at a rally in a park celebrating the news that President Carter had just pardoned the Vietnam draft dodgers. Randy was on the stage playing his drum in a rock band that did a sarcastic version of "From the Halls of Montezuma." I was at the front of the crowd and we were eyeing each other while the tune rolled on. Once the music was over and the equipment hauled offstage, he found his way to where I stood and asked me where I got the stitched woolen purse I was carrying (a Chamula bag from San Cristóbal). He didn't give a rat's ass about my accessories—if I'd been carrying a plastic bag, he would've asked about that—but it got us into a little conversation about places we'd traveled. He'd done the overland trail to Afghanistan. "You don't forget mountains like that," he said. "But cold. And they don't drink! I like drugs as well as the next person but it was a hard climate to handle without alcohol."

"You look sturdy," I said.

"You think so?" he said. "Keep looking. Please."

I'd come with friends, but they dispersed tactfully once they saw what was happening. Randy loped back to the truck where his drums were and had a conference with the guys before we went off for an alleged beer. I got on the back of his motorcycle, with my arms around his waist, trying not to burn my shins when we went roaring away. It was hard to hear him speak, but we understood each other fine, and we drove straight to his crappy little studio apartment and hopped into bed in about two seconds flat. The directness of our ardor made us fall intermittently into comradely laughter, but when things got more serious, he had streaks of elegance I had not expected.

The sweet thoroughness of his methods meant that, after everything hit a naturally spectacular conclusion, I had to leap out of bed to go pick up Phoebe from a third-grader's birthday party. I'd come to the rally in a friend's car, and I was very apologetic about making Randy put on his clothes to take me across town. "Hey," he said. "I'm a lucky man to be your ride." The eight- and nine-year-old girls, who were out in the yard, were thrilled at the sight of a motorcycle with a mother on it. "Hi, birthday beauties," he said. Phoebe wanted to get on board at once. She actually said, "I love your machine." In the name of safety I walked her home; we weren't far. We yelled together—in delight—when we got to our building and there he was (I'd just given him my address). "It's old me again," he said.

And after that he was pretty much with us all the time, except when he was on the road. He was very good with Phoebe—he did silly voices, he played tunes on the table with forks, he nicknamed her shoes—he was goofy and hammy, a happy performer. If we went to the grocery store, he could do a fabulous imitation of the clerk when we got home. He was very quick, a truly sage observer, and only sounded like a dumb rock musician when he was drunk or tired.

His drums stayed at his friend's and there didn't seem to be a lot of rehearsing. His friends were tedious and dopey and burned cigarette holes in the carpet, so I had him see them without me. Every so often the band would finally manage to line up some gigs and he'd be gone for a few months. Phoebe blamed me for this—"Why can't we go to Birmingham with him? Why not?"—and when Randy got around to phoning, it was always two in the morning, after she'd gone to bed.

I never thought he was reliable—I was not entirely stupid—and I did my best not to let Phoebe expect too much. That didn't work either; it only got her incensed at my slander and furious with me. And then he'd come home, puffed up with road stories—who needed to hear about the bass player's swallowing the worm in the *mezcal* bottle or the rainstorm that got them lost in Tuscaloosa? But he brought us hilarious souvenirs—a plastic alligator that sang "Dixie," a toy toaster with prayers printed on fake bread. We were never anything but exhilarated and wildly relieved to see him.

Was I too old for this shit, as Gina, who lived in Austin with Fritz but still phoned now and then, asked. I thought not. It felt perfectly natural. I had a taxing job in a sad, crazy inner city day-care center, I had a high-energy daughter who needed more of me than I could give. Having a fun boyfriend who breezed in and out and didn't ask much was not the worst thing.

RANDY WAS ALWAYS going to take us traveling, maybe to Thailand, so highly recommended by Gina. My high school science teacher had once lived there too and spoken very fondly of it. But we needed more money to do that, and we never had it. I was sort of carrying Randy financially as it was. Another thing Gina resented. "What do you call a rock musician who's just split up with his girlfriend?" she asked me. "You know. Homeless." (Her other favorite was: "What do you call a guy who hangs out with musicians? A drummer.")

But I knew I was lucky, compared, for instance, with some of the mothers of kids at my day-care center. One contingent—the hard-luck moms, some of them still in their teens, with their drawn-on lipstick and their butt-clinging shorts, with bad skin and sandpaper voices and guys who were wrecking everything in sight—eyed me as if it was really too much that someone like me could get what I had.

If Randy came to get me after work, at least one mother would tell me how cute my *novio* was. "Tell your kids to be nice to my baby," he'd say.

Phoebe wanted to know if *novio* meant fiancé. "Only sometimes," I said.

———

IN THE THIRD YEAR we were together, the band had such a long dry spell that Randy got side work with a friend's combo that did weddings and bar mitzvahs. He'd gel back his hair and turn into a twinkling rascal in a tux. He swore he could get the oldest, driest, meanest guests to get out on the dance floor and shake it, and he probably could.

At home we were always giving Phoebe dance lessons. This meant exhibition numbers in which the adults did astounding twirls and leaps and slinks, and group events in which Phoebe named the dances ("Do the cockroach! Do the refrigerator!") or we lapsed into slam-dancing.

Well, it wasn't all so sweet. When Phoebe was throwing a tantrum or bratting out, Randy would curse in snorting disgust and get out of the room fast. Once, when he was taking her across town for ice cream, he left her at the Dairy Queen alone out of outrage.

I didn't want to marry him. My mother asked me what I was saving myself for. "Nothing," I said. "This is my real life now." When I got dressed in the morning and Randy was still in bed, he'd say, "Look at you. I can't get over it. I never will." A man who spoke like a country-music lyric—what was so bad about that? We got along. Perhaps we couldn't have lasted for years without his long spells on the road. I liked those months alone, with no one to please, and then the joyful returns.

His longest time away was a western tour, to Nevada and Idaho and towns I never heard of. The Dakotas?

They were north of what? I tried to train him to phone before midnight. We were having a crisis at work because a four-year-old boy had had his leg broken by his father. Phoebe was very upset when I made the mistake of telling her. She woke up crying, from nightmares that seemed to be about Mexico, which I didn't even think she remembered. So I wasn't always fascinated when Randy wanted to tell me about the giant statue of a potato in some town or the bartender who made margaritas by juggling. Randy himself was too old for this shit, I thought.

I sank to questions about the weather. "Cold here, kitten," he'd say. "Can't wait to get back."

I RAN INTO the bass player's girlfriend, sappy Shelley, while I was buying Phoebe's favorite kind of frozen banana bars to get her through the night. "Long winter without the guys," I said.

"I know," she said. "It's so great to have them back. This month has been a great gift."

This month? This what? I wasn't cool enough to hide my raging astonishment, my thundering openmouthed fury, and I embarrassed poor Shelley.

"He'll come home, honey," she said. "I just know it."

HE DID CALL, as he'd been calling all along, and he was a little mortified but unsurprised to be found out. "Yeah, well," he said. "I took more time." Her name was Nicole and she lived in Billings, Montana, and I wouldn't let him tell me any more. What did he think he was doing? He didn't exactly know. "I wouldn't have lied if I'd known," he said. "You know that."

I wasn't interested. I said that and I mostly meant it. No more. Enough. "You're not a good idea," I said.

"Hey, girl," he said, "is that your worst insult?" He seemed to think he was still someone I wanted to talk to.

My days weren't so different without him either. My life was full of things that had nothing to do with him. At the day-care center, the boy with the broken leg had stopped speaking to any of the other kids or the teachers either. We were trying to get him moved to his aunt's. Phoebe was not doing her homework in middle school— she had decided there was no point. We were so busy shouting about this that she cut back on asking when Randy was coming home. What if he showed up in town with what's-her-name? It was not something I could think much about. It was a stone in the throat, a heel on the chest.

I hadn't told Phoebe the whole story, which grew its own chapters, a network of dank tunnels in my mind. I was a laughable woman who had been tricked by an oily, illiterate drummer, and maybe I had never even liked him either. My anguish was not lessened by my disdain for him. Whether I wanted him or not was not the issue. What was the issue? Nothing you could get a grip on. How long had I been living on nothing?

Phoebe knew what had happened when she saw me

packing all Randy's leftover clothes in a carton. I kept the goddamn rock records. "Was it your fault he left?" she said. "Sweetheart," I said, "it's never that simple. You don't need to blame people." "It was your fault," she said.

SOMETIMES RANDY CALLED ME, out of last-ditch pangs or sentimental greed, raspy-voiced from booze or weed, to tell me I was really the best of all. "Do you know that?" he said. "I just wanted you to know that. Even though." (Why was I talking to this person?) After a while he'd hear that I was humoring him with my thanks—I'd say, "So good of you to call"—and he'd get testy. "Would you please excuse me for taking your valuable time?"

"You're excused," I said. "This time." But I was sorry when he stopped phoning, I was.

AT THE DAY-CARE CENTER, the staff had a mini-celebration in the teachers' room—toasting our diet Sprites—because Byron, the boy with the broken leg, had been moved into his aunt's at last. He still wasn't talking much, but he had been heard singing the toothbrush song in a monotone with the others. I saw the aunt—very fat, very young—picking him up after school, and he went to her, on his crutch, gladly enough.

His plaster cast, with its inky drawings and signatures, had just come off when he stopped coming to our center. The director made a few calls and found out the aunt had given Byron back to the mother. The mother was back with the father and pregnant again, and the sister said they could be anywhere, how did she know, nobody asked her opinion ever, she couldn't do everything.

We left Byron's paintings of space aliens on the wall, and as time went on they came, more and more, to seem like the relics a soldier's mother keeps. The crayoned letters of his name (written by me) were terrible to see, next to the crepe paper turkeys and jolly foil Santas. No one would take the paintings down either and they stayed up till June.

I CAME HOME AT NIGHT tired and spent. But still I met a few new men, mostly in bars and once in a hardware store. I'd have a little sexual enthusiasm for someone— the beginning was okay—but before long I'd lose heart, so to speak, for the whole enterprise. The last thing I wanted was a guy so ordinary he made me miss Randy. Toby, my boyfriend from high school, used to say I had no patience, and maybe he was right. Then Phoebe launched into full-tilt adolescence and I could hardly manage anything but trying to keep her from combusting.

I hated it when Phoebe started stealing. Of all the idiotic objects of desire—what was she even going to do with what she slipped under her jacket? The tacky name-brand sunglasses, the overhyped designer T-shirts. "In Mexico," I said, "a family can eat for a month on what that shirt cost."

"I didn't pay for it, did I?" she said.

"What are you going to do with it? Wear it and look rich? Status for who? I though you knew better."

"I'm not giving it back," she said.

"Look at the *world*, will you?" I said. "Have some imagination. Just for a second."

PHOEBE CUT SCHOOL, she hung out with a snotty girl named April, she did drugs I didn't even know the names of. She wasn't a bad kid but she was nervy and reckless. "You think you know what you're doing but you don't," I said.

"Poor Mom," Phoebe said. "Poor, poor, pitiful Mom."

There was some affection in her mockery. We were dancing around each other, the old-broad mom and the sly little Barbie. Then she trashed a boy's car she shouldn't have been driving, and her father decided she was only going to keep trying to shock me, who was so unshockable, and she'd better come live with him. Phoebe was too flattered to resist this, and I had to relent or make everything worse. This was a very bad time for me.

I phoned Doug's house too often. They didn't want all my messages. Phoebe was a big hit in her new high school—more savvy, more streetwise than the other girls. I wanted her to be happy, didn't I? "Call when you get a chance," I'd tell the machine, Mother Casual. It was not her fault how lonely I was. Any break with a man, any insult or betrayal or sudden shocking reversal, was a piece of cake compared to this.

I hadn't thought my life would turn this particular corner. I came home from work every day surprised all over again that Phoebe wasn't there. All the things I owned—my wardrobe, my furniture, the kinds of music on my records—looked tawdry and half-baked and laughable to me, the trappings of a person who had never known for a second what she was doing. The sight of an ashtray Phoebe had lumped together in day camp could make me soggy with tears.

On the phone Phoebe said, "Tell April she would like it here. They won't let me call her, and you'll see her at the supermarket or something. She would like this school, tell her."

My mother thought maybe I should really think about getting back with Doug, who was single for now. I said Doug was a boob and I hated his house, I hated the smugness of his carpets, I hated all that creepy isolation from funk and riffraff, I liked my own life. "The school of hard knocks, is that what you mean?" my mother said. "Keep knocking around, then. Go ahead."

But it was Phoebe who decided to come back, after six months. She didn't exactly say why. Or she gave too many reasons: the school was full of prissy little jerks, her father had really brainless opinions he was always mouthing, there was no place to eat as good as the Cuban place we went to. She was less noisy when she came home, as if her sojourn into another world had sobered her, and she actually did her schoolwork for a while. We were jokey together again—we had a food fight with marshmallows, we hooted at the TV—but cautious too. Anyone could have seen how cautious.

IN HER LAST YEAR of high school, when things were really quite calm, I began to wake up in the middle of the night from dreams of Randy. A terrible, keening lust for him came bursting out of nowhere, and worse than that, an old, fevered, desperate love. Certain fond phrases floated back. I remembered every eccentric detail, it turned out, every buried endearment. I'd chuckle to myself in bed over hilarious things he'd said years ago.

And no one knew where he was now, which was probably a good thing. This did not stop the dreams, or the haunting that settled over my waking hours. Sometimes I played his favorite groups on the stereo (the Cars were not so bad) or made foods he'd liked (I'd forgotten about Swiss steak). "I must have always missed him," I told Phoebe.

"What are you talking about?" Phoebe said. "You didn't even notice when he was gone. April's mother couldn't get out of bed for months when her boyfriend walked out. You didn't even sleep late."

"Yes, I did," I said. "In my heart I slept very late."

"I bragged to April about how fucking together my mother was," Phoebe said. "Don't tell me now you minded."

I told her I minded, but I believed in having a sense of *scale* about the whole thing.

"Scale who?" she said. "Like on a fish? Like on a map?"

"A map."

"I know. You were thinking of all the poor starving millions who're so busy being fucked over they'd be grateful for just a single spare moment to boo-hoo over being jilted by some asshole."

"Exactly," I said.

"Oh, Kit," she said, which was what she called me instead of Mom when she wanted to act baffled by me, though she was not baffled now at all. She squinted and cocked her head in puzzlement, like the mouse María used to say she resembled, but she was only giving me a hard time (how could she resist?).

It surprised me to think of María like that. I had a sudden memory of sitting on the floor in María's house in San Cristóbal, hooked to a backstrap loom—who did I think I was?—with Phoebe darting around, playing some loud, giddy game she and María's kids had invented. The scene was like a fan flipped down from a folded world. María had enjoyed our visits and been glad for the money, because she had no husband, a fact that had never seemed to us then to be any big deal.

Phoebe said, "I do believe you that we're not the only people on this earth. You think I don't. You never think I know anything."

"Okay, okay," I said. It was the thing I was always trying to say, wasn't it?

A person might not think that occasionally bothering

to remember how fucked up the world was would serve anyone as any sort of comfort. But it did. It made me less stupid, which was really very precious. I might have picked something that stood me far less well, I might have been a lot worse off.

PARADISE

Corinna

WE MOVED TO FLORIDA IN 1924, just as the land boom was taking off. We were not a young family—I was already twenty-one and my parents were in their forties and fifties. What was my father thinking? He was thinking two things, and only one was money. My father worked all his life in a bank in Kingston, New York, but what he loved was to be outdoors. He was a great student of trees and rocks and bugs—a great woodsman and fisherman—and he used to take my brother and me out walking the Catskill trails whenever he could. My brother was the sort of boy who liked to dash up the craggiest heights by taking a running start, but I could clamber behind quite decently. My favorite outing was a trail that was covered in mountain laurel in June and my father used to call it the Corinna Trek.

My father believed that a person who was at his ease in the woods could never be at a loss anywhere else—not in a company's office and not at a full-dress ball—because he would have a sense of the wider reaches of life. He would not be prone to small-mindedness or afraid of petty social wounds because he would carry within him always an inner independence. I was never sure whether my love of pleasant hikes could bring me quite to this level, but I was glad to think of my summer walks as leaving traces I could later use.

My father did not deliberate very long before buying the Florida property. He saw the need to seize the opportunity, though he'd always been a cautious man. And indeed what he bought was worth a good bit more within weeks. My mother was sorry to leave her family and her church—we were from a long line of Unitarians—but in her breathless and mild-eyed way, she was happy at the adventure.

And I was happy too, though I was not the sort of girl who had simple feelings about anything. This fondness for my own varying tints of thought had just caused the end of a long romance that everyone had hoped would bloom into marriage. Ted, who was a nice and reasonable boy and not stupid either, did not like my hesitations, and perhaps he was right. He complained that I didn't find him necessary.

As soon as he broke off with me, I was miserable—I woke every day in a fog of desolation—I hadn't known I would suffer like that. My mother thought I had been very rash. "You were inconsiderate," she said. "Try to consider next time." Ted was never anything more than civil when I met him in the street, and he could not be drawn back by the frankest flirting. I had cooked my own goose. So I was glad to go away, to start again in a new place. My father's Florida was a gift to me, a rescue.

MIAMI WAS A MESS of construction when we got there, but I loved the palm trees. They looked exactly as I had imagined—big umbrellas with arched fronds—but each so intricate against the sky, so gorgeously detailed, I could scarcely follow the fine-cut marks of their plumes. Rows of them lined the road to the sea, as we shuffled along in our roadster. My father said the royal palms and the towering cabbage palms and the little palmettos were native but some others had been brought from other continents. This made us all think of Owen, my brother, who was off working in the jungles of Siam, using his geology skills to help a trading company find tin. The first time I ate a fresh coconut I thought of how Owen had tried to describe it— "It is clean and crisp and unctuously rich all at once."

We stayed in a hotel at first, and my mother and I were excited tourists, taking our seaside walks and watching the waves crash against the shore in their thrilling thunderous way, right next to where cranes and clattering workmen were making their own bustling noise. My father had bought a bare weedy lot, where our house would soon be, and he had bought other land in Miami too. His plan was to sell the other lots, bit by bit. Eager buyers had already snatched up the first few and resold the lots before they had even finished paying my father.

My mother was interested in the progress of the building of our house, but I was not, and I would sit out on the
porch of our hotel and read my books (I was making my
way through anything I could get of H. G. Wells) and I'd
write letters to my friend Helene at home. Helene had
just had her wedding and liked to send humorous
accounts of keeping house for her husband. I was the only
one of my friends not yet married. Sometimes my mother
took me to tea-dances at the hotel and watched while
young men bobbed around the floor with me. I liked
talking to the men, ninnies though some of them were,
but I disliked the hotel's efforts to awe me with its insistent
luxury—Moorish ceilings and swooping satin drapes—its
eagerness to make the tropics feel moneyed. Helene and
some of my other friends at home were Communists or
syndicalists—Kingston was not entirely a backwater. I was
not of a theoretical nature, but I certainly believed that
sharing was better than grabbing or hoarding. But I liked
the dancing, as I always had. I was good-looking enough
to get plenty of partners, which was very pleasant. I liked
the sweating musicians and would have tried to talk to the
mustached fiddler had my mother not been nearby.

I wrote to my brother Owen:

I see why you love the jungle so. Even in this would-be
city, I have the sense that tender vines are growing tree-
size overnight. Everyone is complaining of the heat as
summer approaches, but I like the freedom of less cumbrous

garments and the heavy air feels friendly to me. Am I a
lazy lizard? Our father thinks so. He would like me to be
scaring up a husband. He is on fire with his own projects
however—every bit of sand in Miami will be worth its
weight in gold dust! Every mangrove swamp will have a
palace on it! I shouldn't laugh, should I, since I'm living
so pleasantly here on his prospects. Mother has been lan-
guishing in the heat, but she chatters from her chaise
longue, bringing me gossip of an often delicious kind. I like
it here, but I wish there were more people like me.

AT SUPPER, WHEN HE was not too busy to eat with us, my
father would fret cheerfully about when to sell his holdings. "You know it's only human," he said, "to try to hold
out for the highest profit."

"Is it?" I said. "In Muslim countries, they think it's
wrong to gain money for work you haven't done."

"That just applies to interest," my father said.
"They're against charging for loans. Every piece of bread
that's passed into your mouth, missy, has been from that
interest."

My father always took me down for being spoiled and
airy when I made my gadfly arguments, when I spoke of
other systems, and as long as my own good fortune was
braided into things I couldn't admire, I knew, with some
pain, that he had a point. I didn't know if this point was
something I would ever get over. Couldn't we live without taking things from other people? My friends at home

thought so—there was indeed a whole body of thought on the subject.

My father thought I was a green girl with no understanding of the laws of economics. I did not understand how there could be laws, when each system of thought pleaded from a separate set of truths, like different kingdoms each with its own constitution.

"You know," my mother said, "sometimes I wish we just used stones for coins and squatted in the dirt. Do you think people were happier in those days?"

"We'll never know," I said. I thought the glitter of Florida was perhaps beginning to pall on my mother. She loved company and novelty and conversation, but she was delicate.

We were all more comfortable when we moved into our house. There was much work to do settling in, but my mother and I understood this sort of work, and we both enjoyed the greater quiet. My mother hired a maid and a cook, and then she felt more substantial. Sometimes I slipped off for secret meetings with Artie, the violinist from the hotel band, a Jew from Chicago. He was exceedingly handsome and had been to many places and I might have run off with him if he'd asked, but he didn't ask, though we had long kissing and petting sessions on an isolated tip of the beach, of a more intense and swooning kind than I'd known with Ted. He had a lovely way of cracking clever jokes too but he didn't otherwise know how to talk to me and he may well have had a wife somewhere. It took me a few months to come to that thought.

My brother Owen wrote to me from the south of Siam:

> *Greetings from the jungle outpost. Here I'm alone but not alone. First some villager comes tramping into town to tell us there is a rich vein of tin in some hard-to-get-to spot, and then I go off with my crew—my trusty right-hand man is a Malay who can do all things and my cook is a clever Chinaman, and my workers are anyone I can get. I don't see women except when we go into a village, but to be a white man is to be suddenly quite an attractive fellow here—I have become irresistible! (Don't read this bit to Mother.) I could sometimes wish for someone to talk with as a peer, but the long day's marching on these bush-whacked trails is just what I like, and best of all is the evening in my tent, when I've splashed myself clean from a basin and the cook brings me my supper. Did I mention that Siamese girls are beautiful?*

I MYSELF WAS in a dreamy fever. I'd sit on our patio, where my mother and I had set out pots of red ginger and anthurium and bird-of-paradise plants, and I'd have my secret thoughts of Artie. The bright outsized extravagance of the plants was a kind of propaganda for what nature really was. I wasn't reckless—I had some prudence in me—and some uneasiness about my future too, but I was fond of conjuring heated specifics of what might be.

—

IT DID WEAR ON me to always be so secret, to always have
to tell my mother I was taking yet another long solitary
walk on the beach in the afternoon. "They would get
used to you," I told Artie. "If they met you, they would
understand." My parents did not dislike Jews—truly
not—though I could hardly expect that they would welcome an unprosperous one into the family, a man who
played the violin at night in hotels. It angered me the way
money snuck into my most intimate matters. But they
would be cordial, my parents. My father would try to
draw Artie into conversation about fishing or autumn
hurricanes. My mother, in her shy curiosity, would ask
awkward questions about his faith. I did not even have a
chance to warn him of these things.

"Oh, no, not necessary," he said. "Meeting them, I
mean. Not needed, doll. Not at all."

I knew then that he was going to slip away from me, a
thread without a knot. I pleased him greatly—his dark-
browed face always brightened when he saw me—but he
had no plans for us. I was going to have to watch out for
myself, since I had chosen to go into this unguarded by
family. We were not lovers, but I had to be careful. I relin-
quished all private settings for us. I would only go with
him to a pleasantly underlit speakeasy near his hotel, very
quiet in the afternoons, with its shadowy murals of monkeys and parrots and its thick mauve-brown rugs. At our
dark table, we nuzzled and squabbled; he told stories
about what the drunken drummer in the band said to the

man with a dog. Perhaps he never thought I would linger with him even as long as this. I was a surprise to him in every way.

IN THE SECOND YEAR in Florida my father was always consulting with someone about how to raise funds on property whose value was not what it had been. To save money, we had to let the cook go, and my mother took over the kitchen and made great efforts to fuss over my father. Would he only eat more breaded pork chops? Wasn't banana cream pie his favorite? It was a very tender time between them. My father looked like a weary old lion, squinting in his chair, and my mother cajoled and teased him.

MY PARENTS WERE disappointed when I sent away a young man they'd introduced me to, a real estate investor, who'd proved coarser and less intelligent as I'd gotten to know him. My mother said, a little sourly, that my father was working hard for me—he knew a girl needed a dowry, even a pretty girl—and I wasn't doing all that I could to help my own chances.

"A dowry," I said. "Oh, Mother. That's from a different century."

"I always thought," she said, "that Ted in Kingston might have proposed if you'd had more of a fortune behind you."

"That wasn't it," I said. "Absolutely not."

"Not to you, perhaps," she said. "But who's to say?"

This was not at all like the sweet dullness I'd been raised in, the poky upstate life in which my father read to us from Emerson's essays and much family humor rested on the showy hats and affected speech of our neighbors. What was happening to my family? I loved Florida, but I thought that my mother, of all of us, should not have come.

MY BROTHER WROTE TO ME:

> At first all the people I met here were Buddhists—you would admire their lovely little temples—but it seems that on the southeast coast a good many people here follow the Mohammedan faith. They believe in one God only and think the Trinity is hogwash (just like us Unitarians) and their Paradise (which their prophet dreamed up in the middle of the desert) is a place of lush, ever-watered gardens—just like the Siamese-Malayan jungle I'm in! There the trees droop with delicious fruit, from branches never failing and never out of reach—according to Zain (rhymes with fine), my Malay factotum. I quite like being around their calls to prayer—Allahu Akbar, La ilahah illallah—being a foreigner lets me hear the beauty of it, without anyone expecting anything of me. Oh, the luxury of foreignness! I saw a wedding party in Pattani—no liquor and everyone sitting on the ground to eat. Would you like that for your own nuptial gala, do you think?

I hardly let out any sort of shriek when Artie announced, "Corinna, my girl, I'm moving on. Going to St. Louis with another dinner orchestra." I was a good sport, a champ of a girl. "Poor lamb," I said. "Chilly winters again for you. But business is crummy here, everybody knows." I probably overdid my heartiness in wishing him the best, but I saw no other way not to be entirely absurd. I might have torn my heart out and handed him its pulpy mass and he still would not have stayed.

My anguish was protracted and private, and I stayed home and read novels until I was dizzy and headachy from the marching blocks of blackish type. I sent pressed hibiscus to my friend Helene at home, with blithe remarks about the tropics, though everyone knew the bottom had fallen out of the land market all over Florida. Not far from us was a field of deserted construction sites, dug-up hillocks of dry dirt looking sadly expectant, a street that was not going to be a street after all.

I kept a flask of Cuban rum in my room for the nights when I really could not sleep. I did not like resorting to it, but some nights—especially in the electric restlessness before late-summer storms—it was the only thing that helped. My father, who had nothing but a chain of lying buyers who'd defaulted on his Miami lots, had enough of his own troubles. My mother tried to keep us going with jolly talk and an excess of pie, but when my father wasn't home, she was a morose companion. She said to me, "You've let too much time go by." Where would I find a husband now?

———

MY FATHER HAD taken to blaming the tin-canners. These were the hordes of people who'd driven to Florida from who knew where and stayed in auto camps and lived on tinned food and carried their extra gas and water in big metal cans. "They don't buy land," my father said, "and they're too temporary to contribute to anything."

"Well," my mother said brightly, "they're making the tin company that Owen works for rich. They're his customers!"

"Drifters are a drain," my father said.

"Didn't we drift in?" I said.

"If you can't be civil," my mother said, "I'll have to ask you not to speak."

It was not like my mother to snap at me so harshly, and I understood from this that my father was really not doing well at all. I had my own disdain for his failed cleverness, his solid science that had come to dust, but his suffering was real.

"My girls are pulling together," he'd say, as my mother and I swept the house or waxed the furniture. I might have worried more about him, I might have shown more feeling for the melancholic spectacle of half-built houses on abandoned land, I might have tried to raise my mother's spirits, but I was caught up in my longing for Artie.

I HARDLY DREAMED on those nights when sips of rum with lemon water were my friendly soporific, when the swampy smell of summer weather outside took me into an utter blank until the head-splitting morning. So I was surprised when I half awoke in my bed to the percussive noise of smashed bottles, as if a speakeasy owner were throwing out his trash. When I opened my eyes, the night sky was oddly lit up, and the window across the room was cracked and broken. A gust of wind was flapping at my coverlet, tugging it across the bed. I heard the rain begin then, a beat of heavy drops that sounded torrential within minutes. Water was splashing through the broken window and hitting my bed. People hadn't said a hurricane was coming—or had they? Did I ever listen to anything? Was this what a hurricane was? I could not get my door open—the wind was blowing it closed. When I wedged my way through at last, I lost my balance and fell down the hall. I had to hoist myself up with a bruised shoulder and crawl along the carpet. I wanted to get to my parents.

My mother looked like a ruffled bird, a terrified chick, coming out of their doorway to find me. "Honeybunch! We're all okay! There you are!" she shouted. She was wrapped in a blanket, and my father, in his undershorts, was standing behind her.

"Shouldn't we be in the basement?" I said.

"You're bleeding," my father said. "I think we should stay as we are."

I thought I might attempt the stairs if I went down on my bottom, the way I used to on the steeper mountain trails, but from the top step I saw that our living room was by now under a flood of water. This frightened me more than anything else had. I lurched back to the room where my parents were huddled under a table. My mother said, "What's the purpose of such weather, do you think?" What purpose indeed, what bullying. We had misread the air, the violence waiting in its soft currents, the wet gunpowder in its humidity.

My father got up and tied a sock around the bruise on my shoulder. He tried to keep us calm by pointing out that the last hurricane, in July, had been nothing and soon this one would be too. He put on his robe to wait it out. But I was angry with my father, whose boyish itch for more than we needed had brought us here, where we didn't belong.

WHEN THE STORM ENDED, very early in the morning, we went down to the living room in the early bluish light. The water was up to our knees and our brown velvet sofa was pitched on its side, stained and drowned. There was no electricity and my mother sloshed through the dim hallway with her wet nightgown billowing. In the kitchen she found some oranges for us to eat where we stood. How bright they tasted, no fruit could have been more astounding. I was so grateful to my mother for them. I thought that our shared treat in the ruined parlor was like wartime, and I thought of my brother, who'd been in France during the war. From the parlor windows we could see a house down the lane with its entire roof gone. Gone where?

My father wanted to go outside to see what had happened to our house and to check on our neighbors down the road, and so we changed to our day clothes and put on boots. Under the white sky the landscape was gouged and wrung out—palm trees torn up by the roots and my father's black car upended in a ditch like a giant insect— and everything dripping muddy tears. We all stood speechless at the way we'd been dopey admirers of the prettiness of nature, silly tourists feeding saucers of milk to a tiger cub.

My father walked us toward the main road, though no one else seemed to be out yet. A huge, thick cypress tree had fallen across the spot where our little lane crossed the larger street, and my father thought we should try to roll it out of the way in case a vehicle needed to get through. The efforts of all three of us did not seem to get the trunk to move. "You didn't know your dad brought us here for manual labor, did you?" my mother said. Adversity was rousing her.

"Inspiration is ninety percent perspiration," I said, pretending to wipe my brow, though a breeze was picking up and we were not really so hot.

My father—"our mighty leader," my mother was calling him—was reasoning out another angle for our pushing when the rain started again. "Leave it till later!" my mother called out gaily.

We were splashing our way back to the house as the wind blew the gushing rain back into our faces. My father slipped, and I had a hard time getting him back up. "Too much pie, Dad," I said, but he couldn't hear me over the wind. My mother and I screamed when a utility pole was knocked over and crashed to the ground half a block in front of us. "Go on," my father shouted. I didn't see why we were going straight into the wind, but I did what my father said. "We're the Charge of the Light Brigade," I yelled. The pole rose from the ground as if it wanted to right itself, and my father tried to pull us to the side—until the pole swung into the air before us, a monstrous stick of creosoted wood, twice the height of our house, flying much too close, no matter how we screamed at it.

I WOKE UP WITH a great pain in my arm, and above me was a ceiling tiered with gilded plaster garlands, festoons of sculpted ribbons. I knew that there were other people in the room, and I thought at first that we were at a wedding inside the ballroom of a ship. I drifted in and out of a haziness of sleep, angry that I had been taken to a celebration when I was clearly not well at all.

People spoke to me from time to time, and while they made very little sense, by the time I was ready to open my eyes I had begun to piece something together. I was in the McAlister Hotel, where my mother used to watch me dance, but I was lying on a pallet on the floor with other people next to me. My parents were not there. No one knew where my parents were. A woman in a brown skirt said that someone would come and tell me sometime, but I was not to move.

So I didn't. Why didn't I? I might have shouted and dragged myself up and lurched out of that silk-paneled hotel-turned-clinic to find them. I was unspeakably weary, but I shouldn't have lain there, still as a stone, as if it didn't matter whether they were alive or dead.

It was not until the second day, when I could sit up and eat some kind of thin oatmeal, that I plagued a sallow-faced young man from the Red Cross about the urgency of informing my parents, who would be worried sick. My head ached and my arm was swollen and scraped and some fingers were wrapped in bloody gauze, but really I was fine. "Right as rain," I said. My parents needed to know.

Everyone said my people would find me, but I had the idea, once I was strong enough, to insist that a volunteer drive me back to our house. The water was not so deep in the streets anymore. From two blocks away I crowed to see the roof still on. "My father had a good house built," I said to the man driving me. Then I saw the utility pole lying across the road, and under it was a very large dark leaf, which was not a leaf, when we grew closer, but a jagged piece of the India-rubber jacket my father wore. I knew then—or was afraid I knew—even before our neighbor came out of the house down the lane and tried to tell me what had happened to my mother and father.

SHE SPOKE IN a respectful whisper—a woman I hardly knew, a snappy young matron with spit curls—and it took her a while to explain—she had to say first how happy she was that I was all right—but the words, *So sorry, so sorry, they were lovely people*, were clear enough. Killed. Both. My dear. Oh. She called me my dear.

I covered my face with my hands because I did not like being surrounded by strangers at this moment. I was angry that my parents weren't there to help me, now of all times when I needed them most. I let the neighbor lead me away. What was her first name? I heard myself thanking her.

I WOULD NOT LET anyone stay in the house with me. It seemed indecent to have to talk with strangers. But I did not really know what to do with myself once the others left. All the rooms downstairs bore the marks of flood, furniture swamped against a wall, the Persian rug a darkened sponge. The house, with its smell of dirty water, had no noise in it. I was alone (as my mother would say) with my thoughts.

I sat on the soggy lower step of the stairs and heard my own moaning, an animal sound ridiculous with no hearer but the maker of it. At the bottom of the well where my mind was, I wanted very badly to have my brother with me, which was not possible. I got up to phone the telegraph office, but the telephone line was still dead. The emptiness in the receiver made me feel crazy and I crouched on the floor in defeat. The carpet under me was already turning to algae, to rot; everything human-made had given way, been pulled apart and separated from itself. The house had been churned into swamp, sunk back to its old form.

I rallied myself enough to change into decent clothes, and I walked to the center of town, where the Western Union was. It was a walk of perhaps forty minutes and it was a good idea. The wreckage was so general—buildings collapsed against each other and turned into ancient ruins, mothers leading small frightened children through reeking mud—that it reminded me (though I could not truly absorb it) that mine was not the only woe on earth.

On the way I composed the message that I would send to the Bangkok bureau of my brother's company. I did not know how long it would take to reach him in the south. I had to be as short as I could and yet present the news without cruelty, and the labor of this served me as a form of devotion. Hurricane here. Very bad news.

BY THE TIME OWEN answered me, I was already back in Kingston with our relatives, though I'd had to wait weeks until the railroad was running. His telegram was forwarded to me from Florida. He wrote:

> *Cannot believe. Are you all-right. My dear sister.*
> *Letter coming.*

The letter took five weeks to arrive, and I was very glad to get it. I was settled in with my Aunt Leonie, in her big house by the river. She was a widow, my four cousins were grown, and she said I was good company, though I was hardly talkative. When she spoke of my mother, she called her Francie, and the picture of my mother as a young girl came to me with particular pain. Aunt Leonie liked to distract me with games of checkers. I was too weak to do anything but be polite, but I was seized by a longing to hide. I could not really remember why people bothered to speak to each other, actually. My brother wrote:

> *Two things are much on my mind now. Why did I choose to be so far away? And are earthly ties broken by death? I don't think I should plague you with my speculations (too many nights alone in my tent?) but I wish we could talk face to face. How are you now? I hope you've stayed in Florida. You seemed to like so much the warm climate and the lush vegetation and the subtropical life. I haven't heard about the will (hard-to-find creature that I am) but I assume you are well provided for. Father would want this, we know. But I think you are probably comfortable, if that word can be used at a wrenching time like this. I imagine you having your quiet days, sitting out on the patio you described, gaining strength bit by bit.*
>
> *It is my hope (I think quite a good deal about this) that our father did truly think well of my venturing forth into the tin mines of Siam. I know it was very hard on Mother.*

I READ THIS in my aunt's cozy, overfurnished parlor, with a lap robe keeping off the chill. My friend Helene had told me I had to be careful or I could remain there forever, the maiden niece. My brother was not at all right about my father's estate, which was mired in debt and encumbered by the sale of a house no one cared to buy. I had wanted all the unpaid bills settled and I'd had a dispute with the estate's lawyer, who saw no need to pay anyone who'd worked for my father or sold him anything. He hadn't listened to me, and I couldn't think of anything to do but reason and weep, both of which failed. "He believed it was in your interest to cheat," Helene said. "Any gain seems responsible to such men."

Helene also believed in outlawing all inheritance of money. I had missed talk like that and was cheered to be with her again. I said that I was against greed, and Helene said that was a religious belief, not a political one. Had no state ever tried to put it into practice? "Russia is trying," Helene said.

She brought in more local news too than I could get from my aunt, some of it not so welcome. Ted had gotten engaged over the summer to a person named Priscilla (whose nickname was Prissy and rightly so) and they were buying the pretty stone house with turrets three blocks away.

In my letter to Owen, I said I was depending at present on the generosity of Aunt Leonie, and no one could be kinder, but I did not like to think of my future as a long continuance of this situation. Kingston hardly felt like home. I could be of use keeping house for him in Siam, if he would have me. He knew that I was sturdy, and I had already adapted well to a hot climate. And think of the points he'd gain in heaven for taking in an orphan of the storm!

I wrote several versions before mailing it. What was I

doing? I had no money of my own. I didn't want to stay
with my aunt and I was too timid to try to support myself
in another city. I was going to become more timid still,
more lost to all effort, if I stayed.

Are you sure? Owen wrote. *It is rough here, and there
aren't many other people from America or Europe. The best I
could do would be to set up a house in Pattani, a nice enough town,
but I would be away much of the time. Corinna, try to think
clearly. It's not so easy to go back once you've come.*

I COULD SEE HIS reluctance (and perhaps his Siamese
women already kept house for him) but I saw there was an
opening for me, a hole in the darkness. I saw my chance
and I took it. My aunt kept exclaiming, with some dismay, how brave I was. Was I? I had only the smallest idea
of the place where I was going.

HELENE, WHEN SHE SAID GOODBYE, said, "It's good you
have Owen." And indeed he was all I had, my own boyish, blustering brother (and I hoped he wasn't wishing too
hard I'd gotten myself married). I had a long train ride to
San Francisco, and these days without conversation were
a relief to me. People think being alone is an unfortunate
feeling but it isn't, altogether. On the ship to Singapore, I
liked my tiny stateroom, with everything tucked into its
nooks. It had no portholes, and I awoke the first night
afraid of suffocating in the closeted dark. The fear made
me miss my parents—I had no one to cry out to. In the
morning I was better, and on sunny days it suited me to

sit out on the lower deck with my book in my lap and the great ocean all around. I was still too dulled by loss to be excited, but it freshened me to be where I was.

A woman named Beatrice from San Francisco, who was en route to be married to a pearl trader in Singapore, liked to play canasta with me, though I was a lackadaisical and sloppy card player. She was full of laughter, chatty and quite tickled with herself. I had been more like that once. We bet a few coins on each game, but I stopped this after I lost every round. Beatrice said if I did not have the spirit of a gambler, how was I to thrive in a new place? "Surely," I said, "there's more than one way to be a foreigner in Asia." She didn't know any more than I did, really.

There were men we might have flirted with on the boat—Beatrice did, actually—some British civil servants coming back from holidays and a man going out to a rubber estate in Malaya. For myself I had lost the will to charm anyone. I did expect this to change.

When we docked at Singapore I tried to make out Owen's figure in the crowd at the wharf. I kept thinking I saw him and then I didn't. If Owen didn't appear, I had no idea what to do, on that dock full of strangers. I was not so clever as I liked to think. How silly and cringing I must have looked to anyone nearby. And then I saw a man running along the quay wearing a pith helmet, the green-lined kind the English called a topee. He was sun-darkened and squint-eyed and older, but Owen under the hat. It was a very good thing to hear him call my name.

"I'm here!" I shouted. "Amazing, isn't it?"

"Oh, Corinna. I hope it wasn't a rough crossing."

"It was fun, really," I said.

I could see, as he hugged me, that he was relieved that I didn't seem such a mess as he must have feared. He was my older brother, used to thinking I could hardly buckle my shoes. I was unspeakably thrilled to see him.

We were surrounded by Chinamen—in straw boaters and business suits, in loose cotton pajamas with their hair in queues under conical hats, or stripped to the waist hauling my steamer trunk onto the top of a motorcar. I heard their rapid up-and-down speech and I understood that I was in Asia—Asia!—and I had a flush of being proud of myself. As if I'd never had a second's fear.

OWEN TOOK US to a clean, quiet, small hotel, all louvered shutters and white-painted wood. I had just time to splash water on my face before he had us go down to the lounge for cooling drinks. Singapore was hotter even than the boat had been. I was glad I was enough of a flapper not to wear anything like a corset, but the silk of my undergarments stuck to me. In this place, the liquid of the body was barely contained, a primeval marsh seeping through the pores.

"I'm not used to cities anymore," Owen said. "I bet I look like someone who's just crept out of the jungle on all fours."

"You look all right," I said. "A little toasted and tightened."

"I go days without speaking a word of English," he said. "My Siamese isn't that good—tone languages are hard—but my Malay's really not bad. I learned it fast when I first came and I keep in practice."

"Who do you speak Malay to?"

"Zain, my man, the fellow who knows everything. You'll see how astounding he is when you meet him. And people on the eastern side of the peninsula mostly speak Malay."

"What do you boss your workers in?"

"Most of the workers are Chinese, actually—they seem to pour out of China, looking for work—but they can follow what they need to in Malay or Siamese. And I need Siamese for the villagers in the west."

"And for the ladies too?"

"Yes," he said, smirking a little. "But there's only one lady now, so try not to act as if you expected me to have a horde."

"Will I meet her?"

"I don't think so," he said. "She's in a village, you'll be in the city. There's some English people who have a school and one of the women is going to help you get set up."

"I'm sure I'll like it, wherever it is. Do you feel at home here now, do you think?"

"Me?" he said. "I carry my house on my back, I'm a bachelor."

"On the ship coming over," I said, "people tittered about how the single women were the fishing fleet, come out to hook husbands. It's a very old joke. I told them I was going to live in a tent in the jungle with an orangutan for a fiancé."

"Did you?" my brother said. "That can be arranged."

"An orangutan who plays the clarinet and grows orchids," I said.

In the chairs around us, cooled by the overhead fans, shone the faces of young men in stiff collars and linen jackets. Some of them eyed me from over their whiskeys, as men often did. I was not quite ready to eye them. My brother thanked the waiter in Chinese, which made one table of men murmur in amusement.

"I don't know why they're chuckling," my brother said. "They're in a city where the richest companies are Chinese. Idjits, those men are. That's how they say it. Idjits. I don't, you know, hobnob with Europeans or Americans anymore."

I was going to make a joke about his having gone native, but I had the sense not to be buffoonish. Owen had always been a thoughtful boy, and now he'd had years of nursing his opinions all on his own. I wasn't smitten with the oafs at the next table either, but I hoped Siam had others. It was my bad luck if it didn't.

OWEN WAS EAGER to get out of Singapore, though it seemed quite a fantastical city to me. The Chinese were the most numerous, but on the streets we saw tan-complected Asians that Owen told me were Malay from the interior and other races I could not identify—Tamil from South India (he said) and others. I tried to talk to the Chinese shopkeepers while Owen bought supplies for his treks.

"It's simpler in the jungle," he said.

"I'm going to start calling you Tuan Simple," I said, just to show I, his sister, was not entirely taken in by his scrupulous rusticity. And I had already learned the word in Malay for master, though I felt an American would say boss instead.

THE TRAIN WE TOOK NORTH, up the spine of Malaya, was called the jungle railway, a rickety and dingy length of cars, but it excited me greatly to look out the window and catch sight of the grasslands giving way at last—ah, look—to hillsides dark with palm trees and dense, still thickets of leafy overgrowth. The massed trunks and vines and aerial roots were like a giant hedge veiling out the sun. Here and there I'd spy a slatted wooden house on stilts in a clearing, and once a group of children waved at the train. I could scarcely believe that each time I glanced again I still saw jungle; the word had become a room in my imagination and I hardly credited the swath of deep green with its own reality. I was transfixed at the window, quite out of myself. Owen was pleased that I watched with such interest.

We were two days on the train, sleeping on beds that dropped down like narrow padded shelves. Owen found his too short—he was a tall man here—but I liked mine fine. I liked all this, I liked being with my brother again.

Owen went out at the stations to buy cut fruit and leaf-wrapped pyramids of coconut rice with oily bits of dried fish in it. I was very set on being a good sport, because I was scared every time Owen left me and I didn't want him to know. We stopped finally at the very northeast edge of Malaya, in Kota Bharu, a town where Owen said his man Zain had family.

Owen was looking to the luggage when a slender dark man, wearing a faded cloth suit and white canvas shoes like a European's, walked straight at us. I hoped it was Zain, and it was. He and Owen seemed wonderfully glad to see each other, and he greeted me with a very courteous gesture—he put his hand over his heart.

I wanted to see more of Kota Bharu, which seemed to be a drab provincial city with shops and markets, but my brother hastened us in a parade of rickshaws to the boating dock, and there we waited for an hour with nothing to do until the motorboat set sail noisily along the coast. Under the blare of the engine I tried to converse with Zain. Had he had a good visit with his family? His face clouded, and he said something that my brother translated as, "So-so." He was a stately man, I thought, and good-looking, with the lean cheeks of a cat and a quiet voice. In my head I was writing a letter to Helene about him.

"NOW YOU'RE IN SIAM," my brother said, when we got off the noisy boat. We were at the mouth of a river, a muddy, mosquito-infested shore, and not till I was seated in a rickshaw and had crossed a bridge did I see the city of

Pattani. It looked no different to me from the towns of
Malaya and had (I was told) once been part of a separate
Muslim kingdom with other bits of Siam. I saw pale
buildings with colonnades and vertical signs painted in
Chinese writing and narrow shops all clumped together
and streets full of men—Chinese in their black trousers
and Malay in their neatly tucked sarongs.

The place had a distinct and interesting odor, of muck
and smoke and ripe fruit and briny fish, a dark riverine
odor. My brother directed our rickshaw to the Siamese
quarter, on the other side of the river from where the
Malay and Chinese lived. We stopped in front of a grand
gray edifice. I could tell from the sounds outside that it
was a school, and Asian boys in uniform were chasing
each other in the backyard. When Owen pulled the rope
of the bell, a young Siamese man answered—his words
were all nasal cooing and soft popping sounds, like nothing I'd heard in my life—and then a sweating blond
woman was dashing toward us. She wore a cotton frock
with a belt around the hips, only a little dowdier than
what I wore, and she looked to be in her thirties. "I've
been waiting and waiting!" she called out. "Are you
bushed and done in? You look it, all of you. I can have
them set out a pitcher of lime juice. Are you hungry? Tell
me if you're hungry. She's much prettier than you,
Owen. Much."

This was Dilys, my alleged guide to setting up house
while Owen was on the road, and I was relieved that she
was not quite the starchy Englishwoman I'd feared. She

and her husband ran the school, which was sponsored by the Church of England. "You're a good girl to come and help your brother," she said. I didn't think anyone believed this version of events, but I was glad to hear her say it.

I did not even notice until we were sitting in her parlor, drinking a very nice limeade and eating a lovely greasy snack called curry puffs, that Zain was not with us. He had gone off to the kitchen with the servants. I was disappointed because I had been formulating things to ask him, but Dilys kept me busy with advice. "It's a bit suicidal to go outside without a hat. Servants here don't like it if you hover over them. Make sure your food safe has its legs in paraffin to keep out the ants. Shake out your shoes and the scorpions won't bother you."

I said I planned to scare the scorpions myself. Owen was giving me a look: *Don't mock her.* "You'll be all right, then," Dilys said, a little grimly.

IT WAS LATE AFTERNOON by the time we left and made our way to the house that Owen had taken for us, a few streets away. Before my arrival he had hardly lived anywhere, staying in the houses of village headmen or on the floors of temples or in some wretched rooms his firm rented in another city. The house he had found us here was a wooden bungalow, unpainted outside and in, like a hunter's cabin in the Catskills. Owen made us all take off our shoes before we walked on the floor, with its clean covering of bamboo mats. The luggage had gone ahead of us, and my big steamer trunk seemed the only furnishing, except for some wooden cabinets and some stiff wedges of pillows to lean against, and beds set low on the floors of the side rooms, which someone had made up with beautiful coverlets of gold-threaded brocade. That some-one, it turned out, was Zain, who was having a bright pink fruit drink in the kitchen and gossiping with Ho Lu Ki, the cook. The cook, a Chinese boy who did not look more than nineteen, had a little English and made a friendly speech to me that included the words, "*Tuan* lucky sister." Was *tuan* very lucky to have such a com-mendable sister, sacrificing her comfort to come here? Or did the cook think I was lucky to come to this paradisia-cal country? I wished I knew.

But I liked my new house. I liked the windows look-ing out to what my brother said were casuarina trees, which gave off a piney turpentine scent, and to a neigh-boring yard hung with someone else's laundry, gay printed cottons and filmy scarves. I was sorry my mother couldn't see how bright and sprightly this part of the town was, and how well I was doing for myself, husband-less though I happened to be. My father would have wanted to know about the region's insects—we were burning coils of incense to keep them away—and the birds and reptiles. I was doing my best not to think about the reptiles. I would have liked my parents there, Owen and all of us together. Part of me believed they still waited for me at home.

Owen and I had supper by ourselves, sitting cross-legged over a tasty mess of chicken with soya sauce and rice. In such a small house we could hear Ho Lu Ki and Zain in the kitchen, scraping at their plates, and I thought we were a parody of a mansion. Separate quarters but no indoor plumbing.

"How can it be true," Owen said, "that Dad left you with no money to speak of? You don't think the lawyer duped you out of it, do you?"

"Oh, Owen," I said. "It was Dad's doing—his eagerness to throw all his eggs in one basket. And then the basket broke. Just like that. It did make me believe that money was only paper."

"I wish it were. I wouldn't have to run around in the rain scraping every creek bed in the forest for tin ore."

"And grabbing every tinny plot for your company."

"Oh, the company has suffered—big dip in the tin market a few years ago. Market's up again now."

"I hate markets," I said.

"You sound like a little spoiled flapper after all," Owen said. What did Owen know? He was clinging to what could be lost in a second. I felt superior for the lessons of loss. I was forgetting then that Owen had lost his parents too.

Anyway, I was too old for him to speak to in this way. "If I cared more about money, would I be less spoiled?" I said.

Neither of us wanted to fight just yet. I could see Owen pausing. "I should have sent money home," he said.

"What a horrible idea," I said. "They would have been insulted."

"I should have done something," he said. I didn't want to say: *They would have died anyway.*

"I should have married someone," I said. "They would've been happy at that."

OWEN AND ZAIN went with me the next day to one of the great bustling markets in the street, where I was allowed to buy some woven bamboo boxes for my clothes and some lengths of batik fabric to make the bungalow more human. The lines of crowded booths, with every vendor calling out to us, made me a bit dizzy. Zain did our bargaining—sometimes he spoke in Malay and sometimes in Siamese. I watched his expressions—cajoling and bantering or frowning with feigned shock—as he bargained for me. How was I ever to do this myself once he and Owen were off hunting tin? Dilys would come with me—oh, she was good at this, yes—and I was to be given (Owen actually said "given") a girl who would cook and clean and live in the back of my house.

"*Tuan,*" Zain said, "*lapar, tak?*" He called Owen *tuan*! It made me gasp and want to laugh.

"He's asking if I'm hungry," Owen said.

Various tidbits were purchased—chicken grilled on bamboo skewers, steamed balls of minced fish, and a thick stew of beef in coconut that Owen said was water buffalo. We strolled about, eating all of it with our fingers, like greedy children at a fair. The Chinese buns with sweet pork were Owen's favorite; Zain, who was Muslim, wouldn't take any.

Muslim! I hadn't thought. "And does he want one of those wives who lives forever behind a veil?" I asked Owen.

"Never mind," Owen said. "I'll tell you later."

IN THE FIRST PLACE, Owen told me after supper when Zain went off to meet friends at the night market, surely I could see very well that many Malay Muslim women didn't wear veils or headscarves at all (really, I hardly knew what I was seeing yet). In the second place, Zain had a wife—he'd married young and fathered two children too. His wife had not liked Pattani, because of the troubles, but Zain loved his home district.

"What troubles?" I said.

"Before I came. A big bloody revolt four years ago."

"A revolt against what?"

Pattani, as he'd told me before if I'd only been listening, had once been the capital of a Malay Muslim state. A Siamese king had conquered it some four hundred–odd years ago, and the locals, Owen said, had been revolting pretty often ever since. In Owen's opinion, the more panicky the Siamese got about controlling things—the more they put Bangkok commissioners over every regional bigwig, the more they banned the Malay language in schools, the more every local dispute was decided by an outsider— the more violent outbreaks there were. "Poor bloodthirsty beggars," Owen said. The Muslims pretty much always lost. After the last mess, an uncle of Zain's wife had died in jail in Bangkok under very questionable circumstances. She said she couldn't stand to live in such a country.

Zain said no one could make him leave his home, no one. They quarreled bitterly, and in the end he consented to let his wife go across the border to Malaya, to Kota Bharu, where she had relatives. She was sure British regents were a lesser evil than the Siamese. Only recently had he seen his children again.

"Does he love his wife still?"

"He seems to," Owen said. "Don't make a whole valentine out of this, Cory. But he does, I think."

Owen said that on this trip Zain had brought gifts for his little daughter and son, a piece of pretty silk and a kite and a painted wooden top that he had shopped for very carefully, but the visit had not gone well.

AT NIGHT ON MY kapok-stuffed pallet of a bed, I could feel all of them in the house—Owen in the bedroom next to mine, and Zain and Ho Lu Ki at the back of the house. Men were breathing and sighing and turning in their sleep all around me. I assumed they slept nude, as I did, so we were a house of bare forms, like dolls in a factory. Most of what I could hear, actually, was the thrum of crickets and the occasional *djok-djok* of lizards in the thick air outside, the endless whirring clicking sounds sealing us in, as I was sealed in my tent of gauzy white mosquito netting. My aunt had wondered if I would feel safe here, though truly that category had been taken from me by the hurricane. I was wrapped now in vibrations I could hardly think of decoding, and I liked (as much as I'd liked anything for six months) giving myself over to this strangeness. It was so dark I couldn't see my own hand, and I had a lovely sense of escape.

THE NEXT MORNING, as we were drinking tea and eating rice noodles, Dilys came into the bungalow with the Siamese girl who was to work for me.

"Oh, Owen," Dilys said. "You really couldn't get a better house?"

"It's very nice," I said. We were sitting on the floor, with a cloth set out before us.

The girl bowed with her palms together, as they all did, and backed away, but Dilys continued to loom above. "We'll get some proper furniture made for you when your barbarian brother leaves," she said.

The girl's name was Som and she hardly looked more than thirteen, but it was hard to guess. She wore her hair in the short brushy cut Siamese women here favored, and she was bare-shouldered, wearing a tiny singlet over a sarong whose ends were crossed between the legs to form pants. Dilys assured me she spoke quite a bit of English. When prodded, she did say, "Happy to mee you." She was nothing to be afraid of, at least.

"Perhaps Owen will want to stay home now that he has one," Dilys said to me. She seemed to address one person at a time. I wondered how she taught school in this way.

I DID GET TO SEE the school, in that first week before Owen left. We went to a recital of boys performing an

abridged version of Shakespeare's *Julius Caesar*. An English boy in a white-sheet toga played Mark Antony and a
Siamese ten-year-old struggled heroically with Julius's
lines. If he could learn a language, surely I could. He was
stabbed with a monstrous dagger with a wavy blade that
Owen, whispering next to me, said was a cardboard version of a Malayan kris. Only one Malay boy was in the
production. Muslims avoided mission schools, Owen
said, but the Siamese government had shut all Islamic
schools a few years before, and one parent now sent his
boys here. We clapped wildly when the curtain was lowered, and a young brunette woman teacher in spectacles
came out and curtsied. I had the notion she might become
a friend. Owen said, "Not her. She's leaving."

It did not take much poking to discover that the
woman had been interested in Owen, who was quite a
prize here, where English-speaking men were few and far
between. And Owen had positively fled—"not ready for
a missionary lass." (This made me want even more to see
his Siamese beauty.)

Zain sat in the back row, peering with somber concen-
tration at the stage. I wondered if it made him melan-
choly for the missed years with his own children or was
just a baffling entertainment. He didn't have the sort of
face you could tell from.

AT THE END of the week Owen said to me, "You're fine,
right?" Meaning he really could not wait any longer

before going out on another prospecting expedition. I went down to the river to see them off, as they lumbered their way onto to the boat. Zain directed like a traffic policeman and carried nothing, Ho Lu Ki dragged a wagon with sacks of rice and pots in it, and five Chinese workmen—my brother called them coolies—had huge baskets on their backs or trunks strapped to them, while they pushed wheelbarrows loaded with gear in front of them. "Once we're further into the interior," Owen said, "we'll get elephants to help. They're slow to ride but they jolt less than the buffalo carts."

It looked to me as if he was not coming back in a hurry. "Home in a month," he said. "Think you have enough to do?"

"Plenty," I said. "I'll improve each shining hour. And tell Zain I said to keep you out of trouble."

"He buys my trouble for me," Owen said. "Pretend I didn't say that."

I WALKED BACK to the house by myself, a pleasant morning traipse through the streets of shops and houses. I had to walk around a stubborn sheep in the road, across from one of the showiest Chinese temples. A Malay woman threw up her hands in a charade of frustration and I shrugged in wry agreement. I was so used to behaving calmly with Owen that I was not uncomfortable on my own, despite a persistent fear of getting lost down the wrong side street.

Som waited for me at the house. I had been told not to bow back. She'd made me what I gathered was a favorite lunch of Dilys's—something involving hard-boiled eggs in a dark, sweet tamarind sauce. I had been dreading our poor attempts at an exchange of language, but we both did better than I expected. She responded very well to joking—she was just a girl—and my efforts to imitate the wood rats who lived in our garden and ate all the bulbs (I snuffled and chewed and smacked my lips) produced riotous giggling.

At the end of the week I wrote to Helene:

> *I am installed in my new abode! Dilys the Formidable wanted to have workmen come and build a dining table, but I refused. (Though I'm not as good at sitting on the floor as I like to think.) The whole house is on stilts, with the front veranda a few feet lower than the rest—you would like it. The only room that's dreadful is the bath—you can see through the slatted floor and I'm afraid every morning of what might crawl through—but I wash nonetheless, pouring cool water from a jug, brave soul that I am.*
>
> *My hours are my own. I worried before Owen left, but it turns out I like my regal solitude. It suits me more than the life at my aunt's, where she was so eager not to let me languish. In the cool of the morning I busy myself with walks—sometimes the tiny Som is my chaperone, and we walk as far as the harbor, for the pleasure of seeing the sea—on the way back we hear the calls to prayer at the mosque, and in the afternoon I try to teach myself*

Siamese from a book. They have forty-four consonants in their alphabet, which I think is too many. I read and I look at each tree and lizard in the garden and try (don't shudder) to mentally describe it to my father. He would have liked it here.

Sometimes I dine with Dilys and her husband Gerald and whatever teachers don't have to sit with the whole thundering school of boys. The two male teachers are, alas, not my type—one is timid, one is smug—and the nice female is leaving soon. Not a one of them is as alluring as Zain—cf., my last letter—I am not stupid and know that is a bad idea.

"WE CAN GET MORE boys enrolled," Dilys said at dinner, "if the government keeps sending down Siamese men to work in the civil service. Some of these fellows are ambitious and want their sons to know English. Though it's the Chinese boys who are the really hardworking ones. The Siamese tend to be just a leetle lazy. Not so lazy as the Malay, of course."

"I suppose I think," Tess, the woman teacher, said, "that they're all pretty much the same. Just boys, really."

"Well, at heart they're the same," Dilys said. "They're children of God, of course. But you know the trouble we had getting Ibrahim to learn his lines for the play. You had to practically nail him to the floor and pour the script down his throat."

"I thought he did quite well," I said. "A very decent Cassius."

"He got it at the last minute," Gerald said. "They're not the most organized people."

"Well, Zain keeps my brother organized," I said. "Owen couldn't get across the street without him."

"Couldn't he, now?" Dilys said.

"I don't think you want to know all the things he does for your brother," Gerald said. "Let's just say he introduces him to young ladies."

Tess looked extremely distressed; her whole face clenched. I wanted to hit Gerald, and Dilys looked as if she did too.

"Well, we all loved your Shakespeare," I said. "What's your next play?"

"Once Tess goes home," Alan, the timid teacher, said, "we have no drama coach. Culture goes downhill in Pattani." He laughed between his teeth.

I WAS VERY HAPPY to get back to my little house after the supper. Alan walked me back—I prattled on about the mosquitoes because he was too shy to say much—and I walked through my door with the exhaustion of a sorely tried young woman who's left an unbearable party in a Jane Austen novel. I thought of Artie, who would have had wonderful, withering things to say about the Dilys group. He'd once put me in stitches summing up a table of Miami matrons listening to his dinner orchestra. I had not thought of Artie very much since my parents died; I'd been angry at him for being gone before he might've helped me even a little, and the glow of him had been blotted out by a greater dark. And now I had Zain to brood over. This brooding was my own business and could be kept harmless.

I HAD SETTLED IN quite well. My house had no running water or electricity or gas stove or telephone, but we had great ceramic jars of stored rainwater and nice oil lamps with pierced shades and a good brazier and no one far away we needed to talk to. A person didn't need that much, it turned out, at least not here. I suppose it pleased me to manage so neatly. Thus far I had spent very little of the money Owen had left me with. Som was already paid and our food was cheap enough. I liked to look over the coins, each tical with its imprint of three royal elephants. In Som's village there were people who never used cash at all.

WE OFTEN HAD light rains, a glistening sprinkle that dried at once in the heat. But one day there was an unseasonable burst of heavy rain that lasted for hours. I had never seen so much water fall from the sky so hard—a god did seem to be pouring buckets. We were still in the drier months, but the rains came the next afternoon and the next, though the air never cooled. It was on the fifth day that my brother and his crew came back.

"Don't look at us, Cory," Owen said at the door. "We're a sorry sight."

They were a dank and muddy bunch of men. Their shoes, by the front stairs, were like inky pools of sedge. Zain greeted me again with the gesture (I knew now it was common politeness) that meant I-keep-you-in-my-heart. He looked taut and exhausted. The Chinese workers went off to a lodging on their side of the river, while Zain and Ho Lu Ki waited in the kitchen for their curry.

"What a useless trek," Owen said, alone with me in the living room. "We were lost for days and days—it's very nasty not knowing where you are in the jungle. If it weren't for Zain, we'd still be walking in circles. We were down to eating roasted bamboo rats and ferns for dinner. And Old Wang—don't ask me about him."

I didn't ask, but Owen went on about what a vile and despicable company he worked for—headed, it seemed, by Old Wang. "The whole cold-blooded enterprise," he said, "is enough to give the title Oriental Trading Firm more of the smelly reputation it already has. They might have killed me." I could not quite follow what Owen was incensed about. It seemed Old Wang, that nefarious Chinaman, had plotted to outsmart a nefarious Dutchman, who had in turn duped him, which was how Owen had gotten stuck following a dangerously faulty map. "Small loss to them if we all disappeared in the jungle," Owen said. "They'll milk the blood out of a snail."

"It's very ironic," I said, "that the worst in people is brought out by the lust for tin cans."

"Don't be suave and brittle, please," Owen said. "Now is not the time."

BUT I WAS GLAD to see my brother. I had Som fix dishes I knew he liked for dinner and we had bottles of beer, a hard-to-find treat. "Did you manage without me, then?" Owen said.

"Didn't miss you a minute," I said. Fortunately he thought I was being lively.

"The house looks very nice. You're good at this. Not all women are, I don't think."

"I guess you know," I said. "How are all your girls these days?"

"Don't know. Zain found someone for me in a village, before we got lost. But I really want to go see Noo Kiang. She's the one. Anywhere in the world people would call her beautiful. Next trip I'll get there."

"Do you brood about her all the time?"

"Well, a lot," my brother said. "More than a lot. I can't tell you what we've done in dreams."

"Maybe you're the one who should marry," I said. "If you never plan on going home anyway."

"I didn't say never, did I?" he said.

"I WISH," OWEN SAID later that night, "that our father could've seen this operation I'm part of here." We were standing in the dark garden looking up at a gaudy spangle of stars.

"I thought you hated the firm."

"But we've accomplished really a lot. You didn't see the ingots of tin piled up on the docks in Singapore."

"Do the Siamese get any of the profits from this tin?"

"Our father wouldn't have minded about the Siamese," Owen said.

"Probably not," I said. I thought that my brother and my father were decent men, both of them, pulled along by the machine of greed. The machine had eaten my father.

IN THE YARD the next morning my brother sat out dressing his leech bites with Tiger Balm, the ointment that had made a Singapore family rich. I knew by now that leeches were only tiny black inchworms whose clinging didn't hurt at all, but when they dropped off you bled a lot and had an itchy scab. "Know how Zain keeps them off?" Owen said. "Tobacco paste, smeared on the legs. They hate it. But it washes off if you're wading in the creeks."

"How did the amazing Zain save your neck this time?"

"He was the one who figured out our map didn't fit where we were and we stood a chance of getting stranded for some tiger's breakfast. He was able to find the river—don't ask me how—and our compasses led us out."

"What will you ever do if he stops working for you?"

"Zain is loyal. That's the nature of the man. I don't think you can understand."

"Surely he's not tied to you forever?"

"I've saved his life too, you know, more than once."

"You did?" I said. "That's good you did that, Owen."

NOW THAT SOM was living in the back room, Zain and Ho Lu Ki bunked in a lodging house. I had a secret worry that Owen might bother Som, but those were not his methods. Som was a gentle little gossip; she had worked for Dilys and Gerald and could tell what they had tiffs about (money). She was very playful and we sometimes had water fights when she was trying to help me bathe. Zain came upon us one day in the market—Som loved to go there—it was her chance to see people she knew. We were buying an enormous jackfruit, whose pungent yellow-orange flesh I had grown to like.

Zain wanted to know—he had more English than I'd thought—if I could buy these at home, and I said, "No, but I love them." Zain said he would send them all the way to me in America carried by one of those light-brown sea eagles with black tails. I tried to say in Siamese, "Why I ever go home?" (I only knew simple tenses).

Zain gave me a nice smile, and he didn't smile often. But what he said was, "I think you will go. Anytime you're ready, you can buy ticket."

"Oh!" I said. "I hope you don't want that."

A mix of expressions passed over his face. He had not expected open flirting and was embarrassed—and then more pleased than he wanted to be—and then when he really looked at me, there was quite a lot of sadness in his eyes.

MY BROTHER WAS LAZY the first days back—he ate his morning rice at noon and lay in bed reading the books I had brought. Then his old restless energy returned and he walked all around the town, looking into every shop. He went off on a day trip by boat to Singora, a pleasant journey (he said) to the headquarters of his firm. He came back with orders to go out again, in search of another fabled mountain of ore. I was sorry to see all of them go away so soon. On the dock I watched Zain stepping with agile ease into the narrow longboat and heard him say, "*Ikut, tuan*," which I knew meant, As you wish, boss.

But I was not sad to have the house to myself. When Roger, the boldest of the teachers at the school, walked me home from supper one night, he said, "Our poky little town isn't too dull for a bright young thing like you?"

"Not at all," I said.

"Do you like canasta? I could come by for a game of canasta someday." He cocked his head, with its pomaded pale-brown hair, and smiled.

"The truth is," I said, "I like to be alone in the afternoon."

"A lie isn't necessary," he said. "A simple no, thank you, is fine."

"I say what I mean." This was not entirely true.

"It's not natural," he said, "to choose to go without company day after day."

"Going without," I said, "is very natural to me since I lost my parents. I don't expect you to understand."

This shut him up, though it was distinctly underhanded on my part. Under my snooty tone, I was not really fibbing either. People thought they couldn't go without a lot of things, but the various forms of poverty carried their own instruction. Being an orphan had by degrees made me more self-reliant, and the freedom of this had its own slow-burning pleasure.

Roger went home sulky, but I went in with the bracing sense that an embarrassingly stupid argument had clarified my thoughts.

I STARTED TAKING LONGER WALKS, outside the confines of the town, down the buffalo-cart roads. Any people I passed always greeted me pleasantly. In the heat of midday much of the road was deserted. I was thrilled when I came upon a group of monkeys in a grove, but when they lowered their heads and began to creep toward me, all together, I backed off, alarmed. A group of women, passing by on the road, laughed and put their baskets of fruit down and clapped their hands loudly, and the monkeys fled. As I was thanking them, the women tried to give me fruit. They carried the baskets on their heads, which meant they were Muslim Malay—I knew from Som that the Buddhist Siamese hardly let their heads be touched. "Very good!" the women kept saying about the papayas. "Good eating!"

I thought of Owen always declaiming how glad he was that his work took him into the countryside, where his contact with people was almost enough to make him think well of mankind. The longer he was here, he said, the more he preferred the company of the residents of Asia to that of the selfish, fearful foreigners who had washed up on its shore. If he stayed here any longer, he was going to disappear into the landscape, like a speckled moth against bark, and there were worse fates, weren't there?

—

MY WALKS GOT LONGER, along the roads going inland, with paddies and forest on either side. Often I wanted to bring back a flower or a leafy stalk, but the stems were too fleshy to break, and I had a rational fear of sticking my hand in the foliage. I knew about snakes. What I was really afraid of were tigers, and there was scant chance of meeting one on the roads. Zain said he'd only seen one from a distance even in the deep jungle, and their favorite food was not human anyway. He did hear about a woman bent over to tap a rubber tree who heard a tiger's growl close behind her, but she must have looked like a four-legged animal to the tiger. She got away by climbing the rubber tree, a strategy to remember. Any rustle in the thick growth along the road made me jump. One day I was sure I heard a large animal's heavy breathing behind the trees, and I ran foolishly toward home. The next day I made myself go out again. I had no one to brag to about my fortitude, so I invoked my father.

I would have given anything to be with my father again on the trail. He had loved those Catskill woods, full of hickory and hemlock and oak, a landscape so different from here it was exotic to think of. When I remembered home now, the colonnaded porch of our old house in Kingston, it was incomplete and only half true. And the great swath of the jungle was also incomplete to me, for all its teeming density as I drew near it. I began to think of each spot on the globe as a mere part, the section any lesson had to be broken down into.

—

WHENEVER I WENT to the market, I kept thinking I saw Zain walking by, though Zain was off trekking in the jungle with my brother. In my mind I played out our chance meeting at the market, which featured delightful banter that led to candid and astonishing confessions of hidden passion on both sides. Could he not divorce his wife? I knew that Muslims could divorce. And then I might stay with him, disappear into another city or vanish into a *kampung*, a village where we might live quietly by a river, doing whatever we wanted, night after night.

OWEN STAYED AWAY longer this time. I tried not to think there were good reasons most people lived along the rivers and not in the depths of the forest, where Owen's crew tramped along. I worried for seven weeks, until I heard men's voices outside with my brother's among them. I opened the door to see a ragged and cadaverous line of porters. The corpse with a beard who walked behind them was Owen. The darker figure with a leather face was Zain.

"A bit rough out there," Owen said. I watched Zain unlace his shoes at the foot of the stairs, eyelet by eyelet, as if moving at all were a difficult maneuver.

By the time Owen would tell me anything, the men were all gone, and he was bathed and swilling down Som's galangale soup. "Too much rain," Owen said. The third week, one of the little Siamese ponies hauling a cart had slipped on the bank of a river, and a crocodile had risen up to attack its leg—the men managed to beat and stab the reptile until it let go and sank. But the pony was suffering and useless and had to be killed. Owen never carried firearms, so he'd had to slit the pony's throat, a thing he hoped to never have to do again. Some of the men would eat the meat and some wouldn't. And this same accursed river had led them into a foul-smelling swamp with an especially thick population of mosquitoes. Half of the men had come down sick within weeks, and Owen admitted to being still feverish. But he was excited too— every stream had shown blue-black grains of ore in the washing sieve. He and Zain thought there was ore-bearing ground between the creeks, perhaps richer as you went down. He could hardly wait to go back once they'd gotten a concession for the land. A buried vein of ore was there waiting for the taking.

"Only rest, Owen," I said. "You look awful."

"This could mean quite a lot of cash," he said. "But I know you're not the one to think about these things."

He stayed on the veranda for days, letting Som bring him water and fruit, sweating into his coverlet, and taking quinine. He let me read to him from *Tono-Bungay*, my favorite H. G. Wells, and I thought we were a comfortable household, however temporary. And perhaps we were not temporary.

WHEN OWEN WENT OFF to the headquarters in Singora and I was alone in the house again, Zain paid a visit, which surprised me. He brought me a giant jackfruit—a good two feet long, and not a pretty fruit, with its gnarled shape and its greenish skin covered with bumps. I thanked him profusely. He hacked it open with his knife, and we sat eating its bright yellow flesh on the veranda.

He didn't say much to my questions about his health (fine) or remarks about how the rains had stopped. I tried not to let the silence make me stare at him. I exclaimed repeatedly over the remarkable taste of this remarkable fruit.

Zain in profile looked like a superbly formed monument. He was very still. And then he took an envelope out of his pocket, with his name and an address on it in our alphabet.

"My wife writes," he said. "Someone writes for her, and someone reads for me."

"Oh," I said. "How are your children? Everything all right?"

"Nothing wrong," he said. "But I think is too hard for her. Not natural, woman living without a man."

Oh, wasn't it? How did I live, then?

"Aren't the relatives kind to her?" I said.

"Sometimes the aunt is bossing her," he said. He seemed to want me to know how fine and delicate and commendable his wife was, and how she suffered in this situation. "Doesn't complain," he said. "Not usually. Rare."

"Must be difficult," I said.

"I am sorry for her," he said. "You can see, but your brother doesn't see."

"Yes," I said. How desperate I was, that this flattered me.

"Maybe from you he'll see. You can speak."

And then, with his usual unhasty gestures, he got up from the veranda and took his leave.

When Owen came back from his firm's headquarters, he was fired up about going back to mark out the boundaries of the claim. His face was suffused with a sweating animation which, to me, his sister, did not look like him at all. He charged through town, bargaining for supplies, chatting up every vendor, laughing at his own witticisms. Dilys said he was a fiend of tin fervor.

So it surprised me when he came in to supper one night suddenly glum and slow. "Things are all messed up now, Cory," he said. His voice was hoarse and dull.

Zain had asked if he might have an advance of fifty ticals on his salary so that he might go visit his wife. He had to go at once, he couldn't wait till he got back from the next expedition.

"She sheds a few crocodile tears and he comes," Owen said. "I think she's picked a bad time on purpose."

Owen had refused him the fifty ticals. "I couldn't very well pay him for deserting, could I?"

"Oh, Owen," I said. "You have to let him go."

"Do I?" he said. "I don't think so. I don't think you understand any of this."

THERE WERE NOT MANY secrets among the foreigners in our little city, and over dinner at Dilys and Gerald's school, all the staff told Owen they knew how vexed he must be.

"It's an excuse to avoid going back out on that nasty pestilential trek," Gerald said. "I don't know that I believe that bit about the wife."

"Zain doesn't lie," I said. "He's not like your sneaky schoolboys."

Roger chuckled. "If you say so."

"His wife can write?" Dilys asked.

"Her uncle can," I said. "He writes Malay in the Roman alphabet, the way they do in British Malaya. Zain can't read it, he always has to get someone to read the letters to him. Usually it's Owen."

"Not this time," Owen said.

"They just tend to be slackers," Dilys said. "Lovely people otherwise. A bit violent sometimes."

"He speaks Malay, Siamese, English, and quite a bit of Chinese, he's a brilliant tracker, he can keep maps in his head and he's Owen's bookkeeper too, he knows how to dredge a mine and recite verses from the Koran, and he likes poetry. It's an accident of history that Owen's the *tuan* and he's not."

"I didn't know history had accidents," Gerald said.

"He has a whole life separate from Owen, but Owen can't imagine it," I said. I gazed right at my brother, I wasn't afraid of him.

There was a general pause, not only in the conversation but in the motions of everyone at the table. They had stopped to look at me more closely, to take new stock of my appearance, to guess how long Zain had been my lover. I regretted that there was no grounding for their suppositions.

"Owen has himself to think about," Dilys said. "Don't you, Owen?"

"So it seems," I said. "And is that really admirable? Why is what you all teach against every day in your classes considered praiseworthy in business?"

A rather sweet-faced new teacher named Christopher said, "Yes, well, I think most people are split in two. We've not yet found a moral way to deal with money."

I looked at him with great relief.

"Well, the Communists think they've found it," Gerald said.

We were off on a long discussion of political economy. Was there any morality embedded in capitalism's reward of initiative? Could a country like Siam, where day laborers were known to leave work when they had as much cash as they needed, ever be as prosperous as America or Europe? Perhaps no one thought about Zain at all anymore or Owen's dilemma, though I thought they continued to look at me and to survey my body in its damp blue cotton dress, as if it had a role they had not suspected before.

I WAS NOT KIND to my brother that week—I ended every sentence with a jab against him, with a bit of sarcasm about his once-declaimed kinship with the local populace. Now he had to worry about setting a bad *precedent*.

"I hope you hear yourself," I said. "Look what it's done to you. It's wrecked you."

He waved me away—he hated me too. He moved about like a man in a very black funk.

Christopher, the new teacher, came by one day with a week-old copy of the *Straits Times*. He was done with it, he wondered if we might want to read it.

"Isn't that nice of Christopher?" I said to Owen.

"Couldn't just chuck it out," Christopher said.

"It might cheer me to read about a few catastrophes," Owen said. "Something really horrific with a lot of painful deaths would be just the ticket."

"Zain is still here in the city," I said. "Som saw him on the street."

"Did she?" Owen said.

"If you let him go to his wife, as he's asked," Christopher said, "you'll be able to hire him again. If you don't, there'll be bad blood between you and he can never work for you."

Som had said something similar. I'd thought it a Siamese way to think.

"Well, he's not really going anywhere, is he?" Owen said.

"Neither are you," I said.

AT THE END OF THE WEEK Zain came to the house. His face was closed and he said very little to me, despite my chirruping welcome. I left him alone with Owen on the veranda and withdrew to my own room, where I could hear the rumble of their voices. Neither of them looked pleased when they parted, but Owen raised his eyes to heaven in comic thanks once Zain was gone. "I knew it," he said. "I knew he'd come around."

And the very next day Zain set off with my brother again. It broke my heart to see him directing the workers onto the boat, though he held his head up and his shoulders squared and showed no sign there was any capitulation in what he'd chosen. My brother's face was solemn, with no smirk of triumph on it; he must have been dreading the weeks in the forest with a dour malcontent for a companion. He still trusted Zain—with his life—their dispute notwithstanding. I pointed this out to anyone who started any conversations on the topic.

"Maybe Zain's wife will understand," Christopher said. "He could write to her?"

"There are Chinese scribes at the market who can write to anyone," I said. "They can probably send messages to tigers or elephants if you want."

"Your average elephant," he said, "is probably only interested in conversations about food. And at certain times of the year, less delicate topics." He was the natural science teacher.

"I saw monkeys," I said. We were seated on a sofa in the parlor of Dilys and Gerald's house after dinner. Pretty much everyone had seen monkeys.

"Pig-tailed macaques," Christopher said, when I described them.

"I saw an animal I was sure was an anteater," Dilys said. "It turned out to be a poodle that belonged to one of the Chinese boys. Heaven knows where they brought it from."

"Can an imported creature be happy in surroundings not meant for him?" Alan said.

"We're happy. Some of us," Dilys said. "We imported ourselves."

"Well, imported plants, they say, try to take over. They choke out the native species," I said.

"Do all of them do that?" Alan said. "Do they have to?"

"Ask the poodle if he's happy," Roger said.

Gerald suggested that we interview the animal for the *Bangkok Post*. Did he find the kitchen scraps here too spicy? Did he fancy the local Fifi's?

"Corinna should interview him," Dilys said. "She's very curious about local customs."

I wrote to Helene: *The question about Owen is whether boss is a role that drives out all others. My poor brother, he loved Zain. My opinion of Owen is low at the moment. And my advocacy did Zain no good—maybe it made things worse for him.*

I knew I had cited Zain yet again in a letter, even as I was trying to school myself away from thoughts of him. I had no wish to be silly forever or to indulge in what came to feel like secret futility.

THE MONSOONS STARTED before my brother came back. They were no heavier than some of the earlier rains had been, but they kept on every day, and the streets around the square were lapped by muddy water, the side roads softened to muck. Nothing was ever going to dry out. The city was a sponge, a puddle, a giant waterworks. People moved through the curtains of beating rain with surprising good humor. They were not, of course, surprised. I had the cover of an umbrella but I no longer went farther than the market.

My dripping brother came back at the steaming end of a day when the rain had thinned to drizzle and the light was draining from a white sky. The men set down their boxes and baskets under the veranda—I did not see Zain. "He's gone off already to Kota Bharu," my brother said. "I hope he takes a good bath before he falls into the arms of his wife."

Over supper I heard glowing reports of the new claim. I tried to prise from these a sense of how things stood between Owen and Zain. Owen, at least, was no longer angry. Zain had worked very hard and had been especially vigorous in making sure the men below him did not shirk. He had beaten one Chinaman with a stick for stealing extra rice and fired another for drunkenness.

I really did not want to hear any more. Owen was talking too much anyway, as he did when he was excited. "Did you get to see Noo Whatever Her Name Is?" I said.

"Oh," he said. "I had quite a good visit."

"She's well?"

"Very well."

Perhaps I was too hard on my brother, but his life seemed twisted to me, his dearest friendship a force for ruination, his savor of beauty a coolly limited contract. He could not keep from talking about the final triumphs of his outing—the men had cut frontier lines through hills and gorges and had taken measurements to sink shafts. He was buoyed by his own heartiness and drank more beer than usual, and then suddenly he ran out of interest in what he was saying and his eyelids slid half closed. "It's very late, isn't it?" he said.

IN THE MORNING he did not get out of bed for breakfast. I found him in his room at noon, shivering as if he were in Alaska. "Why in hell," he wailed, "doesn't this house have wool blankets? What do any of you do with the money I bring you?"

I made him take quinine, and I sent Som to the school to see if they knew a doctor. "You're a stupid girl," Owen said. "It's just malaria." Christopher, the science teacher, came later in the day. By this time Owen was sweating and wet-headed and flushed a brilliant pink under his beard. He sat up in bed bare-chested. "Nothing to be done," he said. "My sister's an ignoramus."

Christopher seemed to agree with the first part. He took me aside and told me what I already knew about giving quinine and lots of fluids. The kindness in his tone alarmed me.

THE NEXT MORNING Owen was vastly better—he ate a bowl of rice and joked with Som—but by nightfall he'd fallen into a fever again. His eyes were glassy and his breathing came out as a labored whistling. The task of being sick took all his attention—he was lost to me, staring elsewhere. Where was my brother? How was I to carry on without him?

"Owen?" I called out, and he looked at me with such annoyance that I hated being so afraid for myself, which I would have time for later, whatever later was. Most people did not die of malaria but a few did; I knew that. Everyone knew that. Som had a grandmother who'd died. It hit worst, she said, just at the time of year when people needed to be out plowing and planting.

Each day, Owen had a few good hours in the morning. I made him drink glass after glass of water while he could lift his head. Dilys came by to offer English tea and pandanus-leaf pudding. "Everybody gets this, you know, Corinna," she said.

"Right she is," Owen said. "And Zain always says white men are too fat to die." Owen was far from fat. No one knew how to get hold of Zain.

The nights were very bad. Owen shouted in his sleep and no one in the house slept. I pushed away my mosquito netting and got up and went into his room. I tried sponging his brow with a soaked cloth, but he lashed out and swung his arm at my chest. It seemed to be an illness that agitated its victims, as if the mosquito's bite left a drop of desperation.

In the afternoon, with the rain beating against the shutters, Owen said, "I wish Mother could make something better than this rice. What's the matter with her?"

"I'll speak to her," I said.

Every night I woke to hear his roughened voice trying to yell. His fever was full of protests. "Bugs away! All away!" "I said stop!" "Stupid! Don't ever! Get the box!"

SOM TRIED TO FEED my brother a soupy dessert of bananas in coconut milk. "She's getting old, isn't she?" Owen said. "Her cream pies used to be much better." It was a new terror to me that he thought my mother was hovering near us, like lines from a gloomy hymn my own family would've laughed at.

ONE NIGHT OWEN didn't shout but only whimpered. I wondered if he was whimpering for Noo Kiang, whom he did love, in his way. How useless I was to him. Only just keep breathing, Owen, I thought. In our Unitarian house we didn't do much formal praying at home—we thought God was beyond heeding direct pleas, no matter how ardent they were—but my father used to say it was good to pray now and then to remind yourself you weren't God. My poor brother, look at him, I thought, with all the ardor in me.

In the morning, when Som brought in tea and rice, I asked her if she knew how to summon Noo Kiang. Som gave me a tiny smile. There was very little that Som didn't know about.

And in the afternoon of the next day a young woman in a blue-patterned sarong stood at our door. She was truly very pretty, and when she gave her little bow with her hands together, I saw how scared she was.

"Is it you?" Owen said, when I sent her inside. His pleasure was cracking his beaten face. He said something in Siamese that made her laugh.

"You're not so sick after all," I said from the doorway.

"Not a bit." He raised one eyebrow, a spectral rogue.

AND NOO KIANG WAS a great help to us. She stayed in Owen's room, and she changed his cotton Chinese trousers and his linens all through the day, to keep him from shivering in his own sweat. She slept with him on the narrow mattress and murmured back to his shouts. She led him to the bath and washed him all over and wrapped him in towels. All this bodily closeness, all this intimate tending, could have come from only a lover. I had never had a lover, but I saw the advantage of knowing each other's nakedness. Noo Kiang pulled Owen's robe around him and patted his bony chest.

Dilys did not come to the house anymore, now that Noo Kiang was in residence. But Christopher the science teacher came. He liked me, I could see that. He had an angular, intelligent look and I was getting used to his red hair. He came after dinner one evening when Owen was ranting about the box again. "Don't drop it!" Owen raged from the bedroom. "Watch what you're doing! It's falling in the river!"

"It's his money box," I said. "It's always in peril."

"Do you know where it is?" Christopher said. "Perhaps he'll feel better if we can show it to him."

I was fairly sure it was in the cabinet by my brother's bed. I brought Christopher into the room, where Noo Kiang was kneeling by the bed eating her own supper. She had to put down her plate to *wai* to him, the bow of courtesy. She was looking a little ghostly herself. I opened the cabinet and brought the dented yellow metal box to my brother's bedside. "See, it's safe. It's fine, Owen."

Owen tugged the padlock to check that it was shut fast. He beckoned me closer. "Please," he whispered under his sick breath, "don't let Noo Kiang see where it is. Understand?"

I was terribly embarrassed. "Don't worry, I'm hiding it," I said, putting the box away. I could not look at Noo Kiang, who I hoped had not understood.

"A word to the wise," Owen said, and winked.

"HE WAS A QUIETER boy at home," I said to Christopher. "Growing more sure of himself hasn't been all good."

Som had already gone to sleep and I was in the kitchen trying to make tea. The ants had gotten into the sugar.

"It's not always the best thing for people to be here, is it?" Christopher said. "But I like it so much already." His voice was deep, with an agreeable softness.

"You're planning on staying, then?" I said. "That would be very nice."

He did not break into a smile, as I'd thought he might;

he looked suddenly very wary and uncomfortable. Perhaps he had someone back home, promises to keep.

We carried in the tea for Owen. Noo Kiang had fallen
asleep under the netting, and Owen was sitting up against
the pillows with his eyes closed, moaning about hurrying
up, everyone had better hurry up. "He's the boss of his
dreams," I said.

WHEN I CAME INTO the room the next morning, Noo
Kiang was sobbing quietly. "Oh, no," I said.

"Pay no attention to her," Owen rasped from his pillows. "I was a little short with her and I said I was sorry.
It will pass."

I took Noo Kiang's arm and led her onto the veranda.
I wanted to ask her if my brother was dying, but it
seemed unfair to make her tell me. I gave her tea and rice
and fruit. "It doesn't rain in the morning," I said in my
poorly toned Siamese, "but it rains in the afternoon." She
thanked me for the food. "This is good tea," she said. It
was a fond little conversation.

My brother shouted and shouted all through that
night. "Idiots!" he cried out. "You think I don't see your
tricks?" There were three women in the room—Som
stayed awake—and we spelled each other giving him
water and quinine, drowsing between our turns. We had
one another to be scared out of our wits with, but Owen
was alone, yelling his objections into the dark, making
himself hoarse.

At dawn he fell asleep, and the wheezing rattle of his breathing did not sound good. At around nine he woke and asked for noodles. "You don't give me enough food," he said. "Why is that?"

He stayed alert all day, and at the end of the afternoon he asked if I would read to him. "Nothing dull, please." Christopher had brought a newspaper and I did the news in different voices. I was doing a flutey Mrs. Hoover when the door opened and Zain stood in the room.

"*Selamat petang*," Owen said, and then Zain said something that made my brother snort. "He wants to know," Owen said, "how a man as fat as I am could con so many grown-ups into believing he was dead."

OWEN STAYED BETTER. He was weak and could not do much more than sit up, but I saw him reach around to tickle Noo Kiang under her dainty armpit. A day later he was bouncing her on his lap. I had not seen him play the fool like this. She scolded him merrily and slipped from his grasp. They were radiant now in their silliness. I would have been glad for her to move into the bungalow for good, I thought the two of us could manage Owen well, and I liked to think of having a Siamese sister.

It was not a bad plan, really. Noo Kiang had said she liked our house, which would no longer be just the house of foreigners. I would speak Siamese better, I would understand everything better; my sister-in-law would take me to her village. What an interesting family I'd have. It

made much more sense than my ridiculous hope of elop-
ing with Zain. I would keep my own routines and have
company too. Years could be spent very cozily inside such
a household.

DAY BY DAY OWEN got stronger—he was eating many
bowls of Som's soups and chatting between his naps. At
the end of the week, he made a little speech to Noo Kiang
that made her gasp while he was speaking and get tearful
when he finished. He asked me to fetch his yellow metal
box out of the cabinet; he turned the combination lock,
lifted the dented lid, and gave her some coins. She had
clearly not expected this—she yelled what seemed to be
an insult at him—and then she turned away and went to
her corner and folded the money into a cloth. He was
sending her away. I tried to thank her many times while
she was gathering her few things together to leave. I
didn't imagine she cared. I had wanted her to be my sister,
but that was just a pipe dream.

ZAIN CAME TO VISIT Owen in the evening. I left the two
men alone, and after Zain left, Owen complained that he
was very tired. He was still weakest after dark. I brought
him more limeade, and he sat up in bed, under the white
netting, drinking glass after glass.

"This climate," he said, "isn't healthy for us. We don't
belong here."

"Where do we belong, then?"

"Zain thinks he belongs in Kota Bharu. That's where he's going."

"Ah," I said. "That's an end to a chapter, isn't it?"

"It's a great disappointment. These people can surprise you."

"Well," I said, "it's his privilege to go."

My brother snickered. "You're very charitable." I could tell he thought I was a ninny twice over, fallen and loyal. Generous to a fault. A mismanager of my own accounts.

"Don't you miss winter?" my brother said.

"I do not," I said. "Not at all."

THE NEXT DAY, while Owen napped in the hot part of the day, I went to visit Dilys at the school. Didn't they still need a drama coach? There had been no productions since Tess's departure. I could also teach English—my grounding in American and English literature was very solid—and I had studied four years of French in school.

"Aren't you the useful little thing?" Dilys said. "Well, it's a thought. I'll speak to Gerald. We don't give much salary—it's mostly just room and board."

"Perhaps board," I said. "Meals would be a help."

"I see. Is Owen going home, then? Is that it?"

"He's tilting that way, I think."

"You want to stay on alone? Don't become eccentric, Corinna. It's a bit of a danger here."

"Yes. I'm looking forward to it."

"And at least try not to be a pushover with the students, please."

"THIS PLACE TRIED TO KILL ME," Owen said. "Europeans don't have the constitutions for it. Malaria, cholera, typhus, tuberculosis. Stay long enough and something comes after you." Owen didn't mind repeating every doughty old colonial's stouthearted clichés.

But some days he thought he might, after all, stay on. What had he ever loved as much as those treks, day after day, into rain forest no white man had seen? He could never have as free a life at home. Someone else would be *tuan* to him at home.

But his health was gone. And people had not been loyal. "Time to go back, Cory," he said. "It's come to that. It always does."

He didn't believe I really wanted to stay.

"Don't be ridiculous," he said. "What will you live on? You can't stay on alone."

"A person doesn't need that much here. That's the beauty of the place."

"You're not just lingering to wait around for Zain, are you? Please say no."

"*Owen.* No. Absolutely, no."

"It's not Christopher you're after it, is it? The man doesn't have two cents to rub together. You have to do better than that.'

"You have this all wrong," I said.

"Then who will it be? I won't be here to protect you. It's against nature for you to be alone, Cory."

"Everybody is so sure what nature is. The hurricane in Florida was nature. The crocodile that ate your pony was nature. All the rich people think it's a law of nature all the others are poor. Do I look like some freakish aberration?"

"You will," he said.

IT TOOK HIM two months to gather himself together to leave. He said, "You'll get tired of sitting on the floor like a perennial picnicker. You think the tropics make you free—you and Gaugin—but all that wears off." But he didn't try to order me home once he saw it was no use. "Only come back," he said, "before the sun shrivels you into old-maidhood. Which is soon."

"Who'll rail at me when you go?" I said.

"Perhaps you'll find a nice orangutan to elope with," he said. "Though they're only in Borneo and Sumatra. I don't know what I'll find at home."

"No Noo Kiangs in the U.S."

"I wouldn't say that exactly," he said. "But this place is a paradise for a man. I don't quite know what you see in it."

AFTER OWEN LEFT, my evenings were different. I came back from supper at the school and the bungalow was perfectly empty. Som was back working for Dilys. In bed, I could hear every termite in the walls. I sat up under the gauze net and read my books—Shakespeare, for the students—with the humid ticking spookiness around me. I wandered into the kitchen to eat a piece of jackfruit. I loved the private disorder of these hours, and I thought I had been very lucky to fall into this liberty. I woke very early and sketched a lizard, who posed without moving on my bedroom wall. He was grayish green with yellow eyes; perhaps only a foreigner would admire such a lizard.

I HAD TO TAKE my walks before school hours, soon after dawn. They were shorter walks than I'd had before, but certain spots drew me—I liked the light over the shadowed outer garden of a mosque, I liked a sandy patch on the river where I saw hornbills in the trees, and I liked to watch the market vendors stack their stalls with fruit and greens and squawking chickens. It came as a surprise if anyone spoke to me, because I was so absorbed in seeing that I forgot that I was there—forgot that I, Corinna, was a visible feature of the scene. I liked very much losing track of myself, and I was sorry to be startled out of those moments. I thought how right I'd been to stay on alone.

MY BROTHER WROTE to me from the States:

> I've bored many Americans talking on about my wild
> adventures in the fabled East. But they like me fine at
> Father's bank and seem to think I'm doing my job, though

I probably am not. I can't remember why anyone bothers
with most of what people bother with here.

I MADE OWEN'S old bedroom into a sewing room, and I
sent him a letter with silly sketches of the raggle-taggle
curtains I stitched for the windows. The curtains took me
forever to make—I saw why machines were invented—
and the labor made me think of my mother, who had
taught me to embroider, an art now useless to me.

Sometimes the memories of my parents were very
sharp to me, as if I had spoken to them only the day
before, and sometimes I could scarcely remember a time
when I was not on my own, free of encumbrance and free
of support. I didn't think my mother could have imagined
the life I had at present, which was more satisfying than I
could have explained to her.

SOM COULD NEVER believe that I spoke so blithely about
the prospect of never marrying. It was not an idea that
made any sense to her at all. Owen had once told me that
this simple life I was so entranced with had no room for a
person alone and unconnected. "Villages are made of families," he said. "How else could they come about?" He
always thought I misunderstood everything about Siam,
with my disdain for his work and my sentimental crushes
on the looks of the locals. But he was lonely at home these
days, wasn't he, and I was where I wanted to be. Dilys said
I wasn't the worst teacher either. Much to her surprise.

The boys at the school were allowed (by me) to vote their choice between *A Midsummer Night's Dream* and *Richard III*. I favored the first, in this land of eternal summer, but the murderous connivery of evil Richard won by a very large margin. I did not expect, when I picked a Chinese boy to play him, that there would be an upsurge of anger from the Siamese students on the grounds that the Chinese were always finding their way into everything. "Why do you bother to go to school at all," I said, "if you can't be civilized? What are we teaching you, if not to be better than your worst selves?" They probably didn't hear a word, but my starchy outrage browbeat them into peace. The episode saddened me, but Christopher said the boys' bigotries and alliances shifted all the time.

RECENTLY I'D STARTED thinking about where Artie was, what city he was playing his fiddle in and whether he had a wife. On our secret stretch of beach he had touched me under my dress but I'd stopped him, though I had recognized the shock of contact as happiness. And I thought (but I always thought) of Zain, in Malaya now, sitting on a veranda, near the noise of his children who weren't used to him; I saw him cross-legged on the floor, gazing into the bluish twilight. Who were these men to me? Not my lovers. Perhaps I was never going to be with a man in that way. Perhaps I was going to be a foreigner to the life of the body. That part of it.

—

I WROTE TO OWEN, who was thoroughly miserable at home, about how I'd seen a giant rafflesia flower on the jungle floor—almost three feet across, an orange-spotted thing with a smell like bad meat—and how I was growing orchids in our yard and how I got to see the firewalkers at the big Chinese festival, the one in honor of the Chinese woman who hanged herself when her brother married a local woman and converted to Islam. Did Owen know she cursed the mosque he built and it had never been finished? *The poor brother*, I wrote.

You're staying too long, Owen wrote. *And not getting younger. Your letters make you sound as if you're married to the land the way nuns think they're brides of Christ.*

Helene, in her letters, started calling me the nun of the forest after that.

I DISCOVERED BY asking him point-blank that Christopher did not have a settled attachment to someone waiting far off. "I was under the impression," he said, "that *you* did." Even I knew there were rumors that Zain had left Pattani only to break things off for good with his wife, and that he wasn't in Kota Bharu now at all, but someplace closer, where I could slip away to him for our assignations. "I think he's a remarkable type," Christopher said. "But you're in quite a spot, aren't you?"

"As it happens, I'm not," I said. I wasn't insulted at all by the imputation—no, he needn't worry—but in my attempts to imply just what had definitely not happened, I kept explaining how admirable Zain was—"not someone whose character we should sully"—and I could tell that made my protests less convincing.

I BEGAN TO TRY to sit with Christopher at supper. He was the one decent being in the province, even if the others thought I was chasing him. Christopher asked where it was that I went on my walks—would I show him?

How altered the walk was then, with him on the trail with me. I had always trained my intentness on certain favorite vistas, but now my powers of observation were taken up with what Christopher wanted to show me. He worried about black bears in the forest, but his choices had their delights—he knew a great deal about rattans, a climbing kind of palm that grew all over, and about the social habits of ants, who made their nests in the rattans' leaf bases. While he pointed to the rattans' heavy thorns and said elephants avoided them, the entire landscape was suffused with questions about what was to happen between us.

He did not even offer his arm until we were out of everyone's sight, but then every bit of foliage was suffused with longing and the enactment of longing. Like a very young girl, I assessed any minor touch for signs of interest, but we were neither of us that young and the handholding moved, before much distance had been covered, into the frankness of kissing. He was a subtle and persuasive kisser, and my returned enthusiasm seemed to strike him as a splendid turn of events he could scarcely believe.

So we did not get very far on these walks, only just outside the town and beyond the more crowded roads. We had to take care not to scandalize the locals either and were always interrupting ourselves if we heard anything like voices. Once we almost choked together laughing because we had stopped in panic at the approach of several chickens.

The walks were mostly taken on Sunday afternoons, after our days of classes, so we had to proceed week by week. It took a few months before we discovered an abandoned lean-to, on a hillside beyond a turn in the road—it had probably once been used by someone from the valley watching a few sheep. After Christopher checked the ground, we could sit there, more or less concealed, in our hideaway; we could remove some of our clothes. The slatted wood smelled of ferns and tropical rot, and when I took off my sandals, I thought, I am sealing my fate.

AND SO I DID. Soon Christopher was visiting me more openly in my bungalow at certain hours; soon there was gossip that we were engaged. My brother heard the gossip back home in Kingston. Owen wrote to me: *I suppose someone like you can be happy on a teacher's income, though our parents would be disappointed. Everyone knows Chris is a decent fellow, but I hope this is not happening just because you want to stay on.*

In fact, I was not really engaged—I chose to believe that the rashness of my risk had bonded us, and nature was sweeping us along on a wave of bodily amazement. Christopher did seem as amazed as I was. Luck favored us, in that I still bled every month; I certainly knew very little of how to avoid conception. But I had the sense to worry, and the presence of this worry brought us to more open discussion.

AND HOW SOON SHOULD the taking of vows be done, and what ceremony? We were always standing in the wet garden of my house, waiting out the rain under the edge of the roof, getting giddy together. I was glad to settle myself at last—glad (mostly) that the long suspense was over.

Dilys said, "If you don't settle on Christopher, you might think of going home soon, where no one knows you." She meant: *knows about you and Zain*. Perhaps there was a general feeling that Christopher was behaving handsomely in regarding me at all. Christopher himself only said, "I must've been good in a past life, to have a girl like you in a place like this."

JUST BEFORE OUR wedding there was a note from Zain, of all people—congratulations, *tahniah*, in the pretty Arabic script the Siamese used for Malay. We had to get the student Ibrahim to read it. I never knew how news traveled so efficiently in that region, but Zain had an address now, written on the envelope in block letters in an alphabet I could read.

Som, who was a great fan of Zain's, showed the card to everyone. How could I have imagined an endless future with a man I could barely talk to? What had I been thinking? Of another life altogether. I did hear of people having such lives. Now it seemed like a sealed door, a kingdom under the sea.

After the wedding, Christopher moved into my little house. The back room where Som had slept became his study, and he set up his microscope and a desk and chair where once there had been only a pallet on the floor and a tiny Buddhist altar in the corner. Som's old mattress lay alongside the old one in my room, which was now the room of a couple. In the nights, one of us often woke the other to play out dreamy hungers in humid half sleep. I could hardly remember when my life had been otherwise.

I did not see that it cost more to be married, despite my brother's warnings. Our weekly splurge was sweet snacks from the market, and I saved for fabrics I sewed into clothing. The dress I made was a little lopsided—was I becoming eccentric after all?—but I liked the brightly printed cloth and wore it anyway. The students—especially the Chinese—always had trouble saying Christopher's name, Llewellyn, which was now my name, but they tried valiantly, which I found very touching. I was susceptible to all tender feelings.

———

IT TURNED OUT that the odd fit of my dress was due in part to my being pregnant, which it took me a stupidly long time to guess. Could we feed a third mouth? Dilys, who did not have children herself, actually said, "Oh, dear," when I told her.

The mosquitoes were very bad that season. It was important that they not bite me and give me malaria, because everyone, even Som, seemed to know that quinine was an abortifacient. I had to rely on the mosquito netting and piles of burning coconut husks to keep them away. We'd hear the buzzing outside in the night. How could I be happy here? But I was.

And our beautiful daughter Thea was born very healthy at the hospital in Singora. Som brought me a bamboo cradle, which hung from the ceiling beam by ropes and whose rocking helped shush the baby. I could not have managed without Som. I was so busy coping with the interesting duties of motherhood that I was not even very upset when I read in the paper about the markets' Crash in the U.S. and in Europe.

"What does that mean, crash?" I said to Christopher. "It's nothing but a violent metaphor for the action of paper." We both knew what it meant, but it seemed remote from us in the land of bursting fruit and flooded green paddies. All around us was evidence we were in a place distant from these forces.

—

BY THE TIME THEA was walking, enrollment was down at the school. The teaching staff soldiered on, combining classes, and we did excellent productions (in my opinion) of Jonson's *Volpone* and (at long last) *Midsummer Night's Dream*. At the start of each term, fewer and fewer boys came back. The tin my brother's old company dredged from the ground was no longer being bought overseas. No one needed the local plantations' rubber either. Less cans, less automobiles, less tires. Dilys and Gerald sputtered and struggled and went from petty complaint to haughty valor. I myself did not mind teaching "The Rime of the Ancient Mariner" to a group of three boys, but the Church threatened to close the school.

OUR CHINESE STUDENTS had always been prone to runaway superstitions, and now they spun ghost stories about the Japanese. Reality was bad enough—the Japanese occupied the entire province of Manchuria—but the boys spread their own rumors of demon generals. The youngest were afraid of what might happen to them in sleep, and Dilys and I had to go in at night to settle them. The Siamese boys tended to think the Japanese were not so bad. There were fights with the Chinese boys about this.

I ALWAYS TOLD THEA THAT I was blown to Siam by a hurricane. Lucky winds had carried me across the seas. My father, the king of Florida, had lost all his fortune, and he and his queen had perished. But when I landed in this place, the fruit dropped into my hand without my ever asking, and coconuts fell at my feet, cracking open to show their juice. Som told Thea she'd seen a sea eagle hover overhead just to toss a delicious fish into my frying pan.

IN THE WINTER, in a lucky lunar month, Som was married to a boy from her village. On Sunday afternoons I had myself rowed along the river, with Thea on my lap, on the winding route to the village, which was not all that far away. Som's family made a great fuss over Thea and was nosy about me, and we had many amiable, half-translated conversations, all of them understood by Thea.

I WROTE TO HELENE:

> *Thea likes it that we bring gifts when we go to Som's, and she runs to put a bolt of cloth or some strings of pretty beads in the grandmother's lap. Her rapture in bestowing bounty embarrasses me—I don't want her to grow up thinking she is a local dignitary—but the people here are always laughing and gracious. I don't know how else we could behave, though I always wish I did know.*

DILYS WAS SO SKILLED in making do and carrying on, so remarkable in her frugal tricks, that I was not prepared at all when orders came from England in the fall to close the school once and for all at the end of the term. I didn't want Thea hearing, and she screamed and wailed when she did hear.

But couldn't our little family of three find a way to stay on? Christopher and I had endless, excruciating discussions. "In the villages they live without any money at all," I said.

"Are you planning to work in the fields?" he said. "Or just live off Som's generous relatives?"

Sometimes he said, "They're better off here without us." I'd always thought poorly of my brother for being a colonial, for digging up the country and carting off pieces of it. I suppose I'd thought well of myself, then, for being a traveler, whose task was only to appreciate. And now I'd spent all these years tormenting flocks of boys with Wordsworth's daffodils and the rigors of the English sentence. Good years for me, but perhaps only so-so for the country.

"Home will be lovely," Christopher said. "I miss England. Don't you ever get homesick?"

"For what?" I said. "Only someone who didn't know me at all would ask a question like that."

I WAS BITTER AGAINST going back with Christopher to chilly England. I had a secret dream of staying on alone, of taking Thea with me to Bangkok and working as, say, a secretary for some company. And I had another, wilder, and more vivid notion too, of slipping across the border and staying with Zain—Thea and I in a house with Zain and his family: what was I thinking? It seemed much more real to me than going home.

IN THE END CHRISTOPHER was persuaded to try Florida. "Sunshine and hurricanes. At least I won't need my woollies," he said. Sometimes I remembered that his staunchness was always dear to me.

I wrote to Zain: *I am so sorry that I won't see you if you ever come back to Pattani. I always thought you would.*

Christopher came in just as I was about to walk out with the envelope, and he saw the address. "What are you plaguing the man for?" he said. "Haven't you bothered him enough?"

"Why wouldn't I write to let him know we're leaving?"

"He doesn't care," Christopher said. "It's in your head. You think you can have friends here the way you do at home, as if no one here notices who has more of everything. They coax and cadge you and you don't even know what's going on. It's all a golden haze in your imagination. Thea speaks the language far better than you do."

Christopher looked hideous to me then, with his reddened, freckled face and his sandy hair slicked against his head. All the sweetness in my marriage was not worth anyone having the right to speak to me this way. Jealousy made him pathetic, but I was afraid of him too, of what he might say next. I believed he was wrong, but I could hardly fail to know he was not entirely wrong, and I hated his wanting to smudge and burn the years behind me.

And when I went to visit Som for the last time, after I ate sago pudding with her family and played my last game of tossing stones with the grandmother, and Som walked me to the river where the longboat waited to take me back to Pattani, when Som burst into tears and threw herself against me and we both sobbed and made jokes about our sobbing, a part of me was relieved and triumphant.

ZAIN SENT A LETTER with a farewell poem in Malay! It reached us only a few days before we left, and I was very careful about packing it so that I could frame it later. Nowhere did Zain, who made his living working for foreigners, say how he was getting by. The poem (he was not its author) was some sentimental ditty about the words for goodbye in Malay being different if you were going or if you were staying. Looking at it made me angrier that I had to leave, and I was quite difficult on the boat. I was in the early stages of pregnancy too.

NONE OF US WAS HAPPY at first in Florida, where Christopher taught science to the kids of U.S. Navy men from the base at Key West. I was the only one who had been in Florida before but all of it looked different to me. Thea hated everyone in her kindergarten and cried because we couldn't buy *satay* in the street. I cried because I was surrounded by sappy American dolts who knew nothing about anything, but we all came around slowly to liking what we could. And then I had our new, noisy baby Bob to busy myself with. He was a loud crier and a charming chuckler.

Thea did not remember very much of Siam as she got older. But no one could meet me or Christopher without knowing we had spent time there (by then it was called Thailand, which I never could get used to). We liked to use words in Siamese to each other—not in front of the *dek*, you're looking *suay*—just to remind ourselves we had not made all of it up. Our house was filled with objects—a triangular silk cushion, a wicker ball, a ladle made of coconut shell—displayed in honored spots. We were so notorious for nattering on about the place that Thea's school asked us to give a presentation. With a lantern slide projector, we showed squinting photos of us in front of orchids, and I explained how to extract milk from shredded coconut, and Christopher sang a national anthem that was out of date, and we were such a hit we repeated this every year.

Did I feel silly? Surprisingly not. I was not beyond irony—*au contraire*—but I could never resist the oddly reliable pleasure of trying to explain (though it couldn't be explained, not by me) the elusive connection between place and happiness.

Sometimes parents would say we must be very glad to be in the U.S. now. This was usually because they confused Siam with China, or with some other country bordering Japan (no one believed me that Japan, made up of islands, had no borders). Christopher and I seemed to live in a zone of secret knowledge. This was the zone where we were lovers.

We could not get anyone to seriously think that where we had been was a real country. Our souvenirs looked stagey even to me—the palm-straw farmer's hat like a flattened cone, the broom of dried grass. Despite what I said in school assemblies, I myself had never husked or grated a fresh coconut in my life. We had loved Siam, but we were pretending to a higher level of Siameseness than we had. The pretending was a great joy to us.

MY BROTHER THOUGHT it was hilarious that we gave speeches about Siam. We could not talk about the place without his correcting our pronunciation. I gathered, however, that Owen spoke about it quite a lot himself, muttering his accounts to fellow travelers in bars. He had lost his job in the bank and taken the western sales district for a company that made metal screws and nuts and bolts for airplanes. When he told my kids stories, Siam was a dark forest full of cobras and crocodiles. Thea's favorite tale of his was about a treacherous map and the clever servant who saved everyone by seeing a message in the sky about where the river was.

And Owen hadn't married either, though I'd always thought he would, once he was home. He had not really done well here. Whatever had thrilled and emboldened him there, he'd not been able to carry it back. He wasn't good at being in America. He'd lost his knack, he said.

—

ONCE THE WAR in Europe was on in earnest, Christopher worried a great deal about his family in London. Constant reports of the Blitz hit him very hard and he listened to the radio with his head in his hands. Bob, who was only six, wanted to know when we were going to be bombed. We both said, "Oh, no. Not here," and then I felt as sappy and arrogant as everyone around us.

And they did bomb here, they being the Japanese and here being Hawaii. Within hours of the Pearl Harbor attack, Japanese troops landed on the coast of the Gulf of Siam—they took Singora and Pattani and Kota Bharu. I looked at the map in the paper, with its arrows and underlined place names, and my first horrified thought was: Now we'll never get back.

I was ashamed right away for thinking such a thing, while Zain and Som were in the bloody path of an invading army. As it happened, Zain was worse off in Kota Bharu, across the border in Malaya, than he would have been in Siam, which made its own slippery peace with Japan at once.

The Siamese had no way to resist a power like Japan and wasted no time thinking otherwise. But Christopher was angry at them for not even trying to stop Japan's troops before they came down the Malay Peninsula. He spoke with sarcasm about the famous Siamese genius for compromise. And hadn't Siam been glad to grab bordering bits of *Indochine* back from the defeated French? Hadn't it been happy to see the West lose its grip over Asia, hadn't some people cheered over Asia for the Asians?

The British began at once to lose very badly in Malaya. All these years I had sent my little careful cards every December to Zain in phonetic Siamese—*sawat dee pee mai*, happy new year. There wasn't a stamp in the world that could take them where he was now. *Friends across the water*, he used to write in his notes to me. *Wishing you weather good like we have here.*

It was terrible to hear on the radio about civilian deaths in Malaya, massacres of Chinese there, local men taken captive to cut roads as the Japanese made their way to Singapore—I hated the peculiar privilege of listening to this in the fanned comfort of our living room, with a bamboo rake on the wall as ornament. How had I come to live here? How had that happened? It was an accident, wasn't it, that we were safe and someone like Zain wasn't, though it didn't feel like one.

At night Christopher heard me weeping for Zain, and perhaps my weeping should have been more private. I should not have sighed out loud, "He's *lost*." "You were nothing to him, if you don't mind my saying," Christopher said. Poor Christopher. I told him I was only crying for the country we'd known. And what did it matter which unrequited love I was crying for? Weren't we beyond that now? How was my crying a disgrace?

THE WAR WAS ERASING Siam for my husband. He didn't forgive it. And for me the war did something quite different. It caused me to pray. I pleaded over and over in my head for Zain's fate, and the only holy words I knew that could be for him were in the calls to prayer we always heard from the mosques in Pattani. *Allah u Akbar, Allah u Akbar*, God is greatest. *La ilahah illallah*, no god but God. I had at least those by heart.

ZAIN HAD BEEN right all along that my money (such as it was) would take me home when I wanted, though I hadn't wanted. Christopher said to me, "You can't really think it's so safe here either." They (meaning the Germans) could bomb this coast, this base, and we didn't even have a hurricane cellar. "America's not immune," he said.

I said, "Yes, yes, I know"—I didn't want my sweet, sheltered kids to hear it. But I wouldn't answer them or let them interrupt while I listened to all the solemn-voiced war news and sat sewing a hem for Thea. I was elsewhere anyway, stuck in longing; I saw that I had planned every second to go back. I was so homesick now, hearing the place names over and over on the radio, that the rest of my life seemed like smoke, though I couldn't have said this to anyone. I sang out the right tones to the announcers when they said the names wrong.

ALLEGIANCE

Mike

SOME PEOPLE THINK TRAVEL IS UNSAFE. They don't trust the aeronautic logic of planes, and they think the rest of the earth is more bloody and troubled and roiling than wherever they're from. I'd never been one of those people, though I taught a course called Patterns of Civic Unrest in the Post-Colonial World and I knew more about trouble than most people. No, my not traveling was because I got married young and had kids early on. A lot of kids, as it turned out.

I suppose I always thought I would have a family, though not so fast. I had steady girlfriends from the time I was fourteen, I hung out in their TV rooms and ate dinners with their siblings. My mother was sure for a while that I was going to marry Viana, the girl I took to my senior prom. Everyone liked Viana. Her parents were FOBs, fresh off the boat—they had come from Sicily a generation after everybody else in the neighborhood—and the meals at their house were enough to bring a boy to his knees. Viana herself was fresh and round and smart and sexier than anyone knew, but she went off with Eddie DiFranco that summer. She had never been smitten with me, I knew that.

But Annabel was, right away. We met in an economics seminar my first year at college. She was a nervous but eager girl, quite confident underneath that surface fluster. Much of Annabel's power was hidden; she was a tiny redhead, small-boned and lightly freckled, who trained for triathlons. At the end of our first date we had a long kiss—hungry and inspired—and I thought how particles of lust had been flickering all evening through our fog of conversation. I was ready to go home with these thoughts, as we untangled ourselves, but Annabel, holding my hand, assumed it was time to sneak me into the dorm. I followed in manly silence. She told her half-awake roommate to go sleep on someone's floor across the hall, and then we lay down together, in our lordly freedom. My life was turning out even better than I'd expected.

It might have been my idea, in the early days, that we should pass every day in each other's company, every possible hour. It seemed such a gift, to have a craving you didn't have to struggle against. "Are you my boy?" Annabel would whisper, in queenly gloating. "You're my boy." She seemed so tickled with herself to have found me. By November, Annabel's roommate requested a transfer, and I became known as Mike the guy who was secretly living in the girls' dorm. When I went home for Christmas, it

felt odd to be in my family's old narrow house in Hoboken, a son instead of a lover. I shared a bedroom with my
younger brother Pete, and I still had too much time alone.

Annabel's mother thought she needed to date more people, but blending and binding together so young had advantages. We had some of the dopey intimacy of children—the
playful, messy physicality, the shared private customs,
the histrionic displays of injury. We settled right in. The
fights we had were mostly about money. I refused to let
her buy an expensive box of Belgian chocolates and I
truly believed that car wax was a corporate scam. Annabel
came from more money than I did, though not as much
as I pretended, and I saw her bossiness as spoiled, while
she viewed me as arrogantly mingy. I would call her a
slumming aristo fake-leftie, and she'd call me a macho
poor-mouth show-off. Politically, we were both complicated forms of socialists.

We married at the end of junior year. Back in my old
neighborhood, Brad Battaglia asked me, "How do you
deal with the fidelity thing? You sure you've seen enough
of the world?" Richie Cohen said, "When you get as
much at home as he does, you don't need extra helpings."
I smiled serenely, the well-fed man. I had a wife—what
did I need to talk to these guys for?

There was some pride in me—and certainly in
Annabel—that we'd sped ahead of our friends, formed so
precociously as a couple, learned how to do it before anyone we knew. Capitalism makes people overcompetitive,

I knew that, but I could not keep from crowing to myself, and the zest of victory was real.

When Nicholas was born in my first year of graduate school, my secret fear was that I would lose Annabel to him. The fatigues and fascinations of motherhood swept her along, and she hardly knew I was there. My strategy was to kidnap the baby ("the men will go play in the park") and let Annabel swim or run or bike. I knew that even sleep-deprived she hated to stay still. On my lucky days Nicholas came back zonked and ready to nap and Annabel returned buzzing with endorphins and remembering what sex was.

We were living in Ann Arbor then, where I was trying to write my thesis on shifting constructions of marginality in postwar Palermo and whether Sicilians ever believed they were Italians. I was fired up about it, and would work through the night, the obsessed scribbler. When the baby's crying brought me back to where I was, I'd feed him his breast-pumped milk and try to let Annabel sleep.

Annabel always had deep reserves of energy. After Matthew, our second, was born, she started competing in races again. I'd see her on her bike in that weird swimsuit that zipped to the neck and I'd think how you had to be someone who preferred ecstasy to pleasure to do that. "Honey," she'd say, "you get used to it from practicing." She was very good at focusing, which also made her an ace at statistics, the field in which she was slowly getting her doctorate. And it was her idea to have a third kid. By then we were settled in Bloomington, where I'd gotten a very decent teaching job. She said she liked having a *group* of kids, a full house, and the town was thronged with students who would look after them for cheap. Annabel always pushed things to the hilt, she couldn't stand to do anything halfway.

And I liked being king of our own rowdy boys' club, our principality of noise. I liked scrambling around with my guys, I liked inventing elaborate games in the yard to tire them out, I liked their cockeyed inventions and their weird boy theories. I had to make an effort not to keep repeating their witty sayings to my colleagues in the history department.

The fourth baby was a big surprise, and when I went home to the old neighborhood, I faced the usual jibes about not being able to keep it in my pants. Four was a lot but by then half the people I grew up with had done something weird. Joel Fantini was in jail in Sri Lanka for smuggling drugs, Angie Lindblad had killed herself in a car in her garage, and Viana LoBianco had run off with a Muslim from some country and her parents had cut her off.

I HAD TO QUIZ my mother for more of the Viana story. Viana had always been very tight with her family and got angry with me the one time I made fun of their being gushingly protective and Old-Worldy. I thought she must have fallen in love very hard. She was a sweet girl with a tender nature, and it did not surprise me that she had given herself over to a great attachment. My mother said he was a doctor from Thailand, a very nice boy, who'd come here on a fellowship and had treated Viana for an interesting knee problem. Her parents didn't worry when she was dating him, since he was leaving soon. But then the two began writing back and forth, all the time. It was Viana's father who insisted she break it off. Viana cried and then she did what he said. But she stopped eating, she hardly spoke, she never slept. "A zombie," my mother said. "She didn't even look pretty anymore." When she began writing to the man again, she didn't lie about it. Her parents told her she had to choose. If she wanted him, they were done with her for good, finished. For months she agonized, and then she grew bitter against her family, and she left.

"Poor Viana," I said. My own parents had been only moderately miffed when I married a non-Catholic. My mother was wholly on Viana's side in this saga. "They lost her anyway," she said. "So what did they have to break her heart for? I got news for them. It's a bigger world nowadays."

SINCE I SPENT my working days talking about what kind of world it was nowadays, I went home and looked up Muslims in Thailand. Plenty of them in the south. There had been local outbreaks in the sixties and seventies—protests against poverty, underrepresentation, cultural assimilation, the usual—but things had mostly simmered down; in one province, a die-hard band of separatists was still active. With this scanty information, I worked in a reference to it in my next seminar on minority movements, and I probably blushed when I heard myself speaking all of a sudden about Thailand.

I would have liked to write a book about the great mystery of what allows a heavily outnumbered population to ever stop hating the dominant group. And if the fighting ends, how do old enemies manage to live together? There were people you could still talk to, for instance, about the Italian Resistance and how the Partisans went back to towns full of old Fascists trying to be invisible. How did they all walk across the same piazza? I had notes for this book, a half-written introduction. But I would have had to travel to ask those questions, and I couldn't see myself making any trips soon. How could Annabel manage four kids by herself? But later I was sorry I hadn't gone.

I always felt funny teaching courses in global whatever when I'd never been anywhere. I had some other ideas about where to go too. In the highlands of southern Mexico, an armed leftist band of Indians called the Zapatistas, with a leader who always wore a black mask (my students loved him), had just recently mounted a brief, astonishing insurrection around San Cristóbal, to bring local rule and oppose the takeover of resources by international grabbers. Mexico wasn't that far, and I didn't get there either.

—

BUT I WOULD HAVE given up much more for my boys than that. A secret perk of fatherhood was seeing yourself rise to the occasion, get a little heroic on the job. I still couldn't get my mind around how Viana's family had acted—it chilled me to the bone. To turn your back forever on your own daughter? How would you get up every morning after doing that? I had sometimes wanted to throw my kids out the window—Nicholas especially could be a real pill—but deciding to never see them was not thinkable. And Viana's parents had been regular nice people, as far as I'd ever seen. The house was full of photos—Viana in a starched Communion dress, Viana a gap-toothed baby held by her brother; the refrigerator still had smeared drawings on it she'd done in grade school. When she got her driver's license, her parents had every single relative over for a gigantic picnic in the yard. They turned their back on Viana?

MY OWN HOUSE was a mess of toys and Fritos and juice, the pandemonium zone. The thing about four boys was, they egged each other on. This was the hardest time for us, with a houseful of banshees under eleven. Once the first two moved into early teenagehood, we didn't have to run around in circles every second, and we could lean on Nicholas or Matthew as babysitters. Annabel was good at bribing the older guys with extra privileges if they'd just let her escape now and then. The summer Aaron turned four, two boys were away at camp and one was working, and the house had a staggering quiet. I noticed I didn't like the way the future felt.

On her side, Annabel was seizing the time to train harder—rising early, working late, whittling her pale body to sinew. It was beyond me why she did this, a type of music I couldn't hear. I was afraid one afternoon when she sat me down for a discussion in the backyard that she was going to start talking again about building a pool we couldn't afford. But she wanted to talk about Steve, her coach. She was having an affair with Steve. Well, she had been having it for seven years. "You must have known," she said. She gave me a tight smile with a lifted brow. "You thought I fucking *knew*," I said, "and closed my fucking eyes?" My house was built on sand, on dry granules of nothing, and was about to be blown away. She wanted a divorce.

All I could voice at first was righteous outrage. More than grief, more than anguish. I couldn't believe she thought she could get away with this. I shouted and roared and then I was steely and appalled and disgusted. This kind of rank, flagrant injustice couldn't be railroaded through. Not on my watch. It was the sort of unspeakable maneuver that had to be stopped. Right now. "Don't pretend you didn't *know*," she said. And we went on like this for weeks, we couldn't shut up or keep the kids from hearing, and it only got worse. Annabel had been suffering with me for years. This hideous fact (I had to believe her) burned a hole in my heart, a crater. In the end I agreed to move out, because it seemed the least humiliating alternative. I had the kids on weekends.

THE FIRST YEAR was very bad. Each of the kids freaked out in his own way—the older boys were sullen, the third was a brat, the littlest was screamingly needy. They came to visit a father who looked like a miserable, red-eyed creature-from-the-deep and who lived in a large hovel of an apartment. Self-pity reeked from the malodorous kitchen.

At meals, one boy would suddenly wax sentimental about the buckwheat pancakes I used to make, how great they were, and another would talk too much about what Steve told them about the White Sox, Steve knew a lot. They were like citizens of a country whose borders had changed, confused about where their loyalties fell or on what side their advantages lay.

Aaron, who was still in kindergarten, said to me once over the phone, "Steve's in California the whole week. Don't you miss Steve?" He was so little he didn't entirely follow the new arrangement. It had crossed my mind some time before that by the simplest of calculations, there was a chance Aaron wasn't my son. Annabel and I had never talked about this, and my guess was that she didn't know. I didn't see how it could matter now. I was his father, now and forever, every day of his life. All my efforts on weekends were to get this very point across to him and his brothers: we were bound together for good, even if their mother and I weren't. My job was to repeat and underline this eternally, to make them see the ties between us etched in the air. Maybe they saw.

IN THE SUMMER I had them for a month—Annabel was a bit too glad to be free of them—and I took them to see my parents. "August in Hoboken," Nicholas said, "where the elite meet." Aaron, usually the whiner, developed a blissful crush on an enticing five-year-old he met in day camp. Rosa this, Rosa that. She wore fetching red overalls and pink sneakers and it so happened, according to my brother Pete, that her mother was Viana.

Viana? How could that be? "She's back living at home," my mother said. "A sad story." Her marriage had busted up? After all that sacrifice? "No," my mother said. "Will you listen?" Viana had been very happy with her husband. "I told you he was a nice fellow," my mother said. They lived in Bangkok, which she loved—who could like that hot weather?—where he doctored poor people. She helped in his clinic. She learned the language, which was not an easy language, but she was a bright girl, wasn't she? She even cooked the food whatever way they eat there. She had a lovely, healthy baby who grew into a cute, cute girl. Her parents never wrote her when she sent pictures. One night Viana and her husband and Rosa were in a car driving back from the countryside when a drunk driver came out of nowhere and ran right into them on the highway. The husband was killed at once, Viana blacked out, the little girl wasn't hurt. While Viana was in the hospital, her parents came and took care of Rosa. Then they all went back to the U.S. together. "End of story," my mother said.

It was only a few days later that I saw Viana herself, at a show put on by the campers. She had always been a soft, bosomy girl and she had thickened some, but what struck me was the freshness still in her face. When I saw her in the audience, she was laughing at a child in a caterpillar costume—a pure, wide-mouthed laugh. I found her afterward, and we hugged as if it were a great joke to see each other. "You're the parent of the astounding Aaron superboy," she said. Aaron was busy ripping off his bee antennae.

Two of my other kids were around me, and I introduced them. When Viana spoke, I could see the sorrow lodged around her chin, the downward tilt of defeat. I suggested a playdate between Aaron and the enthralling Rosa. Rosa crowed and squealed something like, "*Dee mak!*" in what I assumed was Thai and she jumped for joy. "Okay, okay," Viana said, and there were more words between them in that secret language from her other life. She had only been a widow for a few months. I wasn't the sort of asshole to come on to her right then, but I thought she could get used to me again.

So I had a nice August. Viana and I took the kids to the park and hung around our parents' tiny urban yards. We discussed my teaching and the book that I might, who knew, someday write. Viana thought she might go to a school nearby to study nursing. "So you'll stay here?" I said. "Where else do I have to go?" she said. I hated the irony of her being stuck with her family again. "You could go anywhere," I said. "Not me," she said. "Not anymore."

One night I thought she needed cheering up, and I took her—don't ask me why I did this—to a Thai restaurant in the yuppified part of town. The waiters, once they heard her speak Thai, could hardly keep from hovering around our table to beam and banter, and they brought us amazing food (though not, Viana said, as good as in Thailand). One of the waiters wore a little white embroidered Muslim prayer cap and was from Pattani, near where her husband's family lived, a disclosure that made both of them cry out in gleeful amazement. Over the dessert of mango and coconut sticky rice, Viana said, "Oh, well. I shouldn't complain, should I? At least I was happy once." What was so awful to me in this sudden bit of bathos was that it showed her trying with all the resolve in her character to have a good attitude.

WE HAD TO ASK our parents to be sitters when we went out, and this caused massive interest on both sides. I was just what her parents had in mind in the first place, and my mother had always liked Viana. I didn't want anyone badgering Viana—hadn't she been pressured enough in her life? And I didn't want to be talked up as the sensible choice. Never a sexy job.

And once I got back to Bloomington, I did no more than send her chatty e-mail messages. *Aaron has learned to stand on his head. If he can get Alex to hold his feet. Love, Mike.*

Am getting through the days okay, Viana answered. *Rosa misses the ferry we took every day on the Chao Phraya and wants to know when we're going back.* I could see I would have to be patient. All fall I wrote my breezy notes, and for Christmas, which I spent in Indiana, I sent Rosa a ballerina outfit and Viana an expensive book on Italian painting through the ages. She sent me a plaid wool muffler, not exciting, but I wore it for months with a nice, itchy feeling of hope.

I was, of course, haunted by hope. I went to bed with hope every night, with its ghostly brightness settled against my delighted self, and I waited every minute for it to turn and show its teeth. Some men are fools many times over, and maybe I was one of them. I was almost sorry I was bothering with any of this.

The next August, when I came back with the boys, my mother invited Viana and Rosa for the first dinner home. Viana acted slightly embarrassed to see me and I wondered if she had someone else. It was not until the last week of that humid and highly fraught August that I got a certain vibe while we were shopping for picnic supplies, and I snuck us down to her family's furnished basement while the kids were at my parents'. She giggled as I led her to an ancient leatherette sofa, and with the most straightforward of moves, we became lovers. I got us across that line.

We had slept together when we were teenagers, and though time had gouged and battered and scourged us since, all the nakedness of sex was much easier than it would have been with anyone newly met. Later I wondered if she was very different from when she was seventeen, but I found I could not exactly remember the details from then. Several times I noticed extra things she'd learned, later-formed preferences. But mostly I did not have to think.

It was not really possible to hide our changed status from our families. "Better than that last one," my mother said. "I never liked her being Jewish." Annabel was the most secular of Jews, a post-Marxist atheist who'd hardly been inside a synagogue. "What kind of rotten thing is that to say?" I said. "Viana's a Muslim, if you want to get that way about it." Viana had converted (a simple process, she claimed) to please her husband's parents and have the ceremony they wanted. "*He* didn't care," she said. "He was very modern, very spiritual in a general way. You know what I mean."

My mother decided the conversion didn't count here, much as Viana's parents apparently gave me a familial dispensation for my divorce. I had to be careful around Viana—in the last days of the summer and in our phone calls after—not to rush her but not to seem less than eager. I was truly eager. My mind was flooded with pictures of Viana. Viana was the view out my window, Viana was the water I drank. I had not thought I would fall into such a haze of pure hunger. I didn't want to be desperate or grabby or too cloyingly grateful, though I was all those things. A corner of me could not imagine starting again, and the rest of me did nothing but imagine it every second.

I became a commuter dater; every month I'd fly out. Since Viana was still living with her family, they were unusual dates for adults, blandly chaste or hotly furtive. Sometimes my parents tried to give us some space—this was a bit hilarious to us. "Let them pick a really *long* movie," Viana said, "and stay to watch it twice." Part of her was happy, I did feel that. I could bring her along slowly, if only the others didn't press her. But they did press. Once she phoned me at my school office in tears because her father had told her a husbandless mother was being unfair to her child; her indignation at her father led her to split up with me for a week. I hated her father then, bullying her in his growled Sicilian, evoking a hinterland of fifty years ago, the village he'd gotten the hell out of, as if it were some scriptural landscape.

Not until late spring did I suggest that Viana come to Bloomington for a visit. And then her fleshly presence in the town where I lived, where I'd undergone my whole fucked-up adult history, was almost more than I could bear, and I was a rattled host, hoarse and nervous and all over her. The one thing I could not have expected was that Viana was moved by this. The sight of me unmoored pled my case. She wanted to help, how could she not help? By the end of the weekend, we were engaged.

—

WE WERE MARRIED in June, in Viana's parents' yard. That first summer felt like endless bounty to me; I lived with a woman who laughed with pleasure when she brought me anything I liked—a tiny pale green frog from under the shrubs, an early cup of coffee, a spontaneous bit of lavish invention in bed. She cooked meals so stunning that even Matthew, a real pain about food, decided he liked fish. I thought of this time as Paradise Regained. When I said this, she brought me dates—one of the named fruits in the Garden of Heaven, she said, in the Islamic afterlife— and fed me a few from her fingers. It was an odd feeling to eat them, to chew the dark, sugary fibers and wonder about her old life, what she ate, what she did, though I did not want to be sour or jealous.

She often got e-mail from a woman who'd been her best friend in Bangkok, a nurse from the clinic with the odd name of Toon. Every so often the message came through in Thai letters that spelled (Viana said) nonsense. "You'd be better off with Morse code," I said. "Dit dit dit dot dot." Rosa, of course, didn't know what a telegram was. I thought of all the dead technologies—pneumatic mail whooshed through Paris in tubes puffed with air, mechanical typewriters, pigeons—and always the dream of mind speaking to mind.

Viana still nattered in Thai to Rosa, though she told me Rosa was starting to forget words. Once Rosa said, "Hold me upside down, I want to swing over the floor," and Viana said, "Niwet used to do that." Niwet was her husband—her first husband. Viana could not say *Niwet*—on the rare occasions she did—without softening her voice. Rosa had grown in weight since he'd lifted her up to hang like a bat, but I did my best.

ON THE DRESSER in our bedroom was a hammered silver box that Viana used for her earrings, a gift from her husband's grandfather Zain. The design was in Arabic script, which was used for writing Malay in that corner of Thailand, and only there. What a great fact, I went around repeating it to everyone I knew—I was trying to get more interested in Thailand. And tidbits like this always pleased me, I was one of those historians who gets high on details. I planned to bring Zain's box in to show my students. The silver lid worked in *repoussé*, the curled and dotted letters. I was trying to like Thailand more.

THAT FIRST SUMMER of my second marriage, I found myself once again working on what I hoped would be my book. It was odd to be deep inside post-Fascist Italy, reading about *partigiani* in the Appennines, while thinking always about Viana, who was so linked to Thailand, and with Rosa, my half-Thai girl, in the house. And maybe I too could become an adept in things Thai. I knew a woman from Bloomington who learned Hungarian (Hungarian!) so her kids could speak what her husband spoke.

Rosa still hated the way Americans wore their dirty

outside shoes in the house and she was always crawling under the table to pull off my sneakers. And Viana's mother, I happened to know, automatically put her stocking on the left leg first, to keep the *mal'occhio* at bay, even after five decades out of Sicily. How careful people were, all over. From my desk it was clear that each separate corner of the world was obsessed with its own set of the familiar, the mass of fine points its residents were sure every human had to know. The whole fucking globe was populated by idiots savants, who knew what they knew very well and not all that much else. I was an idiot too, but at the moment I was a happy one. From my desk, I could hear Viana listening to music—the Pretenders and then Howlin' Wolf—while I worked. Howlin' Wolf was vowing to pitch a wang dang doodle all night long.

WHEN THE SUMMER ENDED, I went back to teaching, and Viana leafed through nursing school catalogues, still dawdling over what to do. I was in my office eating a terrible midwestern bagel when a student ran in with the nutso, hyped-up story that planes had hit the World Trade Center towers on purpose. I was arguing him down when the department secretary came in, and we all spent the next hour looking at the TV set in the lounge. Over and over the two buildings, one by one, spewed black smoke and sank straight down on the screen. I had considerable trouble believing my eyes. Some of the students were crying, and this made me worry about my own kids, and I called their schools (Annabel never liked me to call their schools). I remembered I had a wife at home—shouldn't we be comforting each other?—and I drove back. When I came in, Viana was on the telephone speaking Thai. For a second I was sure that her husband was not really dead at all, on this day of the dead, and she was talking to him. She had her hand on her heart when she said goodbye.

It was her brother-in-law, who had just called the house in Hoboken to make sure she was all right. "Oh," she said when she got off the phone and threw her arms around me, "it's just so hard, it's too much. I hadn't spoken to Winai since I lived there."

Afterward, this was what I always remembered about that day, though I didn't tell it when all the people I knew were telling their where-I-was stories. After that morning, Viana began sending e-mail to her ex-brother-in-law, who could read English just fine—and through him to the rest of her "old" family, as she called them, especially his mother, who mostly spoke Yawi, the Malay dialect written in Arabic. *I am thinking of you in these terrible times*, Viana wrote at her laptop in the kitchen. An entirely harmless sentiment, and I didn't try to read her incoming e-mail either. Though I thought of trying.

Meanwhile, my mother told me over the phone that I should make sure I didn't tell anyone Viana was some kind of Muslim because she wasn't really. "We're both wearing giant neon crosses around our necks," I said. "But my kids have to wear half-crosses-half-Stars-of-David."

"You can joke," my mother said. "But people are afraid for a reason." People were always afraid for a reason—that was what I taught my classes about.

"I couldn't believe it when Niwet's brother called," Viana said, more often than I liked. "Winai was always kind of stiff-necked, a little too fond of himself." Now he was the proud recipient of digital photos of Rosa in tap shoes.

How could I resent someone like Viana writing to her ex-in-laws? The news was full of features about how 9/11 made everyone value old bonds of affection. An attachment is not the same as an allegiance. She could be mine and write a few notes overseas. I had a sweet wife; I had no reason to be a grouchy, possessive jerk.

For my birthday in November she put rows of candles all along the walkway of our building, she held out a *torta di ricotta* with my initials in strawberries, and in the doorway Rosa did a special dance for me in her pink tutu. I bragged to everyone at school, I was an unstoppable moron of contentment.

A few weeks later, Viana said to me, "I always like this time of year. When I was in Thailand, we used to go visit the relatives then, when the rains were over. Zain, the grandfather, had an amazing old house. After Ramadan too there's a big thing of everybody visiting."

I said I wasn't sure long family visits were my idea of a good time.

"It's very beautiful in Pattani," she said.

"I wouldn't know," I said.

"You'd have to see it," she said. "I can't explain."

"Fine," I said.

OKAY, IT WAS VIANA's business if she liked some city on a bilgey river where it was always hot and rainy. In Italian, homesickness was *nostalgía*—if you longed for a place, you longed for another time. Could my wife miss the golden continent of her lost decade and still be okay with where she washed up? Could she have a few different kinds of longing at once? I certainly hoped so.

And this was a good year for us. Viana knocked herself out for my boys, who were sporadically nice to her. That spring she heard that she'd gotten into nursing school, and the two older boys actually brought home a pizza to congratulate her. Viana herself did a handspring on the lawn. Feet in the air, hair streaming on the grass. Who knew she could do that? "That's just something I do when I'm happy," she said. I didn't say I'd never seen her do it before.

SHE WAS NERVOUS about going back to school. "Piece of cake," I said. "You'll ace it." I teased her about being the sexy nurse, every boy's dream of the med exam from heaven. "Right," she said. And once school started, she was frantic and frustrated. "*Why* do I want to do this?" she'd say, pushing away some fat expensive textbook. She had to learn long Latinate terms for the unspeakable processes of the body, its rot and secretions and monstrous attempts at self-correction. I gave her pep talks about how smart she was, I made my old bachelor Boyardee meals for the kids. She was noticeably less interested in what the rest of us were doing. "Tell me later," she'd say.

Alex said, "You have time for your e-mail."

"She can do what she wants," I said.

"Thank you, thank you," Viana said.

"Are the people you write to Muslims?" Alex said. "Are they?"

"Viana's a Muslim," Nicholas said. "She is, I'm not kidding."

Aaron said, "No! She can't be!"

"She's a Muslim who doesn't do any of the things," Nicholas said.

Viana put her head down with her hands over it, the gesture that meant, *Let me alone, for Christ's sake.* For a Muslim she had committed the worst of sins, rejection of the precious gift of faith, grave enough to be technically punishable by death. I didn't think this was the moment to cite that fact.

"Hey, she got married by a priest," I said. "A regular Catholic person in a white collar. The nice fat man from my brother's parish who didn't care who was divorced. Remember, guys? You were there."

"I wore pink," Rosa said. "My dress was pink."

"Remember, Viana?" Aaron said.

IT WASN'T UNTIL her second year of school that I began to worry about Viana. In bed she had become what I would call compliant. She never turned her back, she never refused me, and when I questioned her she always claimed enthusiasm. But I knew. She was a poor liar. The fancier I got, the more determined I was in my attentions, the more unconvincing she was.

I didn't know (how could I?) whether she might have liked any other man better. After Annabel and I broke up, I used to ask myself: What if a person only gets one great love in this life? I didn't really believe that, and people in my place and time generally didn't. But I thought Viana might be the sort of woman who loved only once—his for always, simple as that. A heroine. Whose valor was now being mangled.

THE NIGHT PATTANI was on the TV news, Viana got very upset. "Look what they've done!" she kept saying. "They" were the Thai police, who'd killed a hundred and eight Muslims in the capital of Pattani. Bands of Islamist youth with machetes had attacked police stations and checkpoints trying to steal firearms. (What a crazy idea, who'd thought that one up, the ungunned trying to rob guns.) Special forces, who'd been tipped off, opened fire, and those left standing took refuge in a sixteenth century mosque; when the cops couldn't get a surrender, they killed everyone inside. The TV showed a marble floor gouged by grenades and a Koran covered in blood. "This won't help," Viana said. "Do they think this helps anything?"

I thought she sounded like Rodney King asking why we all can't get along. The oldest of all questions. "It's a beautiful mosque," Viana said. "You can't see in the pictures. It was never finished, because of a curse. It's very famous."

"The whole world will be rubble soon," I said.

"You've never seen it. It's a real place. I know it's not real to you."

"It is to you. More than here."

"You have no idea. You've never been anywhere so you can't imagine."

"I can *imagine*," I said. "Do you think all the time of going back? You want to go back."

"People are *dead*. What are you talking about?" she said. "What's the matter with you?"

"I'm not dead," I said, but even I knew I sounded pathetic.

IT WAS A STUPID DISCUSSION, and what it did (I should have known this, I taught about this) was inspire a deeper loyalty in her to the bloodied mosque, the bullet-pitted brick, the local mourning, her old life. Not a political loyalty, worse than that, a familial one. I couldn't stop either.

"I know you don't like winter here," I'd say. "You wish Indiana was the tropics, don't you?"

"What if I do?" she'd say. "What then?"

"Half the time you don't even know you're here."

"What if I don't? Whose business is that?"

Unlike Annabel, Viana was not much of a quarreler, but the rhetorical questions she fended me off with had threats of separation as their answers. A shadow of possibility had entered the house, though we went on as if it had not. A mere shadow can be lived with. That was what I thought.

ONE FRIDAY VIANA was out when I came home and she wasn't back in time for dinner, though her car was in the driveway. By six all four boys were there, with Rosa, and we waited. I thought maybe her hours had changed at the hospital—a friend might have picked her up—and she'd forgotten to tell me. She was training on the pediatrics ward, which was very high-stress, but how could she forget us? I gave the kids some food, and I called the hospital. The head nurse said crisply that Viana LoBianco was not on duty till Sunday.

My first thought was to hope the head nurse hadn't known I was the husband. In my mortification, I could hardly look at the kids when I hung up the phone. Hadn't I seen the signs? I had, this time. How did it happen that I was a man that two women chose to leave? What had I done? Rosa said, "She better get here soon."

Then I was ashamed of not worrying that something had happened to her, even on the safe streets of Bloomington. She wouldn't just leave Rosa, that was very unlikely. I didn't want to alarm the kids, so I sounded friendly and sheepish when I called the police, who had no news, and then I called patient admissions at Viana's hospital and another nearby. No Viana anywhere, no matter how many times I spelled both her names. By this time Rosa and Aaron were in tears, and Alex was braying at them, "She's okay! She's really okay!" Nicholas had the idea that we should just cruise around checking the streets and the back roads, and I let the older two go off while I stayed with the others.

I plied them with late-night snacks, but no one was hungry and Rosa wept into her chocolate milk. *Don't do this to them*, I thought, a prayer in the form of an argument. They were asleep in front of the TV when the older boys came back at two a.m., having found nothing. I was thinking, after I got everyone settled in bed, that if I'd known life was going to be like this I wouldn't have bothered with any of it.

The phone call came at nine the next morning. All the kids were in the kitchen and I could hardly hear Viana's breathy voice. She was in a detention facility for women in Indianapolis, where the FBI had taken her, after questioning her for hours about her e-mails to the relatives in Pattani. "What?" I said. "What?" My poor girl, she had to repeat it before I promised to call a lawyer. "Kisses," I said to her, dumbly, as her quarter ran out. I told the kids she would be home soon.

IT TOOK THREE DAYS to get her out, which the lawyer said was much, much better than he had feared. When the lawyer and I went to pick her up, she looked wispy and blowsy and spent, but at home in front of the kids she perked up. "It's over," she sang, and perhaps that was true.

"Your father got me out of there," she told Rosa. When she put her hand on my shoulder, I saw she meant me.

For a week, she had no interest at all in leaving our apartment—she said it looked like the world's coziest nest to her. I wondered that she felt safe there, since it was from this living room that the FBI (a man and a woman) had taken her. She said she just wanted to sleep now. Her questioners had gone at her without letting her sleep very much. They had repeated the same questions in many different ways, and they had done their best to scare her out of her wits. Did she like this jail, would she like to stay here a lot longer? They understood how loyal she might feel to her former relatives, but did she know how serious it was to keep back information? Was it fair to her daughter not to give full answers?

Our lawyer had expressed some surprise that they hadn't questioned me too, and there was nothing at all to keep them from coming back. I thought about the men's jail, worse than the women's. I kept this fear to myself, since airing it would only have given Viana more dread, to no purpose. I'd spent my whole adult life reading prison memoirs, prison poems, letters from prison—Nelson Mandela, Cesare Pavese, Martin Luther King. I hadn't thought that history was going to come get me of all people in this of all ways.

Small noises in the apartment made me jumpy—a phone call at an odd time, a branch hitting the window. But I didn't want to walk around quaking in my own home; I didn't want to quail before those fuckheads, or act as if I were not equal to what my wife had just gone through, or get Rosa more spooked than she was. Fear was not a good idea here, but I had my hands full being the steady guy.

In the week that Viana stayed indoors and slept, she liked me to nap with her. Or—she asked—would I just lie next to her until she nodded off? Would I phone her from school later to please wake her up? We held hands over dinner, like a dating couple. She saw me freshly as her rescuer, which was a little ridiculous. Rosa was clingy again too; she would lay her head on my chest while I was still eating dessert. I liked all this, I liked this time. Perhaps it was not such a bad time for Viana either.

I DID NOT EXPECT the delicate intensity of these days to last, once Viana went back to nursing school and became again the overworked woman in white. But something of the generous and melancholic fondness of that time did stay; a shift had been made. For good, it seemed. I could hardly believe this turn of the wheel. It was strange to profit from the scare tactics of a marauding arm of the government, but the oddness of it didn't keep me from being glad.

In public Viana and I were together more too, talking to journalists, addressing rallies, lined up in a delegation to our congressperson, making as much of a fuss as we could. We'd coach each other before and rehash all of it afterward. Early on, to the kids' great astonishment, we were on a local TV station, for about two seconds. When I saw the tape, I was a little startled at how old we looked. Well, Viana looked better; she was the dark-haired expert on regions whose names she pronounced with rippling exactness, while I, her barking professor of a husband, looked on.

Viana was shy under this glaring attention, but her indignation was deep and she was too modern, shy or not, to just let me speak. Underneath her wincing she was proud. After someone wrote about us in the *Herald-Times*, I saw her e-mailing the article to friends in New Jersey.

"So what do they think in Hoboken?" I asked later.

"They think we look like Sonny and Cher," she said. "Just kidding. They're pissed off on our behalf, they can't believe it. In Thailand they're always afraid the cops want money but I told them it's a different problem here."

"You sent the article to Thailand?" I tried not to sound infuriated and shrill with foreboding. I was worried for Rosa. I was worried for me.

"I did," she said. "I thought about it. I did ask Winai not to tell my mother-in-law—she gets upset, she's been through a lot—but I couldn't really keep it from them. You know?"

I didn't know a thing.

"You don't think I should write to them?"

She already had. How often did she send these notes to them? Every week, every minute? More now than before? She gazed up from her computer while she waited for me to answer. I waited too. She had her eyes trained on me, trying to see what I thought, and a terrible expression crossed her face, a look of pained surprise. Was she alone in this after all? Her chin took on its fallen, defeated angle.

"Mike?" she said. I could hardly stand to see her like that.

"Yes," I said. I had principles. A person had a right to send e-mail wherever the hell she wanted. Any jerk could tell her that much, couldn't he? "Of course you should. Are you kidding?"

Viana looked at me happily, though it was not my happiest moment.

And I thought about those photos of us (Sonny and Cher indeed) going out into the world as bright pixels emanating from our kitchen table. I'd never exactly understood cyberspace. But here I was, swimming in it— sink or swim—floating on a lake as big as I ever could imagine, bigger. Look what love has done to me, I thought, but it was too small an idea for where I was.

LOYALTY

Annunziata

Nobody talks about it now, but I hated Americans when I was young. We lived in a town in the mountains south of Palermo. Half the kids in our part of town were my cousins. Giuseppe Sneaky across the street was my uncle's sister-in-law's son, Giuseppe White-Head (who got called that because his hair was sort of light brown) had the same aunt, and every night the boys hung out in the piazza with my brother, whose name was also Giuseppe but who was called Piddu to keep things straight. Piddu was the smartest of my brothers—he could get anybody to do anything—and he kept the cousins from bullying me. "Pick on an ugly girl instead," he said. Our father ran a store that sold anything that didn't have to be fresh—sugar, rice in sacks, bars of laundry soap, powdered bullion, shoes, candles, salted anchovies from barrels, and sometimes toys around Christmas. All of us helped in the store, but only Piddu, once he was old enough, got to ride the train to Palermo to buy supplies.

My father didn't like to make the trip himself and he decided no one could cheat Piddu. Piddu brought me back very good souvenirs—a set of paper dolls, a postcard of the Virgin Mary (I was a religious girl), and once a tiny, beautiful peach made of marzipan.

I have to say: we all liked Mussolini then. We weren't wild devotees—the man was not Sicilian—but he was less of a joke than most politicians, my father said. My brothers were *avanguardisti* in the Fascist youth group and they got to wear black shirts and black fezzes with long tassels while they marched around the schoolyard on Saturdays. My mother heard the government had built very nice apartments somewhere for old pensioners. And we weren't immune to the idea of glory. In school we had to sing rousing hymns about hailing the people of heroes, hailing our immortal fatherland, and I liked the singing.

Piddu was the second oldest of us, after my sister Vincenzina, and he was the first to go to war. I laughed when I saw Piddu in uniform—our Piddu in those boots! He said, "Don't worry, Nunzia, I'm going to Africa, where the people wear white sheets and don't even have guns." I was fourteen by then and not sure if he meant this. When I saw that he was teasing me, I was frightened. But I pulled myself together and waved because I didn't want to be a fool.

The first weeks he was away, I kept thinking I'd forgotten to do something—take the coffee off the flame? lock the cash box?—and then I'd realize it was the lack of Piddu that made everything feel like an unfinished sentence. My mother had a little stone altar in a corner of the house with a plaster statue of the Virgin, and I put flowers there every day for my brother, chrysanthemums in the fall or branches of waxy red berries in winter. The few times I forgot to do this I was seized with dread. At night, in the room I shared with my sister, I prayed over and over with a mental chanting of his name. We all felt better when we got a letter—he was in a base on the mainland, being taught to do push-ups, he said, by an officer with a mustache like pubic hair.

The letters took away some of my fright and bit by bit I began to get used to his being gone. And I had an interest in a boy from the next street who always looked back at me when he biked by. I was done with going to school by then, and our store wasn't so busy that I couldn't watch out the window or stand in the door. The boy, whose name was Umberto, had a maroon-colored bike and his hair was cut so the top of it flopped in the wind.

When they sent my brother Piddu to North Africa, we didn't get any more letters. We wrote to him anyway, jokey messages from everyone in the family, dull news of what sold in the store. My sister Vincenzina's *fidanzato* was going into the army too, and she wanted to marry him before he left. So then we were all very busy with the wedding, sewing my sister's dress and making up the little bags of sugared almonds for favors. Enrico played the mandolin, and I danced with my father. My sister's wedding night was the last night before her new husband went off. His house was on a street with stone steps built into it, and all the way up his friends had pasted signs: GO, ANTONELLO! TAKE IT ALL THE WAY, ANTONELLO! AIM STRAIGHT!—these were wishes for his victories in bed, not on the battlefield. I could scarcely stop thinking about what they meant. The next day he left for his unit, and my sister came back to us.

I was more restless after the wedding. I'd wake every night from the scandal of my dreams, with only the sound of my sister's breathing in the room. My dreams were my own, but it made me feel odd to have Vincenzina so near after what had transpired in my sleep. The room was like a cave, damp with our breath and the smell of stone. In the mornings I woke up earlier than I had before, and I came into the dark kitchen and made the fire in the stove. There was more to do these days, with Piddu gone, and they were teaching me to keep the store's accounts too, since my brother Enrico was going soon.

When my mother came into the kitchen in the morning, she was never in a good mood. Sometimes I could clown her out of it—I'd sweep over her feet with the broom, or I'd tuck oranges in my bodice as a fake bosom—and on Sundays, when we all went to Mass, she was better. I was too. Did we all believe that God was taking care of Piddu? Who knew what "taking care" meant to someone like God, Whose eye saw dying every day?

I had the lacquered wood rosary that I had been given at my confirmation, but since Piddu's leaving I didn't bother to use it for prayers when I was alone. Part of me wanted to promise and plead, to reason with God about how much we needed Piddu. Then I would think, Oh, He knows that, and I would try to think of all He knew, and I saw God's awareness spreading over the sands of North Africa. I wanted so much to feel His presence right in the room; I wanted what probably only saints get to feel. But the thought of His attention like a haze in the desert was some comfort to me.

Enrico left in the spring. We knew from the newspaper that the Italian and German armies had been busy for a long time fighting the British in Egypt. I had the idea that the British were timid, skinny people but I also knew that any soldier with a gun was not a comedy. In the fall we heard on the radio that the Americans were in Africa all of a sudden—they waded onto the shore, trying not to get their guns wet—but our forces gathered together and shot at all of them. My father told me that someone like my brother, who could always get people to do things, was not in the front lines anyway. "He gave cigarettes to the right person, he sent a girl in to the colonel. He's Piddu."

GIUSEPPE SNEAKY TOLD me that Sicilians could adapt easily to North Africa because Saracens, who were Arabs, had lived for more than two hundred years in Sicily and left their blood in us. So, for instance, an Arab mosquito today might give a disease to a European but not to a Sicilian. "The Americans will die of malaria," he said. My father said, yes, he had seen mosquitoes wearing little

black Fascist badges. The mosquitoes were all singing
songs to Il Duce.

I had Umberto, the boy from the next street, always,
always in my mind, but my mother had only her misery.
We had snow that winter, a beautiful light sprinkling on
the mountains, and my mother would not even go out to
look at it. She kept inside all the time, blinking at customers from a stool in the store. People were short on
money and in winter they had nothing to trade but
oranges or knobs of kohlrabi, and they'd walk back and
forth in front of the sacks and barrels. My mother didn't
believe in giving anyone credit and made stock cheaper
only when it was stale or broken. (People waited for my
father, but I never saw him lower a price either.) At home
she swept and mopped and rubbed, as though the table
and floor might speak if they were beckoned fully and say
something better than we could.

We knew from the newspaper that bombs were falling
on Palermo and Messina. My father said it was smart of us
to live in an unimportant town. In the early spring Vincenzina walked around the square with me every day,
when the almond blossoms were shedding and the plum
trees were showing white. We were home eating oranges
when Signor Roselli from the post office knocked on the
door. Anyone could tell from the phlegmy way he said
Buon tarde, with his head down, that he had a telegram.

Piddu or Enrico? we all thought. I tried not to wish
against Enrico—he was a good boy, with hair like a sheep,

who loved pranks—I tried not to ask for anything and to hold the moment like the burning coal it was. We made Vincenzina read the message, and when she said Giuseppe Fabiano Tommaso, my mother shrieked, but I was still thinking, Are those all his names? Couldn't it be another Giuseppe? Why not?

THE AMERICANS KILLED HIM. I knew that at once and later we heard it was true. My mother was angry that the government couldn't send him back to us to bury, and my father said, "What difference is it to Piddu now?" I tried to think of Piddu as someone who'd escaped his body. My mother and I went to church every morning for him. To think about Piddu in the prayers made him feel less gone, so I thought I would do this for the rest of my life. Let God get sick of hearing his name, let Him.

God was always the same, it didn't matter to Him who lived or died. Only we had to live with our smallness. For a while I really could not stand the chatter of other people. I thanked all the neighbors for whatever they said and they just kept saying it. When Umberto came to the house with his family, he was a little scared of me and hovered at some distance. I was a creature in a ditch and could only look at him out of one eye. But when I woke up in my room in the night I still thought of him with longing, and I didn't like feeling despair and lovesickness both at once. I would have forgotten Umberto if I could have.

We kept the store closed for a week, and when we opened it again, one of the customers who tried to wheedle a discount out of me was a neighbor who used to buy plenty before the war, when some uncle in Brooklyn was sending him cash. I didn't like to think I was a spiteful person but I took pleasure in saying no to him.

In May we heard that North Africa was lost—all the Italians and Germans there surrendered to the Allies. I cursed the news—my father said he had no idea I knew those words—how could he joke when we were hearing that Piddu's dying had done no good at all? My mother said it probably meant that Enrico would be sent home. She had entirely forgotten that she'd ever thought about anything but family.

Giuseppe Sneaky was riding in a freight car on the train back from Palermo when planes began to drop bombs on the city. He was terrified that the train might not move fast enough to get away, but it did. He heard the thunder of the planes doing their work in the dark; he saw the smoke and the glow when he couldn't see the city in the distance below. My father said the Americans would be on the ground in Sicily soon, they would land on the shore from their ships. My sister got word that her husband was back in Sicily, on the other side of the island, bivouacked in a church, and wasn't that good news? It was hard to know what was good.

ON A VERY HOT DAY in the worst part of the summer, a man sent by the mayor made us close the store. Everyone had to stay at home because the war was coming to our town. The flies buzzed inside the house with us—my father liked to call this a Sicilian concert. We could hear big trucks coming up from the road below, rattling through the streets. I waited for the sound of shooting, but my father said, who would they shoot at? We were nothing but locals, harmless nobodies. My mother wouldn't let me go out, even when we heard shouting and bells ringing in the piazza. What were they shouting? They were cheering the Americans!

By the time my family let me out, all my cousins had taken every bit of the chewing gum and wrapped candy that the soldiers threw at them, and there were no cigarettes left to take back to my father. But the next day, a soldier in a khaki uniform came into the store. He wasn't tall enough to be an American but he was. And he spoke to us in Sicilian! He said, "Hello, you have sausages?" He wanted food—well, who didn't? He was with a whole brigade from Brooklyn and lots of them could speak. "You have to go to the *salumeria* for sausage," I said. "But they don't have any either." He was an ugly boy with sunglasses, too weak to look into the sun.

My parents didn't let me out very much during the sweltering weeks when the Americans were walking around our town. The little I saw made me wonder whether Piddu had gone with hookers when he was in North Africa. I hoped those women (who in our town were rough and mean) had been nice to him. By the end of July we heard that the king and the Grand Council had fired Mussolini and had him arrested. They could do that to Il Duce? "Well, they did," my father said. The Fascist

Party office near the piazza was already abandoned, like a barn where all the animals had been sold off. By the fall the Americans were gone from our town, chasing the Germans to the mainland.

My sister kept waiting to hear from Antonello, who had been somewhere on our island, but where was he now? No one was telling. In September the king said the war was over, by way of saying we were surrendering. My mother said she had a dream that Enrico was a pigeon on a roof, which meant he was coming home soon.

In Sicily the fighting was done. The rest of Italy was still a battlefield the Germans were killing to keep. One morning my father came running into the store to tell us that on the radio he heard the newscaster say Italy had now declared war on Germany. "What are they *doing*?" I said.

My father said, "They want to be friends with the right people."

No one was angry on behalf of Piddu, but I couldn't stand thinking what a dirty trick had been played on him. Now Mussolini had managed to get himself to the north of Italy and set up his own new republic there. I didn't think Piddu would've run to his side—Piddu wouldn't have done anything he didn't have to—but how could he have been asked (and they were asking) to fight with the Allies? Lucky Piddu: he was beyond it. The dead don't have bodies to pledge to anyone, and we envy them this. None of us knew where my brother Enrico was, or Antonello either.

The invasions had made a mess of the wheat fields, and we had no flour for bread. We made fake coffee from chicory and ugly dried roots. Breakfast was a dismal part of the day, especially in the damp of November. It was on one of these mornings that my brother Enrico—still in his Fascist infantry hat—walked into the house, with his sheep-hair grown bushy and his face much bonier and his jacket wet from the fog, and my mother screamed with delight. When I hugged him, he said, "Look at what a fat bug our Nunzia is," and I thought he was the old Enrico, but he was not.

He let us kiss him and stroke his hair and he laughed silently when we asked questions. My mother made a special dinner—rabbit stewed with raisins and lemon—and she was very happy when Enrico ate a lot of it. Eating it seemed to occupy his attention; you had to call his name to get him to look up. I was going to tell him there was a cockroach on his fork (his favorite trick with me) but I thought better of it. Neighbors came in to greet him while we were having our gritty coffee, and they hugged him with real feeling, but then they hung back and didn't know what to say.

It was the same a few days later when Enrico went back to work in the store. The old women reached over to clasp him and say how well he looked (which was not true), but there was none of the loud, jubilant fuss I'd seen before. No one was putting his medals on display in the town hall either. Enrico shrugged when anyone asked questions and he looked disheartened and embarrassed.

—

IN THE WINTER my sister heard that her husband was alive and unhurt—he was a prisoner of war in America, in a place called Massachusetts (none of us could get this name right). He wrote that the weather was cold but being a prisoner was a lot better than being a soldier and they were letting Italians cook in the dining hall on the air base. He was hoping to be able to stay after the war and to bring Vincenzina over.

My sister was so excited that she could hardly stand herself. All her listlessness was gone; she was a creature of itches and fits and visionary deliriums. A riot of perfections was beaming into her mind—I had not known she wanted all these things or found daily life in our town so narrow and dull. It made me sorry to see how joyous she was to think about leaving the rest of us.

And who would Vincenzina talk to in America? Only Antonello would be her age. All the cousins' cousins over there had sailed before 1924, when the Fascists passed a law against emigrating. "You'll be lonely as a toad," I said. I was never leaving my parents. I knew that much.

IN MARCH WE HAD the Feast of San Giuseppe, my brother's name day, and when I watched the bonfires at night, I talked to Piddu in my head about how smoky it was. We didn't have bread to bake into the shapes of angels and flowers, but all the women in our part of town had made an altar with a bower of myrtle branches hung with lemons and oranges. *Look how nice*, I said to Piddu.

No one knows what to do with the dead and I didn't know either. I kept wanting to give Piddu something, and maybe the shadow of the dead produces in us a shadow kindness. I was a little in love with the beauty of this, but I saw already how it would stay inside my head, all that unused kindness, curling on itself.

MOST OF WHAT WE had to do that year was figure out how to eat. My brother Enrico went out very early in the morning and gathered snails, and my mother and I cooked them with garlic and oil. Along the road outside town were wild greens—scratchy weeds, but why not?—that tasted less bitter with something salty on them. We had dried beans for soup, we were really all right. My sister was the one who complained because she was thinking about eating in Massachusetts.

I thought Umberto forgot about me, and maybe as the months went by I forgot him a little too. His father was a town cop, and who was there to pay him now? I stayed at home more, with Enrico working in the store, and my mother and I had our quarrels about whether I was scratching the floor with my mop. In the next valley people had sacked the town hall and burned all the land records, and everyone knew there were robbers on the roads. My parents were afraid about the store.

We kept running out of different items—matches, flour, thread. Piddu could have found us what we needed on the black market. Piddu would have kept the store safe too; he would've known which men to have a word with. Piddu could have fixed the radio antenna, after a storm blew it down. Enrico and my father rigged up a substitute antenna with the rusted springs of Piddu's old bed, but everything sounded fuzzy. The music too. At least we weren't listening for Mussolini's speeches every week. I had heard his voice tell us the Americans were greedy slave masters whose downfall was coming. Now nobody wanted such a downfall and I supposed I didn't either.

IN APRIL OF THE next year we saw photos of the corpses of Mussolini and his men, shot first and then hung upside down from the scaffolding of a gas station in Milan. Claretta, who they said was Mussolini's mistress, had her skirt tied with a rope so it didn't fall past her knees. Someone had not wanted the crowd to see her nakedness, and this made me wonder if it was better, in this life, to be a woman, no matter what anyone said.

Umberto started coming to the store again; they sent me to the back when they saw him because they knew he was looking at me. His voice was gruff when he asked for a pound of salt. He was a sober sort of boy, upright and quiet. What a beautiful love I had for him, in all my swooning ignorance; no feelings could have been less tainted or more intense. And to him too I was a dove, a flower, a ray of light. It wasn't false either, this untested longing—it was as true as anything and more necessary, the small blue point in the heart of all flame.

———

MY ENGAGEMENT DIDN'T come about till after the war was over. I had just had my seventeenth birthday when Umberto's parents came to talk to my parents. Umberto's father was a policeman once again and had gotten Umberto a job with him. I'd never been alone with Umberto, but I'd seen more of him than most girls did of their intendeds because I worked in the store and wasn't kept in the house. The next day, my father asked me what did I think and I hid my face in my hands. Relief and delight made me act like a dope.

That Sunday, Umberto and I took our first walk together on a path outside town, with the bare slopes of the mountains rising up all around and sheep clogging the roads. My mother and Vicenzina came with us and helped with the conversation. Afterward, I thought about any comments he had made (he liked chestnuts cooked burnt! he didn't like cats!) and I tilted each piece back and forth, a tiny mirror of my future. For the two years of our engagement, I lived in a fog of unspeakable anticipation. Very late at night, Umberto would stand in the street under my window and call up my name, like an owl. I would cover myself with my shawl and let him try to say praising things in his shy, stiff way. He was most touching when he was a little strained, a little out of his element. My engagement was a long introduction to understanding things like this.

NOBODY HAD ANY money after the war. When Umberto practiced shooting at a tree with the other cops, scroungers came afterward and dug up the ground for metal shells they could sell. We were better fed than most people, and we were still eating odd-colored pasta made with bean flour. My sister was waiting to go to fat America. I felt sorry for my sister. The two Giuseppes made up funny stories about Antonello's adventures with American girls.

At my wedding, I had a place set for Piddu. It was just a chair covered with flowers—white and pink roses, very pretty, twining around the back, tied with long satin ribbons—and on the table, his army picture where a plate of food would have been. Everyone in the town understood that I could never have married without this. My father said, "Piddu likes a good party." I got a little drunk and imagined I was giggling at Piddu's jokes. (When he saw Enrico dancing, wouldn't he have said he looked like a grasshopper?) I didn't forget Umberto—he was the face I could hardly look into, the sharp fear and the thrill, the serious side of my wedding.

YOU CAN'T EVER KNOW what being married will be like. I was lucky. Umberto had decided on me a long time before and the quiet obstinacy in his nature met me as devotion. It was very heady to be his lily. And I couldn't have known before that the embarrassment I was so afraid of would fade with the onset of desire. The whole obvious course of things was a beautiful surprise to me.

We had our own house—cramped as a hut and dark inside—and I spent my days keeping it fresh and neat and making foods I thought Umberto would like. Every bit of work I did was charged with the impatience of longing for Umberto, and he was home by midday. At the table he would nod at what I'd made, in his gruff satisfaction, and tell me about the intrigues in the police department and then go off to work again. On days when I did the laundry, I couldn't keep from looking at each intimate item of Umberto's. I didn't know how Vincenzina had endured four years away from her husband.

But our poor Vincenzina had a surprise in the mail. The American Consulate told her she had to come to Palermo for a medical examination—for her visa (her visa!), which was being processed. And what if (my mother said) she didn't pass the exam? Antonello's mother said, "Everyone knows the girl is healthy as a cow."

I was jealous because I had never been to Palermo. My sister went with her mother-in-law and they stayed with a cousin of someone in our town. Vincenzina came back telling us about the churches with domes like red hats and the vendors who had rhymes for what they sold. She was leaving on a ship in a month. Her husband sent her a dress to wear in America; it had shoulders with little pads and a smooth, full skirt. It looked very odd in our town. I thought Vincenzina's excitement was a cruelty to our parents—who already had one son they'd never see again—but I wanted these last days to be good between us. Vincenzina had taught me to sew and recited naughty jingles to me and showed me the steps of dances; she was my only sister.

Enrico said her outfit looked like what a donkey

would wear. I was glad to have him to titter with. And what had taken Antonello so long? I knew I had a better husband, and I was grateful I didn't have to go anywhere. I didn't want to be Vincenzina, not for a second. I had what I wanted, and I knew that was rare in this world.

MY HUSBAND LIKED TO READ. I could read fine, but it wasn't something I did for pleasure. Umberto had gone to school a few years longer than I had, and at night he spent hours with a book he had about the Romans. After Vincenzina left, I was a little bored and went more often to visit my mother. My mother guessed when I thought I was pregnant (she was always guessing, but this time she was right). After all the crowing from her and the hot broth she immediately made me drink, I wondered if I was away from my husband too much.

But I already knew. Umberto was fine as long as you let him be alone when he wanted. If you interrupted, a rougher, meaner side of him came out. He could not have been more gallant and more protective of me in my pregnancy. He wouldn't let me carry anything heavier than a melon and he made me wear a shawl and a hat if there was the slightest breeze. But he didn't want me chattering at him. He said, "A man has to be deaf when a woman is talking." I was petulant sometimes in my pregnancy but I was happy too.

SOME MEN LOVE holding babies and swinging and bouncing them—Piddu had been one of those—and some men don't want to be too close to the smells and the mess. Umberto was a little afraid of our tiny, red-faced, beautiful son, but he sat and talked to him for hours. Not for my ears, but what I caught was nonsense. Umberto singing silly syllables! I would have liked to name the baby for Piddu, but he had to be Calogero, for Umberto's father. To me he was always Beddu, handsome boy.

My sister sent him a little navy blue coat with a cap like one a grown-up would wear. She said America was very interesting (which did not sound good) and they were living in New Jersey, which was not the same as New York but was near it. Her husband was driving a bus. Nobody knew Antonello could drive but now he could.

My mother helped me every day with Beddu, but who would help Vincenzina? My baby was growing nicely fat. I was rounder than before too, plumped with milk. I liked my shape, and when they let me nap, I woke up delighted with everything. My father carried the baby up and down the street while I slept. He said he was teaching Beddu to play cards and smoke cigarettes.

One evening when I came back from my mother's I found Umberto reading a book with lessons in Latin. "I'm married to an ancient Roman," I said. But it wasn't Latin, it was English. I didn't even know he had such a book. "*Ow are you? Fine-a, dank you,*" he read. And why was he doing this? But I knew why before I asked. He was thinking we should go to America.

—

IT DIDN'T MATTER what his reasons were (he wanted our boy to have more chances, he wanted more chances himself) or how I argued my sobbing opinions. *This is how it is*, my father used to say, *the donkey eats oranges but shits corn*, which meant: Whatever you expect, something else happens. Why did I think I knew Umberto? I didn't know anything. It wasn't any use to make trouble with my husband. Everything was already happening.

Not that we left right away. It took months and months. I had time to think: If Piddu's bones were buried in the town, it would never be possible to leave. If the Americans didn't care that my brothers shot at them, why should I care? If other people were happy leaving their parents forever, why wasn't I? I was born in the wrong body: that was what I really thought. But I loved my husband, didn't I? It was my job to catch up to that piece of truth.

WHO KNOWS WHAT LOVE IS? On the boat the baby was sick to his stomach and I was sick too. We were animals stinking up the tiny cabin. Umberto came with cool, wet towels to put on our faces. I gave myself over to his way of helping. When I was better, we went up on deck and the other women talked to me. I had hardly ever talked to strangers before. I was shy, and I leaned against my husband. The women admired my baby, the sea air had a very good smell.

When I saw Vincenzina at the pier, she was wearing a hat like a prune. Antonello and she were standing right at the front of the crowd, as if they knew what they were doing. I turned and saw from Umberto's face, which was trying to smile, that he was afraid. Words about bravery that we had sung during the war—"the valor of your warriors, the courage of pioneers"—came into my mind to rally me, and I waved much more gaily than I felt.

I DIDN'T LIKE America at first, how could I? We lived in a room in the half of a house my sister and her husband rented, in Hoboken. The first few months I stayed mainly inside. The currents of air in the cold seasons were too chilly for the baby and I didn't know how to act outside when people were speaking English. It scared me to be so stupid. Vincenzina took me shopping in stores run by Sicilians or by Pugliesi and I didn't say a word there either. I stood wrapped in my heavy coat and told her what I wanted and heard her repeat it in Sicilian or grammar school Italian. Then we went home to her kitchen with its stove with its own gas inside and her bathroom where you pissed on white china and pulled a chain to make water rinse over it. In our town we had electricity but not these things. I hated to be stupid.

But I tried to make things nice for Umberto. At midnight he went with a friend of Antonello's to clean out all the buses; he slept in the day and went to classes in the evening to learn English. In between he played with the baby and ate meals with all of us. I never said, *Why did we come so you could sweep up dirt?* I never said, *Why do we have to learn everything over? What was wrong with what we knew before?*

I might have stayed indoors forever if it hadn't been for Beddu. I wanted him to know English from Americans, so when the weather got warmer we went out to a park. He played in a sandbox and he chased the other children around and he screeched whatever they screeched. When Vincenzina wasn't with me, I picked up words from the other mothers.

Umberto learned much faster than I did, and I was ashamed to try any words in front of him. I was proud the first time I asked a woman what her boy's name was. (The woman looked like a doll with bangs—you couldn't guess from women's faces that they'd just been through the same war.) Beddu, who was Calogero really, was Gerry in this country. Sometimes I was Nancy. I didn't mind, but Annunziata was my grandmother's name and Nancy had no history. My sister said that was the good part—no mean gossip from a hundred years ago, no beliefs based on some ancestor's pigheaded ideas, no old enemies.

Throughout the first year, Umberto was too tired to talk much, but in the late afternoons we would lie in bed with Beddu and be company for each other. I had our old linens on the bed and on the dresser a brass cup that Piddu had won for soccer, which I filled with straw flowers. These rests with Umberto were what gave me strength to go outside. On the street, I couldn't make the man at the drugstore understand what I wanted, and I got lost trying to find my way back, and I had to ask strangers and not know what they meant. It was humiliating to have Beddu see me like this, little though he was.

I didn't really want to get better at knowing Hoboken things—deep in my heart they didn't interest me—but I learned them, inch by inch, in spite of myself. I didn't have to be reminded of all that we had here that we didn't have at home: hamburgers with ketchup; Mickey Mouse; a trip across the river to New York City, where I walked on the avenues as good as anyone; a son who could sing "You Are My Sunshine." But I would have gone back to Sicily in a minute except for my husband, I never would have stayed except for him.

I HAD MY second baby in a hospital. I didn't like the weird odors or the nosy nurses, but I liked being asleep for the pain. I was carrying big in front, which meant a boy, but I woke up with a girl! We named her Anna, a name Americans understood. By this time, Umberto was driving a bus and we had our own half of a house to live in. I missed my mother very badly. We had more room but I had to do everything.

Vincenzina said that in order to learn English you had to practice all the time back and forth, but Umberto had somehow managed to learn without opening his mouth. He was not sociable or hearty like some of the other drivers, but he watched and he picked things up. Not just phrases—after the second year even I could say a few slangy things like "How's tricks?" or "What is cookin?"—

but also the way things worked. When the fat man from Messina who ran the bus company couldn't get a permit for a new route, my Umberto knew what to do. Someone had to be paid—anyone knew that—but Umberto knew which one and how to find him. It was the policeman side of him that knew these things.

My husband believed he wasn't going to stay a bus driver always, and this was true. Just when Beddu started going to kindergarten, Umberto was given a job in the bus company office, something he wore a necktie for. This made everyone say, *God bless America*, and on Memorial Day Umberto put a big flag in the front window like other people on our street. Vincenzina said that all the flags were for dead soldiers, American ones, but we both knew it didn't matter. Our dead had opinions, but they turned their heads if we were doing well.

I had an easy life. My snuggly Anna was a timid little thing who hardly got into trouble at all, and my gorgeous Beddu was noisy but he listened when you told him things. What did I have to do that was hard? Nobody was born with worms or burning up with cholera. Umberto was fine when you did what he wanted and I guessed better than anyone what he wanted, so he was almost always tickled with me. When I got pregnant again, I was so grateful I made a donation to the church building fund out of household money. I just wanted the Virgin to know I didn't take any of this for granted.

So what did it mean when I began spotting blood? What didn't want me to have this baby? Something didn't.

At home my mother would've given me teas and washes and leaves to sprinkle on the sheets—in America nobody thinks a grown woman needs her mother. I went to a doctor, and I had to describe personal things and let him handle me. And the next day I miscarried. My body's joy oozed out as a puddle of horror. Everybody said, "There's more chances," but I was already sick of starting over.

And in fact I miscarried two more times. My sister Vincenzina gave birth to two daughters during this time, and my brother Enrico in Sicily finally married and had twins right away. After a while I stopped making complicated promises to saints, because it's not good to quarrel about what happens. In our town in Sicily there were poor women (we were not poor) who made vows to the Virgin and licked the church floor to thank her later. Now I understood these women, triumphant with their bleeding tongues, but I didn't say that to anyone.

ANNA WAS ALREADY ten and Gerry was twelve when I found that I was pregnant again. Everybody said I had to stay still and lie down all day like a snake in the sun. I didn't like it. I dreamed on the sofa with my kids' voices around me—I never knew what work it was to stay still—but from this work I had my baby girl. Umberto named her Viviana, for his favorite sister, and we called her Viana from the first.

I didn't think we spoiled her, but maybe we did. Even Umberto let her crayon all over his newspaper. And she had a sweet nature. When I was so afraid that Gerry was going to be sent to Vietnam, she would bring me her best doll so I wouldn't cry. I cried anyway, but as it happened, my handsome Gerry got his nice girlfriend pregnant. He married her at the end of high school and got out of the draft with a fatherhood deferment. I knew that God had a different sense of fairness than humans did, but still I thought He had saved me from another war out of fairness.

We were careful with the girls. We never let Anna go on dates. Boys had to come to the house and visit with us. A serious one liked her right away, so it wasn't a big problem. We were more modern by the time Viana was in her teens. She was taller and bustier and prettier than her sister, so we worried, but then she picked Mike, a neighborhood boy, and he was always in our house, praising my cooking and drinking Averna with Umberto and telling us his long opinions about everything. Umberto was very angry when Viana took up with Eddie DiFranco instead. He said things to her I didn't want him to.

But the years with just Viana at home were very good for me. She went to college nearby, and then she got a job in some office that helped immigrants get settled. (*Who helped us?* I said.) There were always boys buzzing around, coming to take her places. She liked them up to a point and no further. She'd help me cook big dinners on weekends, with my wild monkeys of grandchildren running around, and the two of us would stay up late over the dishes and do imitations of the in-laws and she'd sing to the radio. I'd think, This is why we came, and I'd picture all those immigrants from her job—from Africa, from

Mexico, from who knew where—standing at their white American sinks and being glad they had Viana to be so nice to them.

She had that blooming freshness that young girls have, and it wasn't so bad that she wasn't married yet. I knew we didn't know everything about her, but I admired the way she managed for herself. For all her gentleness, no one could make her do what she didn't want to. I was glad for her that she had this time without a man, this spell of independence.

I ALWAYS THOUGHT there were boys we didn't meet. Who knew what she did with her friends? They went down the shore, they went to New York City. One summer they drove all the way to Massachusetts to hear an orchestra outside. And whose idea was it to go skiing? None of us really saw the point of skidding down a mountain with slats on your feet, but Viana loved it. She kept going to this place in Vermont they all liked, and then, just before Lent, she fell in the snow and twisted her leg and came home on crutches.

It was terrible to see my Viana as a cripple. Umberto had to drive her to her office every day. And even when the cast came off, she didn't walk right. She went to one doctor and another and it still hurt her to bend her knee. And then she went to see this new doctor with a long, unpronounceable name, and right away her knee got better.

WE MET HIM a few times (though not, it turned out, anywhere near all the times they saw each other). What did we know about Muslims? He looked like a Chinaman, only darker, and he came to pick her up wearing a short-sleeved shirt—he looked like a kid, not a doctor. He brought us a box of chocolates, as if we were the date! Umberto asked him questions about the buses in Bangkok—the boy knew a lot, and we could mostly understand him through his accent. He was polite but not shy, and he was going back to Thailand in two months. I could see he liked Viana, and I thought he was going to go home with a broken heart.

AFTER HE LEFT, she sent him all sorts of items through the mail—a pile of Superman comics, a CD of this Bruce Springsteen she liked, a T-shirt that said DON'T MESS WITH JERSEY. And a whole carton of nonstick gauze pads (how much did they cost?) for some clinic he worked in. "Viana," I told her, "don't lead him on. It's not kind."

Maybe they were engaged before he even left. Maybe she wanted him out of sight when she told us. She was probably afraid of what Umberto would say, of the way his face would tighten itself into a knot and his mouth would look as if he'd eaten bleach and he would wait a whole minute before he whispered, *You don't know what you're saying because you're a cow without a brain, and I didn't even know it*. He would say, *The man is a crooked thief and a fag of a coward*, and *A daughter who could do this hates her family*. She'd wanted to keep her Niwet away from all that.

This was when Umberto banned the letters. He did try, in his way, to explain what everyone anywhere knows: you can't trust someone who's not from the world that's your world. Such a person has no reason not to cheat you. Maybe not now but later. You'd think you could guess, but how could you?

VIANA WENT OFF TO WORK with red eyes, she sniffled in her room at night. "See," I'd say, "see what he's let happen to you. Does he care what he's done, this man?"

I didn't want her to suffer. "This will go away," I said. I'd bring favorite sweets to her room—chocolate-chip ice cream, pignoli cookies—and she'd look at me in amazement.

"To ruin your life for love," I said, "is for idiots." She thought I didn't know anything because I'd only known Umberto.

And she thought we were bigots who lived in the Middle Ages. "Everything isn't *narrow* anymore," she said. "You think your own tiny corner is everything but it isn't. I just wish so much you had more imagination."

As if I'd never been anywhere but my nice yellow New Jersey kitchen, my living room with the fat brocade chairs, as if I'd never had to stir myself at all.

"You don't even know how sorry you'll be," I said, "if you leave your family." She didn't believe me. She thought all of us were nothing.

I didn't like to inflame Umberto by saying too much, even when we were alone, but the pain of it brought us closer. "We never should've let her go skiing," he said. He was looking for the turn that could take us back to where we were before.

I liked to lean against him from behind and rest my head between his shoulder blades. Only Umberto knew how hard it was, how tired we were from fighting to keep our child away from the cliff she was so set on jumping from. Only Umberto was weary in his bones the way I was.

Viana said the word Islam meant surrender to God, what was bad about that? I wasn't opposed to other religions for other people. Viana hadn't gone to Mass for years, but that was another problem. She told us everything in all religions was the same. When Muslims prayed, they just said, "There is no God but God." Umberto said the Koran said to cut the hands off of thieves and that men could have four wives.

In our town in Sicily, the men who painted donkey carts had written in huge letters on the wall of their workshop, DIO SOLO È GRANDE. I always thought this meant, don't get carried away with yourself, remember Who's looming over every horizon.

And in the end, after all the fighting and silence and obedience and disobedience, only God *was* great, and He had His own ideas. If blood won't keep people tied, there's nothing to hold them.

BUT I NEVER THOUGHT Viana would leave, until she left. I thought she would send the cab away, when the cab came to take her to the airport. I thought she would go to the airport and turn around and come back. She was always sensible and mild, never a dramatic person.

Umberto said that as far as he was concerned, from now on he no longer had a second daughter. He said it to her from the doorway, and he said it to me more than once. After she was gone, Umberto would not talk about her at all, except when he forgot. Sometimes he said, "Where's the salad set Viana bought us that time?" or "That's worse than that singer Viana liked." He hated those slips, the backhanded torment of them. And perhaps he was right not to have us talking about her. She sent letters, to let us know she was fine, to give us her address, to tell us about her wedding. They were stiff little messages that didn't sound like Viana. They were from a stranger who lived with strangers.

I knew why she believed—with all her heart, it seemed—that she couldn't live without this man: it was because we had protected her from everything. If her life had been harder and harsher, she never would have wrecked herself for love. The idea would have been ridiculous. She would have known better without even thinking.

THE FIRST MONTHS, when I was waiting for Viana to come back, were very bad for me. I couldn't stand it when Umberto gave her car to Gerry. Every day it hurt me to see it gone from the driveway. I closed up her room and I didn't even clean it. But the worst was all the time passing. Anna's youngest went to kindergarten, Gerry's wife went back to school, Gerry was losing his hair, and Viana didn't know about any of this.

My daughter Anna always thought someone like me didn't mind getting older because I was never what anyone here thought was glamorous. But when I saw myself in the mirror, a fattish woman with streaked hair, I saw a person who looked lost and not smart and whose youngest daughter might probably think she'd changed into a baggy, sad thing.

It was a new cruelty when she sent us the pictures of her baby. The child looked like him—Viana was holding a tan baby with silky black hair. Later, when the girl was three or four, I thought (maybe because of the way they had her hair chopped) that she looked like my Uncle Turi, who was always called Turi Africa because he was dark. I looked at the pictures and I threw them away. Umberto wouldn't look at them.

I worried about the child getting sick and Viana too. Cholera, malaria, I knew what those were. Gerry said, "Her husband's a doctor, and Bangkok's a lot bigger than Hoboken." Gerry thought she was living high off the hog—a doctor's wife, with servants—no wonder she'd run away.

I DIDN'T UNDERSTAND the message on our phone machine. It was a foreign woman with a light, peeping way of speaking, "Please to call back, very important, very." Umberto was the one who called back. And while he spoke, I heard myself wailing, before Umberto could make me believe that Viana hadn't been killed, only her husband had. I clapped my hands in joy when I understood we still had Viana, though I never wished her husband any harm.

I NEVER WANTED to go to a place like Thailand. I did it for Umberto, who wouldn't have known by himself how to watch over a five-year-old or how to talk to Viana again. We had to change planes twice, in places I never wanted to see—the airport shops made me dizzy and I would only sit at the gate and wait. When we got to Bangkok, the crowd of people from our plane, who mostly looked like us, went through a set of glass doors and were lost in a sea of Asians. "Stay by me," Umberto said to me. Without each other, we could vanish.

The heat outside was a wet smothering heat, not dry like the baking sun of Sicily, but the taxi was lovely and cool. We went over dingy highways and past patches of palm trees and square flat-roofed houses and along an overpass into city blocks of big whitish buildings streaked with soot. On the streets were thousands of people—small like Sicilians but skinnier—on their way to places whose names we couldn't even say, chatting away about news we'd never heard of, laughing at jokes we'd never get.

The driver might have taken us anywhere, but we reached the hotel. I had been in hotels before—once in the Poconos and once down the shore—but not as fancy as this, though this was cheaper. And I didn't want to go out, once we were in our nice room. I lay on the quilted coverlet and I slept, suspended between the old suffering and the new one that waited for us.

A very sweet woman came to take us to the hospital where Viana was. Her name was Toon, she was a friend of Viana's, and we met her in the lobby of the hotel. "So glad you are here," she said. "Much better you're here."

The hospital was at the edge of Bangkok—an hour and a half away—and I didn't see how we were going to talk to each other all that time in the car. Umberto's eyes were hooded and he wasn't saying a word. It was very possible that Viana was dying, whatever they said, and I was terrified to imagine going back on that sequence of airplanes with my girl's body in a coffin, and how would we keep them from losing her? "You speak so well," I said to the woman. "How did you get such good English? Better than mine!"

Her husband was American. And I learned other things, while she drove. She had a boy and a girl. The girl had just gotten married, and the boy was a monk, for a long time now. A monk! It took a little while for me to understand she didn't mean a Catholic monk. "Famous temple," she said, when we passed a building with a cascade of peaked roofs, carved in filigree and covered with gilt. I'd never seen such a thing, glittering like a very elaborate dream, right on a modern street. "Look!" I said to Umberto. He gazed back at me with his mournful look.

"In a little time we'll be there," she said. "Not too long."

I thanked her for taking us. "No trouble. Nothing to thank," she said.

WHEN WE SAW VIANA, she was propped up in bed. She was pale, with bruises on one cheek and a gauze pad taped to her forehead and dark, woeful shadows under her eyes. She saw us as soon as we saw her. I watched as she took us in—we were yet another exhausting part of her fate unrolling before her. I said, "*Cara*," and I could see her struggling to be equal to the task of being with us again.

"We're here," I said. "Here we are." She looked older, thicker in the chin.

"Yes," she said. She was trying to remember how to care who was there.

"How are you?" Umberto said. "Are you all right?"

Viana made a wry face and said, "I'm hunky-dory."

"Soon you'll be better," I said. "Do you want some water?"

"Soon," Umberto said.

"Your friend says you'll be fine," I said. "Your friend Toon who's a nurse. She says you'll be out of the hospital soon."

They had put her in a pale green gown, like a prisoner. Viana looked down at the bedsheets and she looked up at us. "How was your flight?" she said.

How hard she was working, my girl. "Very nice," I said.

"They fed us too much," Umberto said.

"They gave everybody a package with slippers and a little toothbrush," I said.

"Good," she said.

"Don't you want some water?" I said.

"Sure," she said.

There was a pitcher at her bedside, which was why I'd thought of it. "You have to drink a lot of water," I said. I poured her a glass and she took it from my hand, and a line of radiance went through me, to see her swallow.

A nurse came into the room and said something that Viana understood. While she was taking my daughter's pulse, I could tell Viana was introducing us. Then the nurse put her palms together under her chin, as if she were praying, and made a little bow to us. What had Viana told her? Umberto was wincing and nodding.

"They're very nice here," I said when the nurse left.

"Don't you want to see Rosa?" she said.

HER FRIEND TOON, who'd left us alone with Viana, was our guide to the children's ward, where Rosa was. Umberto was trailing behind us like a slow old dog.

I didn't even know which one Rosa was, among all the children in their rows of beds. But she knew Toon—she was the girl waving like mad to Toon. She had eyes like her father's and her hair had turned wavy like Beddu's— she was fidgeting on her bed and calling out to Toon in Thai. That was her voice, that reedy little hoarse sound. When I heard it, my heart cracked and bled. She was little for five, light-bodied and small-headed, an elf of a girl.

She had no idea who we were, or perhaps she had an idea and was chewing it over in her mind. She was smoothing back her hair, with the careful pride of little girls, tossing her head. Why hadn't we brought her toys? I had missed knowing what she liked. She must have liked dolls, we could have brought a doll. I'd given birth to two daughters and I didn't know that? I was sorry for myself then and sick for the war we'd made, sick for the shame and stupidity of war. I could hardly speak, for shame.

AND SHE WAS a little scared of us, you could see that. "Your grandparents," Toon said in English, "came a very long way to see you."

And then Rosa made a prayer-bow to us!

I felt like a fraud, a criminal disguised as a fancy royal person.

"She is maybe a little shy," Toon said.

Rosa said, "My mother doesn't like the food here. Can you get some food for my mother?" Her English was fine.

THE FOOD WAS actually not the problem. Rosa herself had decided that was why her mother was so glazed when they brought Rosa in to see her, which they did once a day. I was worried about Viana too. Even in Sicily when I was young, there were people who never got up, once they'd been hit as hard as life can hit. I didn't think Viana was one of those, but nobody ever thinks that. She had great stubbornness, but stubbornness could go either way.

We'd flown all the way across the world to pull her to

her feet, but what was that? That was just love. She had
Rosa for that, Rosa squirming and kissing and trying to
climb over her bed. (We saw all this later.) She needed
love—she would have fallen far deeper into the pit without all of us calling out to her. But in the realm where she
was—I knew from when Piddu died—she could barely
hear us, we were nothing. I'd had God to think about (I
didn't imagine He thought about me), but what did Viana
have? All her talk about how all religions were the same.
Did that let her slip away at all? Did that let her leap for a
few seconds out of the unbearable cage of herself? What
I thought was: Whoever God is, it's better not to take
your own hellish troubles personally, because (this is what
the Virgin knows) what's happened to you keeps happening over and over. I couldn't have explained why this was
a consoling opinion. And who could say what thoughts
were in the head of the Viana I didn't know, what views
she had? Whatever they were, she needed them now.

WE WERE IN BANGKOK for six days. Several times Toon's
husband came to take us to the hospital, a pink-faced man
named Toby in his early fifties—it was always a relief to
be with an American. He'd say, "*This* isn't bad weather,"
or "It's a very good hospital," and we believed him. He'd
leave us there for the whole day, which gave us a different sort of time with Viana. I would bathe her neck and
arms with a cool wet cloth, I'd tell her what the other
grandchildren were up to. She hardly talked but I saw
that she was putting on lipstick for our visits. And Rosa

began to get used to us. She made us watch tricks she could do with her toes, she demanded candy. Umberto told her Superman lived in New York and he'd met him several times.

At midday there was no place nearby for us to eat except from the vendors in the street. I was afraid of what they would feed us or charge us, but Umberto pointed and held up fingers and women scooped up hot stews from vats in their carts and young boys fished out skewers of fruit from under glass counters on wheels. I didn't want to eat the food, but people meant well. They'd gesture to say, *Good, yes?* Each lunch was nerve-wracking and made me homesick.

Once, when we came back into the hospital, Viana was talking Thai in her room with two women friends from work. It was always startling to hear Viana making those sounds! Umberto and I backed away and left while they were having their conversation. The women looked solemn and touched Viana's hand. They had known Niwet too. And where was his family?

"It seems so long since they were here," Viana said later. "Since his father came with his brothers to take Niwet's body home."

"The funeral was already?"

"Oh," she said, "they have to have it right away."

She looked as if I were on the edge of affronting her. Her face had closed into its own outrage of grief.

"I said goodbye to them then," she sighed. And that

was the first we had reason to think that she was coming back with us.

In the evenings I stayed inside the hotel. There was a restaurant in the lobby that had food we could eat, and after Umberto had his coffee we could go back to the room. We could make the room as cool as we wanted, and Umberto sat up in a chair and read his paper and did some kind of puzzles in a book. If I didn't fall asleep, I watched the movies they had in English on the TV. A few times Umberto went down and walked around the block. Whatever he saw didn't make much of an impression. "Noisy," he said.

We were sealed in with air-conditioning, but once, when Umberto was asleep, I got up and opened the one window that would move, to listen to that noise. How could so many people still be out? There was the streaming hum of cars and voices calling out their twanged and clipped syllables. People were laughing and yelling and insisting about something. It humbled me, this noise that had nothing to do with us. I saw that I had been vainer than I'd known. Who would want to know that? I felt corrected, and I let the massed sounds wash over me, the unsleeping street.

ON THE LONG PLANE journey home, Viana slept most of the way, but Rosa could hardly keep still. She was very excited. Did they have every kind of ice cream in America? Did they have Game Boy? What other games did they have? "Will you sleep?" Viana said. Rosa did collapse, eventually, in a curled lump settled in her mother's armpit. "It's good she's so curious," I said.

"She thinks her father is waiting in America," Viana said. "She knows better, but she has her ideas."

"Everything looks so familiar," Viana said, not happily, as we were driving from Newark airport. It was a rainy April afternoon. "Everything looks the same." She was blaming the buildings for this.

Hoboken itself had changed a lot, as Umberto tried to point out, but she didn't care. Her arrival was marked by the weight of her discouragement at finding herself back at this spot again. Rosa, of course, had her own disappointments. "Why do the trees look like that?" she said.

There were too many kinds of trees in the world; I was mad at God for making everything so complicated. Too much variety, more than any single human could take in. What had He been thinking? I knew by now (if not now, when?) that such a question was not helpful and would get me nowhere.

"They're *nice* trees," I said.

VIANA COULD HARDLY see her way across the room, those first months. She greeted her friends warmly, but when they left, she barely spoke to us. She was especially sullen with Umberto and Gerry. We kept Rosa busy. We had her playing with her cousins, we let her watch videos, we fed her thrilling delicacies. When she heard Umberto say,

THE SIZE OF THE WORLD · 275

"*Ammuni*"—let's go, in Sicilian—she ran around saying it to everyone. I knew this imitation meant she liked us.

When Rosa went to day camp in the summer, Viana moped at home. She had no intention of feeling better. I'd grown up with widows who wore black their whole lives, so I saw her point and the truth of it, but it was not an American point. And in the tenderness of her loyalty to the dead, she was as furious at us as if we'd had her husband killed.

She never said a word about getting a job all the next year. She took Rosa to kindergarten and she helped me with the house, but she didn't want to do much of anything else. So I was very excited the next summer—I could hardly believe it—when she took up with Mike, her old boyfriend. How fresh she looked, all of a sudden, how much more like herself. What I didn't understand was that she would leave us then and take Rosa with her.

WHY DID ANYONE need Indiana? I though that Mike might want to come back to Hoboken now, but Viana said, how could he, his kids were with the wife. I had a son-in-law anyone would envy me for, but I had been double-crossed by good luck. Every week we talked to our Rosa on the phone, but she chattered about people we'd never met and she was a little older each time we saw her on holidays.

All the same I was very glad—I still said prayers of thanks—at the way Viana's life had turned out. She seemed to me to be proof that mistakes can be made good

again, roads rolled up back to the start. I never forgot to
be grateful that she was returned to us, home safe, after I'd
lost any hope of seeing her again in this world.

FOR ALL THAT WE were back as a family, Viana was never
the same toward Umberto—she gave him respect but she
kept her distance and she didn't ever agree with him—and
maybe that was why we weren't told right away when the
FBI came and took her to jail. I had to hear about it from
Mike's mother, who thought I knew. "What is this crap
with arresting everybody?" she said.

By the time she said this, Viana was home safe—out of
jail, fine, fine, not to worry. I had to be reassured, over
my wails and my repeating every sentence—I couldn't
take any of it in, except by reciting and asking over and
over if that was right. Umberto heard me from across the
room. I'd never seen him so clenched, so grim and red in
the face. *We had a daughter who'd been in jail.*

"What the hell's the matter with this president?"
Mike's mother said.

VIANA WAS SLEEPING when we called Indiana, but we did
get Mike on the phone.

"The FBI is nuts," he said. "We're a Fascist state now."

"And how's Rosa?"

"Rosa," Mike said, "remembers the Thai relatives better than you'd think."

"Of course," I said.

"It's a mess over there, a nasty little civil war," Mike

said. "There was always a group in the south that wanted to separate from the rest of Thailand."

We'd had separatists in Sicily too, before we left. Giuseppe White-Head had punched Giuseppe Sneaky in the nose because one of them was a separatist and one wasn't.

"It's very bloody," Mike said. "First the police managed to suffocate seventy-eight Muslims when they were transporting them, then some Buddhist villagers were beheaded in retaliation, then—this was really bad— Buddhist monks were slashed to death while they were out collecting food offerings."

"Enough. Don't tell me," I said.

"Schoolteachers were killed," Mike said. "Because of the language laws. More keeps happening."

He was interested in the history of it, he explained too much. I didn't want to know. I didn't see why history, even now, refused to leave us alone.

UMBERTO SAID, "Who told her to write those letters?"

"The police aren't supposed to read e-mail," I said. We both knew the police could do whatever they wanted.

"They came to her own house and took her away," I said.

But he thought Viana had chosen. Once again she'd gone over to the other side, taken her place with the people from her other life.

"It's a crime to send pictures of Rosa eating ice cream?" I had to live with Umberto forever, so I didn't say more, but I was bitter against him then, for not moaning in horror, for his daughter's sake. I looked at his glinting eyes, his familiar hawk nose. Why was I married, if I had no one to moan with me?

AFTER WE TALKED TO MIKE, all I could think about was Viana in a cell in jail. I didn't know what jails were like here but there was no way they could be good. I pictured her alone in a dank root cellar of a room, but for all I knew she was crowded in a fluorescent-lit pen with other women. At night she would've been on a cot bare as a shelf.

No jail has any kindness in it. The point of jail is to be mean to you, to break you down. Mike didn't even find out where she was till the next day. The only night in my life I slept in a room alone was my sister's wedding night. Viana must have been better at this than I ever could have been, on her own in a cell. She had the dignity of her stubbornness and she had a hardness from her own life that might have kept her calm. Her friend Toon had told me how she believed (and all the Buddhists were supposed to believe) that if you knew not to cling to what was impermanent, you weren't so fearful. Perhaps Viana thought this too. On those nights. You needed human love, in the worst times, and you needed something that was independent of all love.

"IN ITALY SHE NEVER would have been arrested," I said to Umberto. Mike would have said, *Italy when? Which*

Italy? but Umberto just grumbled. My sister Vincenzina liked to say how extremely well we'd all done in America, as if she'd personally rowed us across the ocean. A very good country, I had nothing against it. But now I did, and I had the old, peculiar feeling that I'd switched sides. In my head, I wanted to say, *Piddu, can you believe this?* except that Piddu was beyond sides, where he was.

I would have liked Piddu to know I'd been to Thailand. *Their temples are gold and they eat frogs like we do,* I wanted to tell him. I hadn't imagined such a place, how could I have? At the time when Viana left, I had thought of her only as gone to a hated nowhere, lost to me, as if she'd dropped off the flat table of the earth. What a stone I'd had for a heart then. How full the world was of such stones.

The great, swarming world—I knew more of it now, didn't I? Even I.

I hadn't wanted to know either. Carried away across it nonetheless, swept up into air. Sometimes in deep night now I liked to tell myself that it was afternoon of the next day on the other side of the world—all that hot glare and bright, bright sunlight—and I did what I could to hold this improbable truth in my mind.

THE OTHER SIDE
OF THE WORLD

Owen

I DIDN'T KNOW I WAS GOING to be so homesick for the life I'd had in Siam, on my own. In Kingston I had plenty of useless connections, men I'd gone to school with, girls who'd married cousins of mine. It wore me out to try to talk to them, to go to their houses for unspeakably dull dinners. How parochial they seemed, and how affected and full of myself I must have seemed to them.

Kingston's bars were still speakeasies then, dens of merry lawbreakers—a seedier and more interesting side of my town than I'd known as a boy. The customers were young marrieds in their smart and daring phase, salesmen being snappy, local hookers, sometimes a farmer in a pressed shirt. Most of the bars were near the river and I'd get that dirty-water smell as I got near the row of them. I loved that smell. At the end of the night I'd walk by the marshy edge and look out at the dark Hudson and the string of electric lights along one of the dingy piers. I would've shot myself the first month if it hadn't been for those bars.

I was not what I'd once been. Each morning I thought that, even when I hadn't been drinking at all. What I did at the bank was imitation work to someone like me, as if I spent each day carrying on my back trunks and boxes filled with nothing but air. I'd catch myself looking at the granite in the portico of the bank building, the white marble columns and the travertine panels, and I'd be hit with nostalgia for the lucid facts of minerals.

Getting a job in a bank in 1928 was not a lucky stroke anyway, as it turned out. After the Crash, my father's friends kept me on as long as they could. When the job ended finally (and none too soon for me), I wrote to Corinna in Siam, *Hallelujah, I'm a bum.* But then I drove to all the nearby burgs—Poughkeepsie and Catskill and Albany—and humiliated myself asking every insurance company, every underwriter, every lowly accounting firm for work.

One morning I could not get out of bed at all. In my rented room I lay in the sheets, nauseous and sweating and shivering. This is the sad result, I thought, of drinking cheap alcohol, and I was disgusted with myself for not having money anymore for better. But by evening I knew it was the malaria coming back. And where was my sister when I needed her? Where was Zain to tend me? I thought about summoning my aunt on the phone, but the thought was not bearable. In the very early hours of the morning, I heard the clatter of a horse-drawn milk truck in the street, and I called out the window and had the driver carry up a great vat of milk. I lived on that for a week.

The fever ebbed while I sipped the souring milk. When I went out, I was still a sight—yellowed eyes and hollowed neck—and I alarmed my grocer. I stayed in my room eating soup out of tin cans and reading Byron and Jack London. I was down to my last hoarded dollars when one of the hookers I knew from the bar sent word that a company in Schenectady was hiring and I should get my heinie over there fast.

I drove to what turned out to be a factory called Universal Screw and Fastener. I thought I'd been sent as a joke, but an office boy inside pointed me to a line of men. The company was hiring salesmen, and I hardly knew why I lined up, since I was hardly a glad-handing sales type. "I don't suppose you know anything about metals," the exhausted interviewer said, and I had the sense to ask what kind of ferrous alloys they used.

So I got the dumb job. At least it had to do with metals and the world of matter—that was how I comforted myself—at least I was being paid to talk about significant particulars. And right away I was on the road all the time, I had a territory to cover. I did like that part.

I liked the roads that curled around the scratchy slopes of hills, I liked the lit roadhouses at night and the eager little hotels in small towns. My sister wanted to know if I could stand such a life if I were married. Female company could always be found, but that was not what Corinna meant, of course. I'd forgotten how men and women talked to one another here. Women were coy or hilarious in ways I never got used to. I could not imagine coming home to one of them.

What did I imagine? Mostly still Noo Kiang. Girl of my dreams, who had married a Chinaman a month after I sent her away. In my dreams she was given to admiring me lavishly, craving me constantly, understanding me perfectly. She lived in the Siam at the end of the rainbow, a place foreign men were notably partial to. We were both younger there too.

TO FIND OUT WHAT screws a company needed, you had to know its true wants—aside from strength, what about corrosion resistance or weight or magnetic permeability? I was good at sorting that out, and I didn't have to tell corny salesman's jokes either. One client called me the Screw Doctor. Holding the world together, one sale at a time.

I made a good name for myself at U-Screw (as we liked to call it) and they shifted me to more demanding accounts, to people who made transport for the Army or the Navy. "As a veteran myself," I would say to some engineer in a tie, before I recited statistics. It was not a lie, but I felt that I was lying. I meant: *An old soldier like me only wants the best for our boys.* Had I gone all the way to France and lived like a snake in a ditch and seen real men get blown to gore just to get a client to believe me? It was a whorish thing to do, but it wasn't lying. No one made me do it either.

I SOLD SO MUCH glittering hardware that my boss asked if I wanted to head the Western Division. Western New York didn't sound like any prize—how many inches of snow in Buffalo?—but he meant California, which pleased me so much it hurt me to know I no longer thought of these things for myself.

From the first, I took to that part of the country. What San Francisco had, first of all, was a Chinatown. I had forgotten most of the bits of Chinese I'd once had, but I still knew phrases you said for politeness or to a girl. It was wonderful to see the girls again. In the streets most of them were dressed like American girls, with short hair combed flat or curled against their cheeks. In the clubs I sometimes saw them in *qipao*, those slinky silk dresses with high collars—they carried fans too! I didn't want to be a slathering Caucasian patron, a gawking male with a wallet, but what did I want to be, then? A man Asians thought was almost Asian, a chameleon with cosmopolitan gifts. I wasn't a boy, I knew how silly that was.

I lived on the other side of the city, but when I had time I liked to walk the blocks that were built to be Asia, the wedged-in shops open to the street, the smell of hot oil and sizzled pork, the hanging lanterns added for tourists. I wanted to stop every resident and brag about what was familiar. And what did I think I'd have when I was with a woman from the East again? I was as bad as my sister, who'd made her lingering crush on Zain a lasting metaphor for the attachment she couldn't fix to a whole country.

But because I was a man I lived out that metaphor. I found a pretty woman who wanted to be called Lily (why did she pick that name? it was hard for her to say) and who was glad enough to have someone like me, not ugly like an old man and not hungry or rough the way young ones could be. The first time I went with her—to a hotel with a pink-red roof like a pagoda—when she held her arms out to me, I was as touched as if she were yielding a great unspoken kindness. No one could have kept her self more separate, and yet I felt that she had yielded, and the honor of it stirred me. She was not at all like a Siamese girl really, haughtier, cooler, daintier, less playful, but a part of myself came back to me, an old rhapsodic alertness. Afterward I thanked her in Cantonese, which made her giggle. "Very nice person," she said to me.

We got along fine. It elevated my life to have her in it. I felt that I was no longer a man eaten up by old ideas, that Lily was my shimmer of farther vistas. One of the men I drank with called her my "armchair travel," which was not entirely wrong. I had Lily's singsong voice to think of, while I was motoring along a dusty road by the coast or on a train across some godforsaken stretch of desert, and I was more interesting to myself because of it.

I wanted to keep Lily for myself, only me, and for two years I paid her enough for that arrangement. But when she asked for more, I had to let her go, she cost too much. She made a face when I told her—a wriggle of disappointment at me and at fate. It stung me to see her so grasping; the ending was hard on both of us. She went on to a richer patron, and the next year I went on to Fu-Rong, a round-bodied girl who scurried when she walked because her feet had once been bound. Fu-Rong still had family in China and lived in great fear that Japanese armies were coming close to where they lived, though she tried not to bother me, her special friend, with this. I pointed to a map in the newspaper—in the autumn of '38, there were X's for battles near Canton—but she couldn't tell, on the map, where her town was.

Sometimes when I gave her money I wanted to say, *For your father, who might be dead,* or *For your mother, whose suffering we can only guess at.* But I didn't. I was wary of being sentimental with her, of taking liberties—she had enough to bear without my alien violations; a customer's decency was to mind his own business. I thought that the money made me less human then, but I couldn't see how else to be.

SALESMEN DIDN'T REALLY get rich, but I was earning more than I had. When I took the train all the way to Florida to see my sister and her family, Corinna amused herself making jokes about what swank suits I wore nowadays. Corinna was a little sour, but her kids, Thea and Bob, really liked me. Their father had made them an elaborate terrarium, with a vast herd of lizards they kept giving me to hold. Christopher seemed very much in his element, squinting into the sun, red-faced and wryly calm, though Corinna said he missed England.

The kids were great fans of my stories, my quips and tricks. Part of me was sorry I hadn't had children. I didn't think I'd missed what life was for, but at times I thought that I had. I was always taking them for long walks on the beach and letting them dangle big ropes of seaweed and smelly hermit crabs in front of me. When Thea complained of sand in her sneakers, I said, "Do you know how many eons it took for the waves to smash the rocks and shells and calcified plants into sand fine enough to get between your toes? Say: *Thank you, dear waves, for making sand to itch me.*"

Thea and Bob made elaborate bows in the wet tidal sand and called out, *Thank you, thank you.* They were too young to be awed or consoled by notions of mineral time, but I wasn't. To be a speck freed me from dwelling on local complaints. Speck among specks! One of the bars I used to go to in Kingston had a hokey sign that said, DON'T WORRY, IT WON'T LAST, NOTHING DOES. The geologist's motto, I always thought. The necessary longer view.

I had reason to want to repeat these sustaining truisms to myself, because I knew that when I went back to San Francisco, I was going to lose Fu-Rong. An old man was coming from China to marry her, and who could blame her for wanting to leave the life she had? I could, but my woe and my protests were no good to anyone. I was a sputtering rogue, a spoiled boy, a leftover colonial in a freed state.

FU-RONG WAS ALREADY gone by the time I got back, swept off to Sacramento by her doddering groom. One of her friends asked if I didn't want to send my girl a red packet to wish her well. Reluctantly, angrily, I folded a couple of twenties in one of the shiny red envelopes you could buy in the district and I mailed it to her in her new name. It was a very depressing way to be a good sport, and it made me feel ancient.

After Pearl Harbor, I was on the road a lot of the time, immersed in a constant emergency of work, the war effort firing up sales. I kept away from any steadiness with a woman. All through those years, we were more afraid that we might lose than anyone would admit later. I'd been in one war, and trudged with my unit in retreat too—not a good memory, *retreat*—but I knew not to talk about it. I thought of Noo Kiang too, and I pictured her demure and polite to Japanese soldiers. I was embarrassed for Thailand, giving way to Japan at once, siding with the Axis the way a child decides to side with a bully, scared, resigned, hoping for favors. But what would I have had it do? No strategy, no bravery, could've saved it.

For a long time the Allies kept losing battles in the Pacific—Makassar, Badung, Sunda—and I woke in the night trying to think how we'd survive if we lost everything. How I would. Countries did lose wars, didn't they? The Jews I'd known all my life would be taken away somewhere. What might be done to the Chinese did not bear thinking about. We knew by now about the live burials in Nanking and the massacres of Chinese in Malaya. And what would the rest of us be, the survivors, the lucky white people?

I dreamed of California under fire, the rocky coast falling into the sea. My city occupied, like Paris. A woman I knew in Reno used to call me Mr. Ready for the Worst. But I drank all night from gratitude when D-Day finally came. I toasted every soldier, every pilot, every sailor. I blew a week's income treating the bar. I went out to the street and gave bottles of beer to passersby.

Later I had a hangover like a hail of stones, my brain was a ballroom of thudding rocks. I was in a movie theater that week watching newsreels of troops landing in the waves at Normandy when I saw footage (who took the photos?) of Japanese rail lines bombed to smoke—in Bangkok! U.S. planes were dropping bombs on Bangkok—and the audience was applauding. I think I applauded too, in wincing astonishment, in victory.

Later that summer, the Siamese changed government and anti-Japan factions from the Free Thai underground seemed to be sharing power with the old guard. Both together? How could that be? *Now they will be all right*, Corinna wrote to me, *when Japan loses. Hurray for the Free Thai! Christopher is not as glad for Siam as I am.*

THE NEXT YEAR, when the A-bombs were dropped on Hiroshima and Nagasaki, the brute gaudiness of the war's end made science seem lethal and glamorous to people. All sorts of men—and women too—thought that because I could explain atomic fission I had an elegant mind and was someone to respect. I'd show off and be depressed afterward.

All I did was talk in the night and drive in the day. I wasn't so pleased with myself the year I turned fifty. I had the inner riches forever of my time in Siam, but what kept me from being another moody old lush stuck on glory days? There was a birthday gathering for me at a bar—a few other sales reps, an engineer I hung out with—and at the end of the night I was given the key to a hotel room where a girl named Pearl waited.

She couldn't have been more than twenty, a Chinese girl, with straight-cut bangs and the world's most delicate neck. When I came into the room, she said, "Hello, hello. Happy birthday, right?" Her voice was American, she'd been raised here.

"Honey," I said, "you're in for an easy night, because I'm too drunk to do anything. Just don't tell the fellows."

"Look at you, an honest man," she said. She patted the bed for me to sit next to her, and I worried that she was going to try her best to rescue me—I actually didn't want that. But she put her head on my shoulder, as if we were teenagers on a front porch, and said, "I'm very tired myself, you can't imagine." They *never* said that. She wasn't a scared amateur either—had a whole new order taken over?

It was just her—the Pearl way of being a working

girl—though I didn't know that till later. She fell asleep before I did, and we both woke at dawn with our clothes on. "It's your birthday until eight a.m.," she said, and I made a joke about rising to the occasion, which I managed to do. I was very glad not to be an old man entirely, trite though that may have been. The next time I woke up she was throwing her clothes on. "You can sleep, my friend," she said. "I have a babysitter waiting."

SO THAT WAS OUR BEGINNING. What an interesting creature she was, and full of opinions (Harry Truman was just a ham actor, Betty Grable was homely, colds could be cured by eating onions). I gave her enough to live on, and I was a much more adorable guy than I'd been in years, less sullen, more breezy. "Hello, chicken," I would say when I called her after being on the road. "Hello, big shot," she would say. She could be satiric and flirty at the same time, a good way to deal with a codger like me. We got along very well.

We weren't always in the hotel or at bars either. We had a favorite restaurant, where she always told me I held my chopsticks like a trained goat. She liked movies, especially thrillers, and she'd gasp or let out a faint shriek in the dark, and I'd say, "Be brave, Pearl Girl." Pearl was probably not really her name either, but it was for me. In the third year I got her her own apartment, a nice place with old wainscoting and big windows. It was really more than I could afford, but I didn't want to nickel-and-dime us out of staying together. She sent her son away whenever I came to visit—that was her own business, wasn't it?—and his room was kept shut, though I was paying for that room. Once I tripped over a box of Crayolas, but he was otherwise a remarkably invisible figure.

I never came to see her without calling first, so it surprised me one afternoon when Pearl was making tea for us in the kitchen and a four-year-old boy walked in out of nowhere. "Oh," Pearl said. "Want to meet Lincoln?"

I shook his hand, which he thought was funny. He was a fat-cheeked kid in short pants. Was he all Chinese? Half Chinese? Why was I checking that out first?

I pulled a dime out of his ear, I made my index finger fall off entirely and then grow back, I let him guess which hand had the Life Savers candy. Uncle tricks, which he was young enough to puzzle over. He insisted that I reperform them.

Pearl's gaze on us was like an X-ray beam in a Superman comic, a slice of blazing light. She said, "Don't let him keep the dimes." How cool she always was.

IT WASN'T ANY BIG deal getting used to having Lincoln around. He was not allowed to be pesky—he had his minutes with me when I arrived, our goofy boy stuff, and then he was sent out of sight, and sent sooner if he was loud or whiny. I was her friend, sure, but I was also her employer. Pearl could not have loved her boy more (her work had been chosen as a way to keep him) but she believed that children had to be instructed in the hardness of the world or they would perish in hellish ways.

I had my own apartment anyway (which Pearl never saw) and I was an early riser from my days on the road, so sometimes I made it out of Pearl's place before Lincoln was up. But usually he trailed me to the door, an imp in Roy Rogers pajamas. When was I coming back? How far was I going? He made attempts to whisper, breathing his kid's breath at me. If his mother woke up, she carted him away.

PEARL, EVER IMPECCABLE, never talked about him when we were out. Sometimes she asked about my work—"Do the people try to bargain for their hardware? Can they cheat you?"—but mostly she talked lightly about the news of the day, whether Queen Elizabeth had proposed to her husband or vice versa and who cut Mamie Eisenhower's bangs that way. She didn't laugh easily but dumb puns sometimes took her by surprise.

I did ask myself, was there something wrong with me that this arrangement suited me so well? What did it mean to be a man who had never married and never would? My friends thought I was just another sly dog, which wasn't exactly what I wanted to be. Pearl and I understood each other as well as people ever do, though a good deal was left out of it. Of Lincoln's father, for instance, I only knew that he'd been in the Navy, stationed in a town she wasn't naming. "Not interesting," she would say. All over the world people lived in families, and I had kept myself out of this most natural of fates. In Siam, Noo Kiang had gone away weeping when I wouldn't marry her. Pearl, however, was not shedding any tears. She could have done a lot worse than me, and had.

Since she kept her mouth shut on a wealth of subjects, Pearl didn't need to bother (as far as I could tell) to invent any lies. Her particular spirit was above that sort of mincey ingratiation. Whatever you could say about our connection, it had the merits of truthfulness. I had a greater horror of fibbing the older I got. You saw how pathetic people looked trying to believe themselves, what shaky ground they lived on, how little it got them in the end.

IN THE LATE FIFTIES, U-Screw kept sending me to Arizona. I was the rep who knew aircraft the best, and there were a couple of growing companies out there making the guts of engines or the piloting systems. I always liked the last part of the long drive from California, where the land gave up being walls of rock and settled into desert, bare and reddish, with the cacti looking like a western's stage set. I hadn't meant to have such a citified life, and driving was my time on the trail. I'd arrive at the companies' offices very calm and clear, a quiet guy who knew what he was saying, and I did well on those trips.

I was always trying to get Lincoln interested in airplanes, but he was mostly obsessed with music, especially country music, of all things. Who ever heard of a Chinese boy who loved Hank Williams? Who wrote letters to Chet Atkins? Pearl wouldn't let me give him presents, only money, which she put away in an account for him.

She did get him a small crappy record player when he was eleven, and he was warned to play it softly in his room. Through his door you could hear Patsy Cline crying about how she went out walking after midnight. It was hell (in my opinion) when he discovered bluegrass and thought Earl Scruggs was amazing.

Pearl thought I should put money in a college account for him, but she thought I had more money than I did. I was a salesman living as if he were Daddy Warbucks, paying rent on two households. "Ever hear the expression," I said, "you can't squeeze blood out of a turnip?"

"Who's a turnip?" she said. "You're a lemon, that's what you are."

Pearl was beautiful as ever, but passing thirty had made her angry with me. She wouldn't have said I'd robbed her of youth, but something had. Her chances were running out. We still had our old camaraderie, but it counted for less.

When she snickered at my teasing we were equals, but when she told me the heating bill was higher she was a cagey market vendor cajoling a stingy big shot. I thought I might be doing her a favor if I let her have more time without me. I had always lost to richer men. Fair enough, or so I tried to think. I thought of Corinna, with her long invectives against the tyranny of the dollar. ("It wants to turn everything into its ugly self," she said. I used to say, "Go be a monk then and never carry it.")

One night, in a decent attempt to be festive again, I took Pearl to a pricey restaurant with Polynesian décor—

fishnets and stuffed sharks on the wall, drinks served out
of pineapples—and I hated it. Something about it made
me ashamed to have ever been a colonial. Pearl ate her
pupu platter with only mild amusement, but I railed
against the fake tribal carvings turned into party trappings, the invitation to be tropical conquerors taking
their pleasure like children. Who did I think I was, a man
in his sixties with a tender-faced mistress, getting
offended by Trader Vic's?

I COULD SEE THE FIGURE I cut, nothing to brag about,
and I didn't want to stand in Pearl's way. It was an odd
sort of sacrifice, to stay away more and more from Pearl,
but I seemed to have to do it. I took longer trips to other
states, I kept indoors at home and watched TV like the
rest of the country. I missed the boy.

Not that I didn't pop in every now and then—I was
still paying the rent—but only at very neutral times of
day. Anyone seeing us would've taken me for an out-of-
town uncle. I gathered from certain things the boy said
that there were other men around. One of them took him
on a duck hunting trip when he was fifteen, a week near
some lake. "He's so lazy," Pearl said about Lincoln. "The
world's been handed to him on a silver platter." It had?

After the duck hunter was out of the picture, Pearl did
the last thing I expected, she signed up for a course in
bookkeeping. She did this somewhat grimly, out of a
feeling that you couldn't depend on anything. When I

asked her how she liked the course, she said, "It is what it is." The next time I saw her, a couple of restaurants had hired her to go over their books in case the IRS had a nosy spell. She said, "Now I know the secrets buried in every won-ton." You could see she was brightening a little.

I HAD NEVER known her to be much of a Buddhist, but she went to a temple in the neighborhood to coax Heaven for Lincoln's success in his school exams. He was a perfectly smart kid, but he didn't bother with subjects he didn't like, which was a lot of the curriculum. She wanted him to get into a community college or a tech school at least. She certainly didn't want him getting drafted. Pearl had him wearing a charm around his neck all during exam week—a carp turning itself into a dragon, success in transformation.

I WAS IN ARIZONA a lot that winter. U-Screw had a new product they were pushing hard, and they were eager to underbid all the companies trying to get their wares into planes being built to soar over Vietnam. My sister hated the war (well, who liked it?), and told me what I earned was blood money. I said the U.S. had to watch its back. She said we were only greedy and the domino theory was hooey.

And why wouldn't I want the reward of a fat commission? My softness for Pearl had kept me from any kind of savings. The new product pretty much sold itself. It was a brilliantly cheap screw in a steel alloy with a new and astoundingly tough protective coating and the impact strength tests looked very good and so did the shear testing. I had to present it to a bunch of engineers in a gloomy office, pointing to the shining evidence in my sample case, while they asked smart questions and had to hear me say, "As a man who's fought in a war." And two weeks later the contract from Bydex Guidance Systems came back signed.

MEANWHILE, THE AMULET hadn't done a thing for Lincoln's performance in school. He said the teachers didn't like him. "Why would they?" Pearl said. She issued orders against his seeing certain friends who were never going anywhere and only wanted to drag Lincoln down with them.

"That won't work," I said.

"Is anyone asking you?" she said. "I don't think so. Just because I take your money doesn't mean I listen to your opinions."

We were both stunned when she said this, and we stared at each other in bitter recognition. She had always been decorous—not fawning, but always offering the rights due my station; I suppose I thought it was a matter of honor. But now we were inside the rawness of money, the acid clarity of power. Pearl wanted me to know just how far she was bought, where the bargain ended. I had to ask myself then if things might have been different between us if I'd never paid her a dime. Not that she would have talked to me without my dimes, a man my age, but I hated money at that moment and was sorry I'd ever had more than Pearl had. I was disgusted by the taint of obedience around it, the notion that Pearl had had to oblige me to live. I was sick with resentment against money for what it had done to me.

IT WAS A MOMENT we couldn't undo, and Pearl probably wasn't surprised when I really did keep away after that. I kept on paying her rent; that was *my* honor, it seemed. I was fine. I went back to reading Tacitus, whom I'd had to read as a boy, and I liked Mary Renault and Nero Wolfe.

In the late spring Pearl phoned me to say that Lincoln was threatening to enlist in the Navy after he graduated. He wanted the Navy because his father had been in it.

"He doesn't know anything," Pearl said. "I gave birth to a dope. A dope moron goof-off."

Even when she was crying, Pearl cursed like a four-year-old.

Pearl herself was in favor of the war. She hated Communists, for what they had done to China, and she thought that killing was all that certain people understood. This did not mean she wanted her son anywhere near the killing. She saw no contradiction in this.

She must have railed and berated him for days before he left, but once he was gone, Pearl tried to be okay about it. I gave her credit for that. And she had some basis for cheer. First Lincoln was in training on a base in San Diego, looking very photogenic in his white sailor's cap, and then

when they sent him overseas, he lived inside a ship, a
destroyer, that floated off the south coast of Vietnam. He
told his mother that his feet didn't touch land, except for
recreational visits to Saigon. "He says it's boring," Pearl
said. "Isn't that the best thing you've ever heard?"

There were soldiers in my war too who were never
under fire, even in France. A person could have luck. I
tried to picture the coast of the South China Sea, where
Lincoln was, farther east than I'd ever been, and I wondered if being a young man in Asia had any good in it
for him.

OUTSIDE PHOENIX THERE was a roadhouse where they
knew me, and I got so ripped one night I left my sample
case in the parking lot while I was pissing in the bushes.
When I came back the next day, some joker on a motorcycle had run over it and flattened a trail into the mangled
leather. I unzipped the battered case that night, and I had
to laugh at the wreck it was—the foam padding mashed,
and screws all over, with the protective plating chipped
off some of them. Silvery flakes in the foam, and the
screws striped with darker patches of naked metal. Too
much party for the hardware.

Plating had chipped off? They were screws for *aerospace*,
they weren't for doll furniture. How much did anybody's
motorcycle weigh? The tensile strength of these screws
was supposed to have been tested at thousands of pounds
per square inch. I kept turning them over in my hands,
hoping for better news.

How many of these screws had I sold? The next morning I called the vice president for design and development, whose secretary would hardly speak to me (a sales rep, a nobody from no place) until I invoked the term *defect*. Later that day I made my little speech and dumped an envelope of chipped screws on the man's desk.

"Oh, no," he said. "Holy Jesus. No."

"There're a lot of them in planes too," I said.

"Not anymore there won't be," he said. "Who let this through? Poor old U-Screw. It was always a good company."

"They'll recall all of them?"

"Of course," he said. "Jesus. Of course."

WITHIN A WEEK they discontinued the screws, with a suggested alternative at somewhat higher cost. A manager at Bydex a few months later called me to ask why he couldn't reorder the old ones. "Are you crazy?" I said.

No one had bothered to tell anyone at Bydex to take all the screws out of their guidance systems.

"They're in *planes*," he said. "They're gone."

"You have to get 'em back," I said.

"Who's *you*?" he said. "Not me. I'm not the one. And, with all due respect, no one's going to do it just because Owen the salesman said so."

IT WAS THEN I understood the muck I was standing in. I had sold those screws so well, I had pitched them so intelligently. We all knew where the planes were, didn't we?

The white skies of Asia. I wanted to go at once to Pearl, waiting at home for Lincoln's letters, and kneel at her feet, to flatten myself full-length and touch my forehead to the ground three times. In Siam once a year the senior monks begged the youngest monks, with prostrations, to forgive them for ever misleading them. I had tricked myself, I had tricked all of us.

THERE HAD TO BE records of which planes had the screws in them. Every company had a whole department of bean counters who kept track of those things. It wasn't impossible to hunt down the rotten screws and just screw in better ones. The drama of this heroic effort could make the company look good. U-Screw goes to the ends of the earth! The phrases for this plan grew in my head—I thought I could sell it, and I wrote a detailed, persuasive letter to the CEO of U-Screw, who was in Schenectady. *I consider correction imperative*, I wrote, *as a veteran myself.*

An attorney for the company sent a brief, friendly response, praising my concern and explaining how thoroughly everything had already been handled—*a fully corrected screw is now available, to meet market needs*—and suggesting no further thought on the subject was necessary from me. I wasn't *tuan* here, that had never been clearer. What was I, then? A cog in a corrupt machine, and what was the big news about that?

AND I WAS STILL going to work every day, driving the highways in my silver-blue Pontiac. I had a new sample case, brown cordovan. I had never been a showy sales-man, but it was hard to present even the most basic facts now (facts, my eye). I sounded decrepit and mumbling, or I whipped myself into doing better and I spoke like a souped-up jackass. A man has to make a living. I had only to keep my head down and just put one foot in front of the other, but I wasn't as good at it as I might've thought.

The problem was the television. It showed too much of the war. To the rest of the country the rain pouring down on rice paddies looked like the set for a movie called the war, but to me it looked like a place I knew. Once when the camera showed a gathering in a village, women and children squatting under a lean-to thatched with palm, I caught myself looking for Noo Kiang. Who would be a grandmother now anyway. It didn't help when I turned off the TV either. I had my own silver screen of the brain, my own beams and pulses and signals.

AND HOW HAD IT HAPPENED, that a company let screws that lethally crappy be put on the market? Someone must have known or guessed—my trial by motorcycle couldn't have been the first sign. I spent a lot of time thinking through the chain of steps. Engineers in the company must have known—not right away, of course, but they knew. Maybe they said it would take another six months to figure out the problem, and somebody in management thought that was too long, the product was already listed or already selling, and anyway probably (the manager thought) it would be okay. The more he thought of how far things had gone, the more he distrusted the prissy obsessiveness of engineers and the surer he was that the screws would be fine. There were more and more men like that, who really, really didn't want trouble and whose reasoning was habitually abstract.

I'D WORKED FOR SOME dirty trading companies in Siam, so I don't even know why I was so outraged, but I was. If I'd been younger, if I'd had more of a skin to save, I might have just *stuffed it*, as Lincoln used to say. Maybe if I'd been a family man I wouldn't have stuck out my neck. I knew what I was doing when I wrote to the managing director of Bydex, pointing out what U-Screw hadn't told them. *It is imperative that measures be taken*, I wrote, *to remove the faulty hardware from aircraft. I would urge these measures as soon as possible.* No one was going to thank me, I was reasonably sure.

WHATEVER AMERICANS were fighting for was a matter of life or death, but we couldn't afford to be so absolutist about a few screws—the clash of those two points was a conflagration in my brain. It made the nightly news uglier. I had a vision now of people in command as panicked, greedy, and given to lying. What I couldn't stand was the way the government kept sending in new soldiers—*escalating*—when it didn't know what it was doing or why. The slipshod crookedness of it shamed me. So on a nice San Francisco Sunday I walked in a peace march with other veterans against the war. I wasn't a dapper old relic in his uniform (who knew where *that* was?) but I made my slow way behind the young vets in wheelchairs, with their bandannas and their fatigue jackets and their dog tags. We were glad to see each other—they gave me glances as if I knew something other people couldn't. I didn't, not the way they thought—I'd only been in France a few months and missed most of the worst. I hadn't understood then that desperate old windbags of statesmen, too hardened and wily to scruple about lying, thought it was a fair bargain to let me be roasted alive. You could see from the faces of the men in wheelchairs that they had taken that in.

PEARL WAS VERY upset when I told her I'd marched against the war. "I can't believe you did that," she said. "It *helps* Hanoi."

There was no way for her to hear my arguments, though I argued anyway. "Were you ever in the Navy?" I said. "You have no idea what Lincoln's life is like."

"I know the Navy," she said. "As it so happens." She must have been very angry, to make any reference at all to Lincoln's father.

"That's not knowing anything," I said. "That's not what they call it."

"My boy sends me letters," she said. "I don't see him sending you any letters."

We really could not be around each other at this time.

—

I NEVER HEARD FROM Bydex after I wrote. I might have written again, I might have flooded a whole masthead of executives with unwelcome protests. I might have done more. What I did was very little. But my minor burst of flash-in-the-pan outrage was enough to make U-Screw decide to take out an injunction against me. I was not to write any more letters and I had to hire a lawyer and wait to go to court, and my salary was, as they say, frozen.

At night at the bar I kept asking, "What does a person need money for anyway?" Most people said, "I like to eat every day." I thought of what else I'd always needed it for. To make people listen to me, not to have to listen to them. A person without change in his pocket has to put up with a lot of crap. In Siam I used to look at my silver ticals as if they were trophies, cheers from an admiring horde. Tokens to win women to me. A man with money can show himself in a better light.

But I'd been fine too with just a rucksack on my back, tramping through the jungle. I could still live simply. I had plenty of ways to be simpler, if it came to that. First I stopped drinking Jack Daniel's and slipped down to house bourbon—much hilarity about that economy. I didn't have to keep the leather-bound sets of Tacitus and Byron when they could so easily be sold, and some coins from Siam were actually worth something. I could make do fine with the clothes I had. It was not that big a deal to trade in the brand-new, bulging Pontiac for a tinnier, more road-worn car.

This went on for more months than I had planned. I'd always liked being a decent sport, and I hated the penny-pinching and the petty tallying, the waits for bargains. Every two-second phone conversation with the lawyer was a dent in my budget. My deepest monthly expense was Pearl's rent. It was my honor to always take care of that for her, no matter what we said or didn't say to each other. Our ties were much more permanent than our passing relations. We had both always understood that, and that understanding was worth everything. There were moments when a blur of resentment rose in me while I was eating a bologna sandwich for dinner. What the hell was Pearl eating? But I was glad to be keeping my word, glad for the luxury of still having that part of me. In this I was still *tuan*.

I managed each month by robbing Peter to pay Paul, putting off one debt to settle another. A person might think there wasn't money in the account to pay my rent and Pearl's too, but a person might get by through not believing this. I recalculated and adjusted and made allowances. I had everyone pacified in small amounts, I never kept the same ones waiting. Until the check for my own rent bounced, returned with a sullen note from my landlord.

And then I did turn hotly against Pearl for always tak-ing the rent money from me. How many years? And now we hardly spoke anyway. I tried to keep myself angry in order to do what I had to do. My note, telling her I was no longer paying, was direct and plain. I might have been a utility company turning her off.

She didn't answer either, but why would she? I couldn't get used to being a man who'd done this. It ate into my heart, and then I was another drunk without a heart, which every bar is full of. In the afternoons the other patrons entertained themselves advising me on the chances of my lawsuit. U-Screw had deeper pockets to pay its legal help than I did, but who knew how far it could go? In the end (as my lawyer had predicted) the charges were dropped, just before we went to court, and the company was satisfied just to take away my pension.

I hadn't deliberated very long before I sent the letter to Bydex, but I'd had plenty of time to mull it over since. I had always assumed my big adventures were in my years overseas. I trekked those perilous jungle trails just to find the glint of ore in a mound of earth or the particles washed out of streams—eons of earth's compression spilling bits of glitter into our sacks. I had thought my life here, on the highway to peddle hardware, was duller and weaker in risk, and yet I, Owen the rumpled suit, had now managed to spectacularly combust decades of gainful employment and blown the income of my golden years to smithereens. Who knew I had it in me?

Quelle surprise, as Thea used to say. When I was in Siam, I was always irritated by the English and the other Europeans, and I used to sneer at the laughable puffery of the self-righteous, but I could see now that self-righteousness had its rewards, its consolations. I liked my own virtue (it was mine to like) and I tried to like my sacrifices too. I could see why Dilys had been so confident and brisk, so cheerful under adversity. I was still not sure she'd done any Siamese any good, but I felt some degree of kinship with her and with the bracing effects of principle. Me like Dilys! If you live long enough, everything happens to you.

WHAT I DID DECIDE, once the thing was definitely over, was that I had to have a rule against drinking at home. Otherwise, without a job, I was going to just flush myself down the tubes. I had no other prospects, and if I was going to get by on Social Security, I was going to have to be more careful than I liked to be.

I woke up every day with a policy. Why didn't I subscribe to a Malaysian newspaper so I could get back into the language again? Why didn't I go on rockhound walks with organized clubs who hiked around the hills with hammers? Why wasn't I planning strategy as an elder statesman among antiwar veterans? I believed I would do at least one of these things very soon.

I'd been told at my favorite bar that I couldn't say, "Screw those screws," one more time. I said that was enough to make me switch bars, but I didn't. Booze withers some people right away, and others it seems to fuel. I was one of the fortunate ones. I wouldn't have had my accident if I hadn't decided to take a detour home because

I didn't want to walk on a deserted street at that hour. This prudence caused me to get confused at a crossing, and in turning to orient myself I slipped in a puddle and knocked myself out.

AT THE HOSPITAL THE nurses found the old ID card from Universal Screw and Supply in my wallet, and I overheard them tittering about the company name. I wanted to tell them it was run by wolfish thugs, but I was in no shape to speak. On the back of the card was Pearl's number as an emergency contact, and I thought I heard them read it aloud, but I slept on and off, so when Pearl showed up at my bed, I felt I had dreamt her. She had a new short haircut and a bright scarf tied around her neck in some complicated way.

"The haircut's good on you," I said.

I was afraid I was dying, that was why she had come. It scared me to look at her.

"What are they feeding you?" she said. "You want me to get some egg drop soup?"

"Can I eat?" I said.

"Of course you can eat," she said. "You don't have to go to medical school to know a person has to eat. You want it from Double Happiness? They don't make it too salty."

I felt ridiculous asking the nurse if I could eat. I didn't like Pearl seeing me so cautious and whispery and banged up. I had a concussion and a terrible headache. "I bet I look a hundred," I said to Pearl.

"You've looked better," she said.

The nurse wouldn't let me eat. With a concussion, they have to watch you awhile, to make sure you wake up if you sleep. I stayed another night at the hospital, and then Pearl decided she was going to be my watcher.

THE HOSPITAL MADE me leave in a wheelchair, and I had to lean on Pearl's arm and let her help me slide into the seat of her car. I was fine, she didn't need to hook herself under my shoulder to walk me into her apartment. She gave me the room that had been Lincoln's room. Jerry Lee Lewis was murdering a piano in a poster over the bed. "I bet there are old copies of *Playboy* under the mattress," I said.

"Don't check," she said. "You're not supposed to get too thrilled."

When I woke up in the night, I thought I was sleeping in the street. I was curled up under a bridge, wrapping butcher paper around me to keep warm. The paper kept blowing away. In the morning Pearl was standing over the bed.

"It's *alive*," I said, rising up with my arms out stiff. The line was from a horror movie Lincoln liked.

"Nothing wrong with you," she said.

PEARL TOOK CARE of me without any nonsense, the way she had Lincoln. I had not been tended by a woman since the days in Siam. "I was more lordly then," I said. "Servants were cheap cheap cheap." I was kidding, but not entirely. She'd already heard all my stories anyway.

"Young girls fanning you with banana leaves," she said. "Coolies begging you to hire them."

They did beg. Even after I fired them or docked their pay for laziness. It's not always a pleasing thing to remember one's youth. I'd been glad enough when Zain beat a coolie with a stick for being too drunk to work one day. I thanked him for thinking to do it! That was the way of it then. I had not been exceptional.

This was the first time in my life I'd gone against the way of it. My own quixotic effort. My father, I thought, would have been sorry to see me end my life with so little money to my name. Though my father had been stripped of his holdings too, duped by lying debtors. "First rule always: don't believe what people say," Pearl said. Nothing in these stories surprised Pearl.

I thought then of how Chinese Pearl was, after all—unshockable, hardheaded, tuned for survival. (I knew now she'd been raised in Los Angeles, where her family still was, and that Lincoln's father had fought in the Pacific and had a wife and kid.) How hard she'd worked all her life, in ways that didn't always bear thinking about, to have something to hold on to—coin of the realm you could bite to test—and now her sure thing had failed her. I was the theory that had fallen through. In school they used to make us read poems about doing what we ought and ne'er counting the cost. I had not counted the cost, actually, in this most recent phase—not added or prefigured or seen ahead—but now I had too much time to think. I was afraid of my lessened value to Pearl, and I didn't hold it against her either.

PEARL HAD NEVER been much of a cook. While I was there, I could make meals from cheap things—chicken livers and lamb neck and baked bean casserole. The new frugal Owen. Bachelor with a spatula. "Who knew you were so handy?" Pearl said.

I took a bus to the market I liked—I hadn't had a car of any kind for while. Pearl thought it wasn't right that I was carrying bags of groceries up and down the hills. All by myself, how did I do it? "The buses are fine," I said. "You just have to be patient." I had to keep telling her over and over I wasn't going to blow a fuse and have a stroke every time I walked up the hill. It was a sore subject.

So I got ready to go back to my own apartment. Only, that week, Pearl needed me to let the plumber in if he ever showed up. And then it was too hard to get me moved during several days of terrible rainstorms. "Relax," Pearl said, "and stop hopping around. I don't see why you're always in such a big hurry." She had a box of books picked up for me from my apartment, so I had stuff to read while I waited. Once I was through the first layer of books, the prospect of my leaving appeared to both of us to be an unnecessarily violent solution

We kept out of each other's hair. At night we were often in our separate rooms. I hated what she watched on TV. Once I was well enough, I went off a few nights a week to drink at my old local, and Pearl wasn't even awake to check what state I was in when I came home. What was it to her? And I liked the leisurely days on my own, the hours all to myself, taking sandwiches to the park, walking along the wharf while the light changed. When I showed up for an antiwar demonstration in Golden Gate Park, I didn't feel a need to tell Pearl.

MY BUDGET WAS a little better once I let my apartment go, but I had to watch myself about spending. The last thing I wanted was to lean on Pearl. The injustice of sudden rises in prices made me nuts. Pearl said I developed an entirely new streak as a killjoy. I was the one who groused about how much a movie cost, the one who said, "None of my beeswax, but you might be sorry at the end of the month," when she came home with a cashmere coat. "Relax, my friend," Pearl said.

Lincoln's letters were chatty and short. You would have thought the war consisted of nothing but hot weather and homesickness, to read them. In March, just when Pearl was busy with tax season, the letters suddenly stopped coming. There was nothing in the mail one week, or the next week, or the next. Pearl phoned whatever office she could at the Navy, but no one knew a thing.

"You'd think they would *tell* me something," Pearl said. I was more and more afraid of what they weren't telling her, the bits no one wanted to say. After work she went to a temple in the neighborhood. To chant, she said. Chant what? The name of the Eternal Buddha. Over and over. How could someone like Pearl want to do that? "You don't know a thing," she said. "How did you get to be so old and not know anything?" But in the evenings she liked to play poker with me, or Scrabble (my innovation), and once in the pause between rounds she took my hand and drew it to her mouth and kissed the knuckle. I was so startled I chuckled in embarrassment.

THAT NIGHT I HAD a dream about my own war. In my dream I was surprised to find that it was all still going on. I was in a miserable, rain-soaked ditch in France, with no weapon. I was hoping Pearl didn't know where I was, since she had enough on her mind. Then it seemed that in the muddy ditch with me was a crocodile. I saw its bulging eyes above the water, the rough ridge of its back. And I got hold of the idea that I shouldn't be afraid, because I was already so old, what did it matter? Ah, it's not a problem, I thought, and I was glad of it. When I woke up, I thought with some amusement how few crocodiles there had been in France. Hardly a lizard even. I wished I could die for Lincoln. I was more than ready to trade my body in a minute, why not, why not, and the unfairness of it being not possible was hard on me.

THE NEWS CAME in a phone call. I was out walking on Ocean Beach and when I came home, Pearl was sitting at the kitchen table with her head in her hands. From behind her cupped palms she said, "It's not what you think." Lincoln was in a hospital in Da Nang. His ship had been "shelled by enemy shore batteries"—whatever that meant—and shrapnel had lodged in his thigh. Once he could be moved, they were flying him to a hospital in the States.

"He's coming home," I said.

"I know," she said. "I was so relieved I didn't ask enough about the wound. Is that terrible? That's terrible."

THEY PUT HIM in a hospital in Texas, of all places, and Pearl stayed in a motel nearby for a month before they came home together. When I picked them up at the airport, Lincoln, who was walking with a crutch, said, "Hey, the place is still here." His voice was flat and he had a haircut that made him look pinheaded.

"Your town," I said. "It's been waiting for you."

It was Pearl who looked really bad. Her face was blurred and pinched, even under her careful makeup. "Have to get this boy home," she said.

"Chop-chop," he said.

He was edgy and quiet, but he wasn't as bad as I'd feared. I'd cleared my things out of his room, and when he sat down on the bed, he said, "I guess everybody has a mother, right?"

"If you're lucky."

"Lucky boy home come."

He was sarcastic about almost everything, but I thought he was entitled. His first meal, on his request, was porterhouse steak and baked potato. I was the one who cooked it. He made a big joke out of trying to eat it with chopsticks. "Messy boy," Pearl said. One thing that was new was his making fun of being Chinese.

I WAS A LODGER in Pearl's bed again, and we lay awake at night talking about Lincoln. "He could have come out of this in a lot more terrible shape," I said.

"You didn't see the hospital," she said. "You think I don't know?"

It was the hospital that had undone her, and it was a decent hospital, clean enough, with okay nurses. The massiveness of it had been its horror, as far as I could tell, the floors upon floors of other people's sons.

"You think you know things but you just know your own little corner," she said.

"Yes," I said.

LINCOLN HAD DEVELOPED a new sentimental fondness for American TV (he spent hours watching *Laugh-In* and reruns of *Rawhide*) and he ate nonstop, which we thought was good. At his request, I made crusty pans of mac and cheese and tuna noodle casserole. He hadn't really eaten that with Pearl, but he certainly wasn't going near any chicken feet or jellyfish now. He said he hated the smell of sesame oil, and pushed away the stir-fried beef with green onion that Pearl brought home. "Just don't," he said. "Don't bring it anywhere near me."

Okay, okay. Whatever he wanted. My sister Corinna,

who phoned when she could, said, "He wants to be home. Not tasting Asia." I got along better with Corinna these days. "So he's not like me," Corinna said. "Always wanting to be two places at once."

I MADE EFFORTS not to get in Lincoln's way those first weeks. But sometimes he wanted company. He'd hover around me in the kitchen or he'd ask what I was reading. We were the two unemployed males in the house. When I said I was going for a walk on the beach, he said he wanted to go with me.

Ocean Beach was foggy and cold, with the shoreline smell of brine and drying kelp. We looked out into the silver-gray water, toward the jagged shape of Seal Rock. Lincoln could walk on the sand with his crutch, but not well, so we just stood gazing.

"You used to have money," Lincoln said. "They took your money away?"

"Yep," I said. "Screw those screws." (I didn't say: *I did it to save myself. I did it so I could stand to be around you and not fall to my knees.*)

"Fuck," he said.

"Oh, I'm not starving."

"No," he said. "I've seen starving and that's not what you're doing."

"In southern Siam people in the more remote villages— this was a long time ago—got around fine without any cash at all. They grew stuff, they fished, they traded.

What did they need coins for? You would have liked that part of Siam."

"Well, in Vietnam they used money," Lincoln said.

I thought of how I must appear to Lincoln, the geezer with his Technicolor tales of the fabled East, his mother's faded benefactor. I was still thinking about the Siamese villages and the way the families used to come out to see us when we arrived by the river, people walking out of their houses, the children yelling, men and women in sarongs and tucked trousers and none of them with pockets.

Lincoln was leaning on a post and poking the sand with his crutch, drawing doodles in it. He drew a naked woman, the same figure with humongous breasts and wild pubic hair that all boys draw. I didn't actually think the reason Lincoln had been returned safe was because something had forgiven me. But people like thinking that sort of thing, I couldn't help it.

The sight of Lincoln still flooded me with joy. If he'd had the stuffing knocked out of him, if he'd lost the sly look he'd had as a teenager and his snappy walk would never come back, at least he was here. We weren't asking what he'd seen, what he'd done. I thought of him on the ship, sweating in the reflected heat, surrounded by the blue South China Sea, and I thought of him as a dazed boy in the port of Saigon, peering at the rows of shophouses, with people calling to him in the streets.

On our California beach the wind was coming up, blowing our jackets against us. Enough of the fog had burned off so the water below the horizon was darker than the white sky. Beyond that was Japan, if a person could see far enough. The line between air and sea got clearer as we looked.

"No wonder they thought the world was flat," I said.

"From up in a plane you can sort of see more curve," Lincoln said. "Ever notice?"

I said I thought I had. I could feel the horizon staring back at us, daring us to say we knew what was on the other side. Lincoln, who must've felt something similar, set his cane against the post, and made circles out of his thumbs and index fingers and held them up to his eyes, fake binoculars. "I'm watching Honolulu," he said. "There's a girl in a grass skirt. I don't want to tell you what she's doing."

"Wave to her for me," I said. "It encourages them."

In fact we were looking into the most abstract of land-scapes, dove-gray sky, steel-gray water, pale sand. A flat-ness you could fall right off of, the edge of the earth—how could it really be a curve that ran in a loop for more than twenty-four thousand miles? But it was. "Aloha, okay?" Lincoln said into the wind. I was trying to think of the size of the world. More than I could think about, more than I could imagine, necessary to imagine.

IN "ENVY," THE MONK'S BIOGRAPHY THAT TOON READS is *Venerable Acariya Mun Bhuridatta Thera: A Spiritual Biography*, by Acariya Maha Boowa Nanasampanno, translated by Bhikkhu Dick Silaratano (Udorn Thani, Thailand: Forest Dhamma, 2004).

While the characters in "Paradise" are my own invention, information about the life of a tin prospector has been drawn from *Impressions of the Siamese-Malayan Jungle: A Tin-Prospector's Adventures in Southern Thailand*, by Hans Morgenthaler, first published in 1921 (Bangkok: White Lotus, 1994). I have also been greatly helped by *Village Life in Modern Thailand*, by John E. de Young (Berkeley: University of California Press, 1955); *Friendly Siam: Thailand in the 1920s*, by Ebbe Kornerup (Bangkok: White Lotus, 1999); *Tales from the South China Seas: Images of the British in South-East Asia in the Twentieth Century*, edited by Charles Allen (London: Futura, 1984); and *History of the Malay Kingdom of Patani*, by Ibrahim Syukri, translated by Conner Bailey and John N. Miksic (Athens, OH: Ohio University, 1985).

For "Loyalty," my understanding of life in Sicily during and after World War II has been informed by *Sicily as Metaphor*, by Leonardo Sciascia, translated by James Marcus (Marlboro, VT: Marlboro Press, 1994); *Sicilian Lives*, by Danilo Dolci, translated by Justin Vitiello with Madeline Polidoro (New York: Pantheon, 1981); *Words Are Stones: Impressions of Sicily*, by Carlo Levi, translated by Angus Davidson (New York: Farrar, Straus & Cudahy, 1958); *Sicily on My Mind: Echoes of Fascism and World War II*, by Joseph Cione (1stBooks, 2003); and the excellent essays on language and history in bestofsicily.com. Special thanks also to Chuck Wachtel.

ACKNOWLEDGMENTS

For sage advice and utter generosity during all stages of this manuscript, I want to thank Myra Goldberg, Chuck Wachtel, and Andrea Barrett. Kathleen Hill and Rattawut Lapcharoensap gave invaluable final readings. I am very fortunate to have Carol Houck Smith as editor and friend, and her presence throughout this project has meant a great deal to me. I am ever grateful for the good luck of having Geri Thoma as my agent. Special thanks as always to Sharon Captan for her friendship. And thanks to the MacDowell Colony for a residency during the writing of this book.

Parts of this novel have appeared previously in magazines. A section of "Envy" appeared (under the title "War Buddies") in *Land-Grant College Review* and was included in *The O. Henry Prize Stories 2007*. "Allegiance," in slightly altered form, appeared in *Ploughshares*.

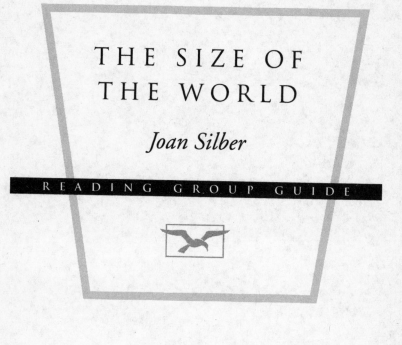

THE SIZE OF
THE WORLD

Joan Silber

READING GROUP GUIDE

THE SIZE OF
THE WORLD

Joan Silber

THE AUTHOR ON HER WORK

I like to think that traveling, which by its nature turns you into the dope who doesn't know how things work, also makes you consider what's incidental and what's elemental. This book came out of brooding about just that. I've been to the places used as settings here—to Asia in recent years, and to Sicily and Mexico in earlier times in my life. Nearly all the characters are invented, but I began the book after a trip to Vietnam and thought much about the time my older brother spent working there as a civilian during the war. I saw, as I wrote, that I was interested in the moments when people are lured from or forced out of parochialism, which is the natural belief that reality consists of what a person knows already. My mother, like many mothers of her era, used to say, "You're not the only pebble on the beach," which turns out to be quite right, always hard to remember, and crucial to remember in an ever more connected world.

DISCUSSION QUESTIONS

1. Vietnam, Thailand, Mexico, Sicily, and the United States all figure as settings. How do the different characters react to the experience of being foreigners? Whose responses did you admire the most?

2. Notions of alliance and loyalty figure strongly throughout the book. Mike, in the chapter "Allegiance," listens to his kids talking at breakfast after their parents' divorce: "They were like citizens of a country whose borders had changed." How are families like countries? Where does this book make you see this, and which family borders seem most fixed, and which most shifting? Can countries be seen as behaving like families?

3. What is the role of romantic love in this novel? In "Independence," Phoebe says that her mother's sense of "scale" means remembering all "the poor starving millions who'd be grateful for just a single spare moment to boo-hoo" over a lost lover. Do you think that a larger consciousness makes romantic problems seem smaller? Or is this a distorted view? For which characters is love the most important and how do they fare? How does the chapter title relate to the dilemmas of cross-national lovers?

4. In "Paradise," when Corinna is walking through Siam and remembering her childhood hikes in the Catskills, she thinks, "I began to think of each spot on the globe as a mere part, the section any lesson had to be broken down into." Does the book's division into parts help show this? Do you think the form of the book is successful? If it didn't meet your expectations for a unified novel, what unities did you see in it? Where were you most surprised by connections? What was the effect of that surprise?

5. Toby, in "Envy," struggles with a longing for solitude, although he is married to a woman he loves. How else does this longing figure in the novel? Is this a neglected craving of our time? Toby is not always happy to be so closely surrounded by his wife's family—is his attitude especially American? How do his Thai relatives compare, for instance, to Nunzia's Sicilian family? Some characters—

Kit, Owen—improvise lives outside the usual forms of marriage or family. How do you view their choices and the results?

6. Corinna, in "Paradise," criticizes her brother for his behavior as a colonial "boss." Corinna is later troubled by how to act toward Siamese friends: "Thea likes it when we bring gifts when we go to Som's . . . I don't know how else we could behave, though I always wish I did know." Is it impossible to behave well as a "colonial"? Where does this behavior have the most consequences? What is a "colonial"? How does Owen's moral test, in the last chapter, play out against these questions?

7. Are there characters you initially felt no sympathy for but later felt differently about? How did the shifts in point of view make this happen, and were there other factors? What was the biggest change you felt toward a character?

8. Each character's chapter covers a long span of time. And the novel as a whole moves through different historical time periods. How does the author manage these leaps and compressions of time convincingly? How did it make you feel as a reader to move through so much time? Is there a particular sensation when finishing such a book?

9. War is an element in parts of the novel—the Vietnam War, World War II, and the Patriot Act, linked to 9/11. Did these repeated images of wartime influence your final sense of the novel? How would the book have been different without them? How did you feel about the characters—and countries—who switch sides?

10. Is a novel like this one, where different narrators tell different (but linked) stories, particularly right for our time? Have you noticed other books that are in a category between novels and story collections? Or films with several storylines? Do you think there will be more such works?

ABOUT THE AUTHOR

Joan Silber is the author of five other works of fiction, including *Ideas of Heaven*, a finalist for both the National Book Award and The Story Prize, and *Household Words*, winner of the PEN/Hemingway Award. Her stories have appeared in *The New Yorker* and have been included in the *O. Henry Prize Stories*, the *Pushcart Prize*, and *The Scribner Anthology of Contemporary Short Fiction*. In 2007 Silber received a Literature Award from the American Academy of Arts and Letters. The *Seattle Times* picked *The Size of the World* as one of its top ten fiction books of 2008. Silber teaches at Sarah Lawrence College and lives in New York City.

*Available only on the Norton Web site: www.wwnorton.com/guides